W9-BXQ-525

The Mushroom Man

The Mushroom Man

STUART PAWSON

This edition published in Great Britain in 2004 by
Allison & Busby Limited
Bon Marche Centre
241-251 Ferndale Road
Brixton, London SW9 8BJ
http://www.allisonandbusby.com

Copyright © 2004 by STUART PAWSON

The right of Stuart Pawson to be identified as
author of this work has been asserted by him in
accordance with the Copyright, Designs and
Patents Act, 1988

This book is sold subject to the condition that it shall not,
by way of trade or otherwise, be lent, resold, hired out or
otherwise circulated without the publisher's prior
written consent in any form of binding or cover other than
that in which it is published and without a similar condition
including this condition being imposed upon the subsequent
purchaser.

A catalogue record for this book is available from the British
Library

ISBN 0 7490 8385 9

Printed and bound in Great Britain
Bookmarque htd, Croydon, Surrey

STUART PAWSON had a career as a mining engineer, followed by a spell working for the probation service, before he became a full-time writer. He lives in Fairburn, Yorkshire, and when not hunched over the word processor likes nothing more than tramping across the moors which often feature in his stories.

Also by Stuart Pawson

To Doreen

Chapter One

Father Tudor Harcourt had a problem. At such times he found it a great comfort to have a silent, somewhat one-sided conversation with God. Occasionally, the Almighty showed him the answer. He was not an impatient man: had he known that he was pencilled in for a personal audience in the next fifteen minutes he would have waited.

He'd reached the part of the lane where the county council had regravelled the road. Why on earth did they waste the taxpayers' money every year resurfacing perfectly acceptable country lanes, used only by agricultural vehicles and elderly clerics on equally elderly bicycles? The three-speed Raleigh didn't roll as freely on the new surface, so he had to pedal more. Then there was the increased risk of a puncture. He winced as loose chippings, picked up by the tyres, rattled under the mudguards. The gravel was deepest along the edges of the road, so he steered into the middle, where the small amount of traffic had worn a smoother passage.

The problem, for which he needed the guidance of the Almighty, involved Father Harcourt's imminent retirement and his friendship with Miss Felicity Jonas. Miss Jonas, a petite and charming member of his flock, 'did' for him three days a week. She cleaned his house, washed and darned his socks and ironed his vestments. She also kept his diary up to date, arranged his appointments and filed his sermons. Sometimes he would discuss a sermon with her, if he felt he had to use his position to comment on a particularly pressing social issue, and he found she had a down-to-earth wisdom that sometimes pulled him back from taking a too holier-than-thou standpoint. She gave him much more than all this, though. She was, he believed, his friend. His best friend, his only friend. The only proper female friend he had ever known. And she gave him a constant, aching reminder of the only woman – the only other woman – he had ever loved.

Fifty years ago it had been a long, hot summer. Young Harcourt was kicking his heels before going to theological college. He would be the third generation of Harcourts to take the cloth – via a line of uncles, of course. A Harcourt had been tortured and executed after the Popish Plot three hundred years earlier; he was the last of a long, proud line. Never had he held a moment's doubt about his vocation, his calling, until he met Mary Hemsby, and now, fifty years later, those same doubts were creeping back.

Mary had been sixteen. She took him on long walks on summer afternoons, in those optimistic days after the war, through the wheatfields that loaned their golden colour to her hair and long, bare limbs. She showed him secret places, and promised pleasures that caused him to lie, sweating and sleepless, through the sultry, tormented nights. He was saved from making the hardest decision of his young life when her parents sent her away. They, he believed, apparently not realising he was a Roman Catholic, had not wanted her to marry a clergyman. He often wondered if she had found happiness.

The truth was more prosaic. Mr and Mrs Hemsby sent their daughter to a relative in Wales in something of a hurry because it was becoming increasingly obvious that she was pregnant. The butcher's boy had banged her up one wet April afternoon, delivering rather more than the half of stewing meat and some polony that his basket held. She'd had a lasting, but not happy, marriage, and now lived less than fifteen miles away.

Father Harcourt puffed with the exertion of pedalling. He could see the black and white chevrons of the barrier marking the bend in the road, a quarter of a mile ahead, where it reached Peddars Dyke and turned abruptly right to run alongside it. Not far beyond that bend was Miss Jonas's cottage and afternoon tea. What was he going to say to her? When he retired he would have to leave his home. A place had been reserved for him at St Jude's Retreat, near Walsingham, and very nice it was too, but it was not what he wanted. What he wanted was to move into Rose Cottage with Miss Jonas. Ideally, he would like to marry her. That would offset one scandal, but would it create another, within the Church? At the very least he'd need a dispensation from the Pope, which could take years. God wasn't coming up with any answers. OK, he'd accept the wagging tongues and the moving curtains when he walked through the village: *Just let me find the right words, and may Felicity's response be favourable.*

He'd reached the bend. Oh dear! A car was coming the other way, its roof visible above the hedge from his vantage point on the upright Raleigh. He pulled over towards the side of the road, where the loose gravel had been swept into a swathe, like a sandbank round the outside of a bend in a river. The stones rattled staccato under his mudguards, as loud as hailstones on a greenhouse roof, and the bicycle wobbled alarmingly.

Reg Davison was having a good day, a bloody brilliant day. He tapped his fingers on the steering wheel in time with Radio Fenland's current chart-topper and mused on the vagaries of his fortunes. The only cloud was the fact that he was way over the alcohol limit for driving and still twenty miles from home. That was why he was on this back road instead of racing along the A47.

'Take the old Roman Road,' Edgar Johnstone had advised him. 'No fear of being pulled over by the traffic police along there.' It was advice Reg had taken gladly. His licence already displayed ten penalty points, picked up for speeding offences; a drink-driving rap would be the end of everything he'd worked for.

It wasn't going to happen, though. He was on a winning streak. He listened to the gravel chipping off the paint under the car and luxuriated in the comfortable feeling that a company vehicle generated. No large garage bills for him. Next week he'd suggest to the boss that they trade in this old tub. The new, twenty-four-valve model looked good, and, by Christ, he'd earned it.

The winning streak had started the day before. Reg chuckled at the thought of it. He'd never know how he'd managed to keep his face straight when old man Wimbles had taken him to one side and given him the news that Julian wasn't coming home, but was marrying and settling in America. For fifteen years Reg had struggled, virtually singlehandedly, to build up Wimbles Agri Supplies. Being sales manager was all right, but he'd been promised a directorship. Then, one fine day, young Julian Wimbless had breezed in, fresh from university, and demanded his birthright. Reg was back on the road; a thousand miles a week, in rain, fog or snow.

The old man had sent Julian to the States to study methods and gain some experience. Well, he'd done just that. Reg's body jerked up and down in time with the music. Rarely had such a mundane tune been so joyfully received. Julian had fallen in love with a rancher's daughter in Utah. He'd converted to Mormonism and was going to marry her. They were building a house on Daddy's land.

'Oh, you must be very disappointed that he won't be taking over here,' Reg had said sympathetically when Mr Wimbles told him, but in the privacy of his own office he had danced a jig round the desk, before collapsing with paroxysms of glee into his executive chair.

That was yesterday. That was only for starters. Today he'd entertained Edgar Johnstone and the committee of the North Anglia Farmers Cooperative for lunch and obtained their signatures on a three-year feed contract. Eighteen months of hard slog had come to fruition with the biggest order Wimbles Agri had ever taken. And there could be more. Next year the seed contract was up for grabs, and Reg had made some good contacts, shaken some interesting hands.

He belched and farted at the same time. For a horrible moment he thought he'd messed his pants. Too much success was bad for the digestion. Duck a l'orange, accompanied by a gin and tonic, two pints of bitter, nearly a bottle of Beaujolais and two brandies wasn't good for it either. That thought tickled Reg, and he threw back his head and laughed.

Live hard and play hard, that's the way to do it, he said to himself. He glanced at the yellow blur of the oilseed rape racing by to his left, and the extensive acres of barley off to his right. 'All mine,' he said out loud, 'soon you'll be all mine,' and he laughed again.

He was going far too fast when he reached the bend where the road turned sharply away from the drainage dyke. It would be kind to say that old Roman roads are not expected to make sudden right-angled diversions, but the truth was that Reg Davison was in no fit state to be loose in a motor car. He hit the brakes and swung on the steering wheel. The back of the car skidded out. Instinct took over as Reg corrected the skid, but this took him wide, into the deep gravel round the outside of the bend. For a second he was convinced he'd made it, but then he saw, or thought he saw, the figure on the bicycle. There was a clatter of metal against metal, and Reg glimpsed a black-clad apparition flying towards him, like a geriatric Batman. The figure hit the windscreen with a hollow *ker-clump*, and then it was gone.

Reg sat there, bathed in cold sweat, knuckles white around the wheel, as sober as a tightrope walker. He reached down to switch off the radio. What had happened to him? He looked around. The road looked the same. The barley was still waving seductively in the breeze and the rape was as cheerful as ever. Nothing had changed. Or had everything changed? He prayed that his imagination had been playing tricks, as he got out and walked round to the front of the car.

There was nothing imaginary about the bicycle, with its bent front wheel and handlebars twisted sideways. Or about Reg's smashed headlight. But where was the cyclist? Reg knew the answer. He reluctantly accepted the reality of the situation as he tentatively looked round the back of the car, to where Father Harcourt lay in a ragged heap.

'Christ!' Reg exclaimed. 'He's a vicar. I've killed a vicar.' He rested his forehead on the roof of the car, realising that his lucky streak had rolled clean off the table, possibly for ever. He thumped the roof three times with his right fist, saying: 'Shit! Shit! Shit!' Then he repeated the gesture with both fists, sobbing: 'Fuck! Fuck! Fuck!'

His initial reaction was fairly honourable. He ran back to the bend in the road to see if any help was approaching. It wasn't, thank goodness. Although he felt sober he knew that he'd still measure the same on a breathalyser. It wasn't just his job that was at stake, he could go to jail for this. Well, he'd got himself into it, he'd have to get himself out. Dispose of the evidence, that was the priority. He unlocked the boot lid and opened it. The crumpled body was lying face down, with a small, sinister pool of blood forming under the head, bright against the new gravel. Reg hooked the fingers of one hand under Father Harcourt's dog collar and grasped a handful of trouser material with the other. As unceremoniously as if he were loading a fifty-kilogram bag of weaner pellets to help out one of his customers, he heaved the cleric's body into the boot.

Now for the bike. There wasn't room in the car, so it would have to be hidden nearby. The neighbouring field was the obvious choice – the oil-seed rape was over a metre tall and wouldn't be harvested for another six or seven weeks. Reg crossed the road and looked over the hedge. At the other side of the field he could see a small, isolated cottage.

'Mmm, better make it the barley,' he decided. 'It would be just my luck for some old biddy to be watching out of the window.'

He wasn't wrong. In Rose Cottage, Miss Felicity Jonas was glancing anxiously down the track that led to her home, awaiting her cue to put on the kettle. Father Harcourt – Tudor, as he had asked her to call him on these informal occasions – was never late. She was wearing a new blue dress, and had dabbed on her

wrists some of the expensive perfume that her niece
had given her two Christmases ago.

The barley would be harvested before the oil-seed
rape, but not for at least another month. Reg cast an
expert's eye over the crop. It was good, probably destined for malting before being transmuted into beer or
even whisky. He stooped and squinted across the tops
of the waving fronds, looking for. the telltale signs of
wild oats, standing higher than the rest of the field. He
knew that in the next week or two the farmer would
walk his lands, roguing out any oats that contaminated
the crop. Reg couldn't see any – he was safe.

He carried the bike about fifty yards into the field
and carefully laid it down, trying not to compress the
tall stalks beneath it. He spent a few minutes teasing
them through the spokes and stepped back to admire
his handiwork. From ten yards away it was invisible,
and in a couple of days the barley would straighten
itself up again to conceal it even more. He dusted his
hands together with a sigh of relief and walked back to
the car.

Stay cool, Reg, he told himself. Stay cool and calm
and think clearly, then we can get away with it.
Remember the old motto: He Who Dares Wins. He'd
never been a soldier, but the SAS were his heroes, and
the saying appealed to his gambler's instincts. There
was just the matter of the broken headlight. He found
the scattered glass amongst the gravel and picked up
as much as he could. Any bits remaining were so small
as to be unidentifiable. After a final look around he
climbed into the car and drove off. Two hundred yards
up the road he turned round in a gateway and went
back the way he'd come – he'd had an idea about
where he could dispose of the body.

Peddars Dyke was part of the drainage system that

had transformed this area from a good-for-nothing bog into the most productive arable land in Britain. The marshes had vanished, taking with them the fen orchid, the bittern and the otter, to be replaced with horizon-stretching vistas of barley, wheat and oil-seed rape. Reg had noticed the ditch running alongside the lane he had so recently travelled. At intervals a culvert would take it beneath a turn-off leading into a field or to a farm. He would shove the body into one of these.

He quickly found a suitable place, and parked in the gateway above the dyke. So far he'd been lucky that no other vehicles had come this way, but something was bound to, before too long. He'd pretend he'd suffered a puncture, and had just finished replacing the wheel. The lifting jack was kept in the engine compartment. He pulled the release lever and the bonnet sprang open.

Reg removed the jack from its resting place and moved round to the back of the car. He wasn't relishing what he had to do, but he acted with the purposefulness of the desperate. He opened the boot.

The lid rose smoothly on its hydraulic struts, and as it did, so too did Father Harcourt. He sat up in the boot and clutched imploringly at Reg's sleeve. His face was a scarlet mess and his eyes were white orbs, the uncoordinated pupils barely visible, one pointing up and one down.

Reg screamed in terror and tried to shake his arm free from the old man's talons. He wouldn't let go.

'Get off! Get off!' shrieked Reg, but the fingers tightened their grip. Reg was holding the jack in his right hand. His arm rose and fell, and the jack crashed against the parchment skull of the priest. Again and again the jack came down until the claw-like grip relaxed and Father Harcourt fell back, to keep his appointment with the Lord.

Reg forced himself not to be sick. He sucked in great lungfuls of air through his open mouth and acted like a robot. With one movement he flung the jack into the boot and grabbed the priest under the armpits. Ten seconds later the body splashed into the shallow water. Reg jumped down after it and, standing astride the ditch and clinging to the bridge, managed to push it with his foot until it was out of sight.

He climbed back up to the road. He'd done it. It was over. Then, and only then, did he renew his acquaintance with the duck a l'orange.

Traffic was heavy on the A47, but the risk of being pulled over for a driving offence now seemed trivial. Reg knew a car spares shop on the far side of Norwich where he could buy a new headlight. He'd obtained one there a couple of years previously, after a confrontation with a slurry trailer in someone's yard. He shuddered when he remembered the price of it; thank goodness he had his gold card with him. No, that was no good – he could be traced through that. He'd have to withdraw a hundred quid from a cash dispenser and use real money. He gave a smile of satisfaction – he was thinking well.

It was about six p.m. when he arrived home. This was about his normal time, but much later than he'd planned on this day of days. His wife gave him his meal and he told her about his triumph with the feed contract. She remarked that he looked strained, but Reg explained that he'd had to do some hard negotiating: it hadn't been as straightforward as he'd expected. Later, he went into the garage and changed the headlight. The refuse collection men were due next morning, so he dropped all the broken glass into the dustbin. Come nine a.m. it would be lost for ever, mixed with the jetsam of a thousand other homes. Then he'd be in the clear.

* * *

The bin men came dead on time, as reliable as a quartz watch – the one owned by the manager of the company that had subcontracted their services from the local council. Reg gave them a cheery 'Good morning' as the week's avocado skins, yoghurt pots and murder evidence was tipped into the back of their lorry. Then he climbed into his car to drive to the office, thirty miles away.

First of all he had to give the feed contract to old man Wimbles. Then they had a busy day ahead. All the cash flows, projections, stock control, orders – everything needed completely rejigging. They were big league now, and the credit was all his – all Reg Davison's. And there was the little matter of his new car, he'd bring that up, too.

The traffic of the suburbs thinned out, but Reg kept his speed down. Normally, when sober, he drove with the skilled efficiency of the professional driver, but he'd decided that a low profile might be a good idea for a few weeks. The bicycle would be found in late August when the barley was harvested. Presumably they'd find the body soon afterwards. It would be as obvious as a giraffe in a dance band that murder, or at least manslaughter, had been committed, but by whom? The police were good, but not that good. He tuned in to Radio Fenland to see if the vicar had been missed yet.

There was a lorry in front. Normally he would have zoomed past it, but it was doing over fifty, so he kept his position. A few spots of rain fell on the windscreen. Passing through one of the many small villages on his route he noticed that the road was wet, with big puddles along the edges. They'd had a downpour in the last few minutes.

That should help the barley along, he thought, with,
a satisfied smirk. The lorry's nearside rear wheel
bounced along the gutter, sending a shower of muddy
spray over Reg's car. He extended the fingers of his
right hand to switch on the windscreen wipers. The
glass in front of him cleared, as the wiper swished back
and forth, like waves on the beach, ebbing and flow-
ing. He turned left here. The lorry was going straight
on, thank goodness. He glanced across as he swung
the car round the tight bend. It was difficult to see out
of the passenger's side of the screen. Something wasn't
right. He straightened up and looked across to see
what the problem was.

He only had one windscreen wiper. Oh Christ! Oh,
Jesusfuckingchrist! The entire left-hand windscreen
wiper arm was missing.

Chapter Two

My phone was ringing. Two pairs of beady eyes fixed on me, anticipating the boss making a fool of himself. It was the moment of truth that could be delayed no longer. After a couple more rings I grabbed the handset, clamped it to the side of my head and spoke:

'Awake! For morning in the bowl of night
Has tum ti-tum ti-tum the stars to flight.'

'That's no good!' protested Detective Constable David Sparkington, owner of the beadier pair of eyes.

'No, it's not. It has to be original,' concurred Detective Sergeant Nigel Newley, possessor of the other pair.

The female voice on the line lacked their assurance: 'Um, could I please speak to Inspector Priest?' she asked.

I was reasonably certain it was Maggie Madison, the office practical joker. I said:

'Charlie Priest is my name,
Feeling collars is my game.'

'That's more like it,' confirmed the beady-eyed ones.

'Is that you, Charles?' asked the voice, hesitantly. Oh God! It wasn't Mad Maggie, it was Annabelle, Annabelle Wilberforce. Now it was my turn to go to pieces.

'Oh, er, hello. Is that you, Annabelle?' I stuttered.

Across the office the pair of them did an impression of the Wise Monkeys, without the silent one, after a successful raid on a banana plantation.

'Are you all right, Charles? What's happening?' she asked.

I dredged up what was left of my composure. 'Yes, thanks. How are you?' It wasn't the best opening gambit I'd ever made.

Annabelle laughed: 'It sounds like a madhouse in there. What are you all doing?'

I gave them two fingers and swivelled my chair so that my back was towards them. 'Oh, it's just a silly game we're playing.'

'A game? I thought you were busy fighting crime.'

'We are. It's for charity – the Baby James Appeal at the General Hospital. Every time you start a conversation you have to speak in verse. If you don't it costs you a pound.'

'Goodness, that could be expensive. How much has it cost you so far?'

'Nothing yet. There's a maximum of ten pounds, so I suppose we'll all end up paying a tenner. Hearing from you is a pleasant surprise. I'm sorry about the concert last month; did you enjoy it?'

'It was wonderful – you missed a lovely evening. It's a shame you had to work, but I know how busy you are. I was wondering if you are free tonight. I'm afraid it's rather short notice.'

Free? Well, there was the washing-up; cook a meal; wash the car; do some weeding; mow the grass; clean the windows; iron a shirt. It would be a sacrifice, but I suppose they could all wait. 'That's OK. Providing nobody robs the Nat West I should be available,' I told her.

'Only the Nat West?' she asked.

'Only that one. I bank there,' I answered.

She didn't laugh. That's the trouble with women who have a sense of humour – they're hard to please. 'Fine. In that case you are invited to supper. A couple of friends I knew in Kenya have dropped in unexpectedly for a day or two, so I thought I'd practise my culinary skills – do something special. Will that be all right?'

'It sounds super. I'm already doing my impression of Spot.'

'Spot?'

'Pavlov's dog.' Still not funny – I was trying too hard.

'I see. Good. Seven thirty for eight, shall we say? Oh, by the way, they are both "Church", but you'd never know it.'

'No problem, I'm looking forward to meeting them.' And to the meal. And you. Most of all, you.

We said our farewells and I replaced the phone. I sat gazing at it for a few moments. It was a simple collection of electrical components and plastic, but it could change a person's world in a few seconds. For some it brought tragedy, for others, more rarely, happiness.

I'd met Annabelle over a year ago, but my pursuit of her would have disgraced a Galapagos Island tortoise. I made Chi-Chi the giant panda look like Young Lochinvar. The fact that her late husband had been a bishop didn't help. Sometimes I wished that she wasn't so attractive. She frightened me. I was scared that, by chasing her, I'd lose her. In twelve months I'd taken her out four times: one meal, two concerts and one visit to the theatre. On three other occasions I'd had to cancel at the last minute because of the job. My wife, Vanessa, left me, she said, because of the loneliness. I don't think I could take that again.

I spun my chair round to face the others, and with an expansive gesture towards the window, said:

'The curfew tolls the knell of parting day,
The lowing herd winds slowly o'er the lea.
The ploughman homeward plods his weary way,

And hopes it's not... brown bread again for tea.'

'Isn't love wonderful?' Sparky sighed, looking at Nigel.

'Yes,' replied Nigel, 'but that will cost you a pound.'

We made it through the day, although Good didn't score any victories in the war against Evil. Several other members of the public were not impressed with their encounters with poetic policemen, but we raised a couple of hundred pounds for the appeal. I hit the ten-pound limit well before lunch, but kept on with the vile verse just for the hell of it. It was fun. About four o'clock the phone was ringing yet again.

'If you're having any trouble,

We'll be with you at the double,' I said into it.

It was the Control Room.

'Then grab your pencil and your book,

And you might just catch a crook,' growled the Sergeant.

Our busiest time is late afternoon, early evening. Kids come home from school, grown-ups from work, and find that their home has been turned over during their absence. This one fitted the pattern.

'I'm all ears, Arthur. Give us the details.'

'It's The Firs, Edgely Lane, off Penistone Road. A couple of Jehovah's Witnesses rang in. They went up the drive to sell their tracts, or whatever, and the door was smashed in. They ran to the next house and phoned us because they felt someone might still be inside. We've a car there, but the birds have flown. Place has been well and truly ransacked. Problem is, the owner's not home yet.'

'They did it!' I declared. 'Chuck 'em in a cell and we'll talk to them in the morning.'

'Can I leave it with you?'

'Oh, OK then, Arthur. We'll look into it.'

'It's the very last house. Will you arrange Scenes of Crime, Charlie?'

'Will do. Thanks.'

I glanced round the office at the gallant body of men I call The Troops. One or two had drifted away, but Dave Sparkington, Nigel and a couple of others were still here. I waved the sheet of paper at Sparky and he came over.

'If that's what I think,

I've just gone for a drink,' he said.

I'd worked with Sparky for years. As far as I was concerned he was the best DC in the force. 'It's a burglary,' I told him. 'Do you want me to send someone else?'

'No, it's only saddle of lamb in red currant sauce for tea; nothing special. Besides, I thrive on work. Let's have a look.' He grabbed the paper and I told him the little I knew.

Nigel had wandered across and was listening. 'I'll go, if you want. I've nothing on tonight,' he volunteered.

'In that case, both of you go,' I suggested. 'It's a posh address and you might recover some of the credibility we've squandered through the day. And take a SOCO with you, they don't know about it, yet.'

Sparky tilted his head on one side for a few moments, then said:

'Away with the SOCO and my trusty Sarge,

We'll catch the burglars but he'll get the credit 'cos he's in charge.'

'It doesn't scan,' said Nigel, testily.

'Well that's what we're collecting for, isn't it?' responded Sparky.

'What?'

'A scanner.'

I couldn't help wondering how well they would
work together. Sparky was a local lad, and always
claimed he'd worn clogs as a kid, but nobody
believed that. After twenty-odd years in the force,
he'd developed a carefully refined brusqueness with
strangers that he loved to display when least expected. Nigel was university-educated and from deepest
Berkshire. After three years he outranked Sparky.
Another three and he could outrank me. He'd never
hold the title of the longestserving inspector the force
had ever had, though. That was mine, and mine
alone.

On the way home I bought a modest bunch of flowers and an extravagant bottle of claret. I had a short
nap, interspersed with pleasant daydreams, while the
water heated, and then showered. I whistled a few
tunes and rubbed great dollops of some smelly blue
jelly over myself. Life was good. God was in his heav-
en. All it had taken was a phone call.

I was ready to leave, resplendent in decent suit and
gaudy tie, when the phone rang again. It was Dave
Sparkington. 'Sorry about this, Charlie' he said, 'but I
think we need you.'

'Why, what's happened?'

'We're still at The Firs. The householder – he's a Mr
Dewhurst – arrived home about thirty minutes ago.
Apparently his daughter is missing. We've made the
obvious enquiries, but we've drawn a blank. It's looking bad.'

If Dave said it was looking bad, then it was. 'How
old is she?' I asked.

'Eight.'

'Oh dear. OK,' I told him, 'I'm on my way. Tell me again what the road's called.'

It could be a false alarm. If we found her in the next hour I could still make it to Annabelle's. On my way out to the car I took off the tie and stuffed it into my pocket.

Edgely Lane is about two hundred yards long. The houses, all rather magnificent and extremely detached, are down one side only. The other side is open country, the view broken by a row of huge beech trees. The lane ends at a farm track, which leads out into the Penistone Road further along. I parked so that I was blocking off the track. Sparky's, the SOCO's and the squad car were all in the road. A fourwheel-drive Nissan Patrol stood on the drive to The Firs. The house probably derived its name from the fifty-foot-tall leylandii that flanked the grounds on three sides. I'm a founder member of the Society for the Abolishment of Leylandii in Suburban Gardens.

I had a quick look round the exterior, then went in. It was easy to see how entry had been gained: the door at the side had been jemmied. Someone had made quite a mess of it. Mr Dewhurst was sitting in the kitchen talking to Sparky, an untouched mug of tea in front of him. The kitchen was large and well equipped, but untidy and not very clean. A bit like mine. Sparky introduced me. Dewhurst surprised me by offering a limp handshake. He was about six feet tall, with short-cropped dark hair and designer stubble. My immediate impression was that he couldn't decide which era he belonged in.

'Where's DS Newley?' I asked Sparky.

'Talking to the neighbours, sir.'

'Good. Where are we so far?'

'According to a little girl a few doors away who goes to the same school, she didn't attend today.'

I turned to address Mr Dewhurst. 'And should she have done?' I asked.

He nodded a yes. This was bad news.

'I see you've already provided DC Sparkington with a photograph.' It was lying on the table between them. 'Do you mind if we borrow it for a short while, sir?'

He shook his head. 'No, of course not,' he mumbled.

It was a school photograph, enlarged and in a decent frame. It showed a dark-haired little girl, wearing spectacles. 'Thanks. Dave, send whoever we've got to City HQ with it to have it copied. We need to get moving before the light goes. And rustle up some extra help.'

Sparky went out with the picture and I sat down opposite Mr Dewhurst. 'First of all, sir, what is your daughter called?'

'Georgina.'

'Nice name. And she is eight years old?'

'Yes.'

'I know you've been through it all with my sergeant, but I'd like you to tell me everything that's happened today. First of all, when did you last see Georgina?'

'This morning.'

'Go on,' I invited.

He looked at the tea, realised it was cold and pushed it away. I didn't suggest making another pot – I wanted to move fast. 'Do you think you'll find her?' he asked. 'There's so many madmen about. The papers are full of...'

'It's a bit early to be thinking like that, Mr Dewhurst. At the moment we're hoping that there's a simple explanation. She's probably at a friend's house, drinking cocoa and watching TV. If you'll just answer a few questions we might know where to look. Tell me about this morning.'

He stared down at the table as he spoke: 'I took her to the bus station in Heckley, like I do every morning. She catches the school bus there.'

'Which school does she attend?'

'KGP.'

King George Preparatory. Fee-paying. 'Pardon me asking, sir, but is there a Mrs Dewhurst?'

He shook his head. 'No, she died over two years ago. Leukaemia.'

'Oh, I am sorry. Can we go back to this morning, please. What time did you drop Georgina at the bus station?'

'About five past eight.'

'And what time does her bus leave?'

'Eight fifteen.'

'Did you see her on to the bus?'

'No. I usually do, but... there was nowhere to park. I was in a hurry. I never thought... never expected...'

'Don't blame yourself. You weren't to know...'

Nigel came into the kitchen. 'Anything from the neighbours?' I asked him.

'No, sir, except that it appears she didn't go to school today.'

'So I heard, but we can't rely on the word of a neighbour's child. Have someone check with the school. Do you know the name of Georgina's teacher, Mr Dewhurst?'

'Yes, it's Miss Aitken.'

Nigel went off to deploy someone to track down Miss Aitken. As he left I asked him to arrange for the farm track to be taped off. There were some good tyre marks on it.

'Is your daughter happy at school, Mr Dewhurst?

Can you think of any reason why she might have played truant?'

He shrugged his shoulders. 'No. She doesn't like school very much, but neither did I. She does fairly well. I don't think she's being bullied or anything.'

'OK. Have you a sheet of paper?' He produced a shopping-list pad out of a drawer. One of those with a pencil attached that looks like a good idea but never gets used.

'Right, sir. I want you to spend the next few minutes making me a list of all these names.' I started writing on the pad.

'I've given the sergeant the names of Georgina's friends,' he said.

'Fair enough, but you might have forgotten a few.'

I wrote:

Close friends at school
    Local friends
    Neighbours
    Relatives
    Favourite auntie or anyone she might turn to if she was unhappy
    Any friends you disapprove of
    Any other names she's ever mentioned
    Favourite places (amusement arcades, cinema, riding school, etc.)
    Where she plays (any dens, favourite walks, etc.)

I was racking my brain for further inspiration when Paul Scott, the Scenes of Crime Officer, popped his head round the door.

'Excuse me, Mr Priest. When you get a minute can I borrow Mr Dewhurst, please?'

'Sure.' I gave Dewhurst the list and gestured for him

to go with the SOCO. I walked outside to my car and rang the Superintendent. The clock on the dashboard said ten to eight.

'Hi, Gilbert,' I sighed wearily, when he answered. 'Sorry to disturb you, but I think we've a heavy one.' I filled him in on the details. While we were talking another squad car and a SOCO van pulled up. Gilbert agreed to arrange for further reinforcements. The idea was that tonight, what was, left of it, we'd hit everyone we could think of with photographs of the girl. In the morning we'd cover the bus station. She had to be somewhere, and somebody knew where that was.

'Gilbert?' I asked, hesitantly, when we'd finished. 'Could you do me a little favour, please?'

'Of course, what is it?'

'I'm supposed to be at Annabelle's at eight. Give her a ring and tell her I'm busy. It'll sound better coming from you.'

He agreed. If the truth were known, Superintendent Gilbert Wood is just as ga-ga about her as I am. Fortunately, he's happily married.

When I went back inside, the SOCO was taking Dewhurst's fingerprints, for elimination purposes. He explained that they would be destroyed in six months, and that Mr Dewhurst could witness this, if he desired, or sign to say he authorised the SOCO to do it in his absence. I don't think he heard a word of it. When they'd finished I sat down and had a long chat with him.

Dewhurst told me he was managing director of his own company, called Eagle Electric. They supplied components to industry and acted as agents for several big manufacturers. In the last few years they had diversified by importing fancy light fittings and sup-plying them to the major department stores. They were designed in this country and made on the cheap in the Far East. It was this side of the business that Dewhurst was most personally involved with.

Every morning he took Georgina for the school bus. In the evening a child minder met her off the bus and looked after her until Mr Dewhurst called for her. Yesterday Georgina hadn't been on it. His mother-in-law, Georgina's grandma, spent a lot of time with them and helped look after her, especially at weekends. She'd been the first person he'd contacted when he discovered that his daughter was missing.

'She's worried sick, same as me,' he said. 'Will it be all right if I go and pick her up? She has her own room here. She's a widow and idolises Georgina. She's her only grandchild.'

'Doesn't your mother-in-law drive?' I asked.

'No. She's quite old and has bad arthritis. I always have to collect her. Thank God I didn't go to Birmingham.'

'Birmingham?'

'Yes,' he sighed. 'My first call this morning was at Ashurst's in Manchester. I got a puncture in their yard. So much for all-terrain vehicles. It put me behind schedule, so I cancelled a couple of late, calls in Birmingham. Otherwise I'd have been home much later. Georgina would have stayed with the child minder.'

'I see. Would you like me to organise a car for your mother-in-law?'

'No. She'd be frightened. It's better if I go, and it'll give me something to do. This waiting's getting me down.'

I wouldn't have sent one with a blue flashing light on the top, but he was probably right. We all have our individual ways of reacting to situations. Dewhurst looked shaken, but he was taking it well. He was grown-up, he read the papers. I refused to discuss the possibilities, but he knew as well as I did that they were frightening. He didn't want me to call his GP for a sedative.

It was nearly one when I arrived home, and I was back at Heckley nick by six-thirty. We had a team meeting in the big conference theatre at ten. Gilbert outlined what was happening, for the benefit of the reinforcements we'd drafted in, and then handed over to me.

'So far,' I told them, 'we've had an astonishing lack of success. The enquiry has been in three main areas, namely, amongst known acquaintances last night; at the bus station this morning; and there is an ongoing physical search. What the link is between the burglary and the missing girl, we do not know. Possibilities that spring to mind are that she came home and disturbed a burglar; or maybe she was abducted in town and then brought home; or maybe there's no link at all. Sergeant Scott was the SOCO. What can you tell us, Paul?'

Paul raised himself from his chair and perched on the corner of the table so he could be heard more clearly. He went straight into it: 'We looked for fingerprints, examined the MO and had a thorough general look-round. We also took plaster casts of tyre tracks in the bridle path at the end of the lane. All prints have been eliminated as belonging to members of the family; the burglars were apparently wearing gloves. We did find suitable smudge marks, and have lifted some glove prints. The most recent set of tyre tracks were made by Mr Dewhurst's four-wheel-drive van. He says he uses the bridle path occasionally to get out on to the main road. The method of entry is interesting. The side door is a double-glazed, PVC effort. Most of our clients can jemmy one open in about three seconds. There are six different sets of marks on this door where the burglar had attempted to gain a purchase. It wasn't a very determined attack. Inside, he had ransacked all the bedrooms. The contents of the drawers were strewn on the floor. I asked Mr Dewhurst to identify where stuff had come from. It appears that the top drawers were emptied first. This is the natural way you or I might act, but, as you all know, not the way a professional thief would do it, In short, gentlemen, we found nothing of any forensic value, but, for what it's worth, I'd say we are looking for an amateur.' He sat down on his chair again.

I stood up: 'Thanks, Paul. Has anyone any questions?'

'Was there an alarm?' someone asked.

'No,' I replied.

'He might bean amateur in practical terms,' someone else suggested, 'but he seems to be well genned-up on the theory if he's got away without leaving a trace behind.'

'Good point,' I said. 'I haven't told you what he stole. It appears that the only thing missing is a small quantity of jewellery, sentimental value only.' I knew what they were thinking, so I said it for them: 'And one little girl,' I added.

Nigel was next in the limelight. He told us about the frantic efforts of the night before to get as many people as possible on the streets armed with photographs. We'd enquired in all the places where she might have been seen and all those where we hoped she hadn't. Nothing.

Acting Detective Sergeant Jeff Caton had supervised the raid on the bus station earlier this morning. Sparky and myself had been there, too. I invited Jeff to say his piece.

'Morning,' he began. 'The KGP school bus is run by Carter's Coaches. It arrives at Heckley bus station at about eight and leaves at eight fifteen, prompt. Yesterday was no exception. The missing girl did not get on it. Her father dropped her off in Bridge Street, right outside the station. Sometimes, if there was a parking space, he would walk through the station to where the coach waited, a distance of approximately seventy-five metres. Yesterday he couldn't find a vacant place, so he double-parked to drop her off. He nipped to the newsagent's kiosk to buy a paper and then left. The proprietor of the kiosk recognised the photograph of Georgina and remembers exchanging pleasantries with her father. He sees them arrive most mornings. Georgina sometimes buys sweets in another shop, but didn't yesterday. Fourteen other people who use the bus station every morning at that time recognised her face. Only two claimed they saw her yesterday. None of the other kids who use the bus saw her, nor did the driver. Somewhere between her dad's car and the school bus she vanished without a trace.' Like a snowflake that falls into the palm of your hand.

Superintendent Wood read a press release he had prepared and told us that he was planning on recording an appeal on television tomorrow morning. None of us felt optimistic as we left the meeting to make our individual contributions to the search. The simple explanation had not been forthcoming; now we were contemplating the grotesque one.

Chapter Three

I went up to Gilbert's office and had a coffee with him. 'Strong, black and preferably with caffeine,' I requested.

'Coming up. Would you like a tot of something stronger in it?'

'No thanks. Did you ring Annabelle?'

He placed the coffees on two mats on his table. 'Yes, she said she understood. She'll realise what it's all about when she reads the papers.' He dunked a digestive biscuit and manoeuvred the soggy mass into his mouth just before it collapsed.

'That's a disgusting habit,' I protested.

'One of life's little comforts, Charlie. Help yourself.' He swallowed the remainder and went on: 'Annabelle's a nice girl. Too good for you, if the truth be known. You'll lose her if you don't watch it.'

'Thanks for the vote of confidence; it's just what I need.'

'No, you don't understand. It's not you, it's the job. Just look at yourself; take stock. You went to art college, got a degree in batik dyeing or something –'

'It was in art.'

'OK, art. You pretend to like decent music, appreciate good food. The fact that you listen to jungle drums and eat rubbish is due to circumstances. You could look reasonably tidy if you changed your clothes more often –'

'I change my clothes as often as anyone,' I protested.

'Well, you always look crumpled. Sometimes I don't know if you're supposed to be a Hell's Angel or an out-of-work violinist.'

'I like looking crumpled. I feel comfortable when

I'm crumpled. And look at yourself. You had that shirt on yesterday.'

'No I didn't.' It was his turn to be indignant.

'Yes you did.'

He looked down at it. 'Did I? Must have picked the wrong one up this morning. Blame it on the early start. Anyhow, we're not talking about me. The point I'm making is that you've some hard thinking to do. Charlie the Artist could just about pull Annabelle. Charlie the Policeman never will. She needs more than you can give her as you are at present, but she's worth the effort. If I were you, I'd make it.'

I hadn't a clue what he was talking about. 'Are you telling me I ought to resign?' I asked, incredulously.

He shook his head. 'No, of course not.' He dunked another biscuit. 'But outside that door all hell's breaking loose, and I'm in here trying to sort out your love life. Last night, if I'd been in your shoes, I'd have gone round to Annabelle's for supper.'

I stared at him for several seconds. 'No you wouldn't,' I declared.

'Yes I would, if I wanted her.'

'I don't believe you. I don't believe you and I think you're wrong.'

'Maybe, maybe not. Now, what are we doing about finding this kid?'

I left Gilbert concocting a speech for the television cameras and drove round to see Mr Dewhurst. A patrol car was parked in the lane. I pulled in behind it and had a word with the driver:

'Is he in?'

'Yes, sir.'

'Any problems with the press or passing ghouls?'

'No, but it suddenly seems a popular road for dog-walkers to use.'

'Does it? Is anybody talking to them?'

'Yes, sir, we are. Most of them say they *didn't* come this way yesterday, but the few who *did* didn't see anything.'

'Fair enough. Keep at it.'

There was a Toyota Supra parked on the drive as well as the Nissan. The registration plate bore Dewhurst's initials, MJD. Personal number plates should be compulsory – they are a lot easier to remember. I glanced round the garden at nothing in particular, then pressed the bell push. I was just considering whether it would be polite to ring again when the door was opened by an elderly lady. I fished in my pocket for my ID card.

'Good morning, I'm Inspector Priest. Is Mr Dewhurst available?'

'Have you found her?' she demanded, and for a brief moment her face lit up with hope.

I shook my head. 'No, I'm sorry, we've no news yet. You must be...?'

'Mrs Eaglin. Georgina's grandma.' Her face sagged back to the hopeless expression it had borne a moment earlier. 'You'd better come in.' She took me through to the sitting room and invited me to sit down. 'Miles is asleep,' she told me. 'We waited up until about four o'clock this morning and then I insisted that he take one of my pills. Do you want me to wake him?'

'No, I'll catch him later. If we have no success today we're thinking about making a television appeal tomorrow morning. We'd need Mr Dewhurst down at the station at about nine thirty, if he agrees to it. Sometimes they produce good results. I'd be grateful if you could forewarn him.'

'What do you think's happened to her, Inspector? She's such a lovely girl...' Mrs Eaglin's eyes filled with tears and she sniffed into a tiny lace handkerchief. Her fingers were clenched as tightly as the arthritis would allow.

When she'd composed herself I said: 'We're hoping that Georgina played truant from school and became too frightened to come home; or maybe she got lost. We're talking to any other children who were absent on Monday. Alternatively, she may have been abducted by, say, a childless woman who wants her for her own daughter. That happens more often than you'd realise.'

I didn't mention that we were dragging the canal, and that the helicopter was scouring the fields and woods with the latest heat-seeking technology. We also had a long print-out of sex offenders, and were slowly working our way through it. Silly men who'd led blameless lives after flashing in the park thirty years ago were having their pasts raked up in front of their families. It hardly seemed fair, but we were grasping at the wind.

'Mrs Eaglin, how did Georgina seem when you last saw her?' I asked.

She lowered the hanky and thought for a few seconds. 'Perfectly normal. In fact she was looking forward to going to school because they were rehearsing for the end-of-term play.'

'Was she in it?' I enquired.

A smile briefly made an appearance, then fled. 'No, but it disrupted lessons. I think that's what she liked it for.'

'When did you see her?'

'Over the weekend. Miles picks me up Friday evening, straight after collecting Georgina from the child minder. He works Saturdays and likes to have a game of golf on Sunday. My husband, George, died nearly seven years ago, so I love to come here and look after Georgina. I sometimes visit through the week, too, especially when Miles has to stay away overnight.'

'And when did you go home?'

'Sunday evening, about seven. They both took me. After dropping me off I believe they were going for a pizza. Not really my cup of tea, and far too late for Georgina, but I'm old-fashioned.'

I declined a drink and left after proffering more empty reassurances. It's a thin line between false hopes and premature gloom. As long as we didn't know, we had to assume she was still alive. Any other attitude was pointless.

On the way back to the station I had a flash of inspiration, so I went via St Bidulph's on the Top Road. Annabelle lives in the Old Vicarage, near the church. In the door pocket of the car was a bottle of claret, and the back seat held a rapidly fading bunch of salmon-pink roses. I stood on her doorstep, bottle in one hand and wilting blooms in the other, rehearsing my lines: 'Sorry I'm late, I was held up.'

But she wasn't in.

Wednesday morning we filmed the TV appeal. The crew set up their cameras and lights in the conference room and the producer went through the scripts with Gilbert and myself. Gilbert introduced me as Acting Chief Inspector Priest.

'What's this Acting Chief bit?' I whispered to him at the first possible opportunity.

'It goes down better with the public,' he replied in a hushed voice. 'Gives you a bit more status.'

'I don't want to be Acting Chief,' I hissed back.

'Well you are.'

'Officially?'

'Yes.'

'Paid?'

'Yes, bloody well paid.'

Our whispers were growing louder and faces were turning towards us. 'Are you trying to get rid of me, Gilbert?'

The Super's face was red with frustration and he thumped a palm with a fist.

'For Christ's sake, Charlie, I thought I was doing you a favour!'

'Oh. Well, thanks.'

I liked being the longest-ever-serving inspector. I'd been as young as it was possible to be when appointed, and then made no further progress up the ladder. It was a record I was proud of. Out of the corner of my eye I saw Mr Dewhurst going into the toilets.

'Excuse me,' called the producer. 'We'll begin if you're all ready. You first, Superintendent. Quiet, please.'

'You're on,' I said to Gilbert, adding: 'You won't mind if I go to wave Willy at the wall, will you?'

In the gents', Dewhurst was standing at the wash-basins, running water into one of them. He looked up as I entered and we exchanged polite but grim nods. He left as I was having my pee. I washed my hands in the sink next to the one he'd used and followed him out.

There was another delay for some reason. Mrs Eaglin was standing with Dewhurst, giving him support before his ordeal by television. He had the worst part of all. Eventually they were ready and the producer called for Gilbert again. As he was leaving me I told him: 'Your hair's sticking up at the back, Gilbert.'

He gave it a perfunctory wipe with his hand.

'No,' I said, 'it's still sticking up. You ought to comb it.'

'Bloody hell, Charlie!' he hissed at me. 'It's not a frigging game show. What's got into you?'

Gilbert had one minute to tell the story so far; then Dewhurst did his bit. It was harrowing. He broke down and wept and couldn't finish off what he wanted to say. Nearly everybody in the room was crying with him, some openly, some internally. Then I had to go on and tell people where to come with their information. I don't envy newsreaders: I felt shagged-out when it was over.

The film was shown locally on the lunchtime news, and broadcast nationally in the evening. The response was phenomenal. We imported extra staff to man the computers. Over the next three weeks every single lead was followed, and every one of them took us up a dead end. Georgina Dewhurst had vanished from the face of the globe as effectively as if she had never existed.

We checked over three hundred alibis and made thirty-one arrests. Of these, only two reached the 'helping us with our enquiries' stage. 'Georgina – Man Detained' screamed the headlines in the tabloids. We were only going through the motions, though. The first was Billy Sunshine. Billy stands just outside the bus station most days, rocking gently backwards and forwards on the balls of his feet. He usually has a bottle sticking out of his jacket pocket and a big smile for everyone who passes by. There had been one report of a little girl being seen hand-in-hand with a man heading away from the area. A scruffy man – it could have been Billy. He'd been shown the photo on the Tuesday morning and said he recognised her. We kept him in overnight and gave him breakfast. He had a better alibi than

Nixon when Kennedy was shot, so we handed him over to the detox centre.

The other one was more like it. It wasn't as a result of fine detective work – someone wrote us an anonymous letter. Terry Finnister lived in Workington, but had delivered a lorryload of bathroom equipment to a company in Heckley early that Monday morning. And, the letter-writer kindly advised us, he was a convicted sex offender. They went on to give us some advice on how to treat his sort. I took Nigel to Workington to have a word with him, and we brought him back to Heckley.

It was a mess. When he'd been a teenager his mother had remarried. Her new husband had a young son. Finnister served five years for buggering the child while baby-sitting. During the interview he told us that his stepfather had raped him, and that his mother had died of an overdose while he was in jail. At the time of Georgina's disappearance he'd been off-loading two dozen avocado, low-level, easy-flush toilet pedestals, and he had the invoices to prove it; plus a receipt for his breakfast, eaten shortly afterwards. We asked the local SOCO to give the cab of his lorry a going-over, but we lacked enthusiasm.

The Reverend Gerry Wilde, vicar of St Peter and St Paul's, was annoyed; or as annoyed as he ever allowed himself to become. His hatchback crested the brow in the road where he gained his first view of St Peter and St Paul's. He always looked forward to that dramatic moment. First the trees loomed up out of the ground, then they appeared to swing to one side as the road curved, revealing the majestic prospect of his church. Normally, the Union flag, taut in the stiff breeze, would have added an extra *frisson* of delight. The

Reverend Wilde was firstly a man of God, and secondly a patriot. Not that he would have separated them in that way. For him, the two conditions were so tightly intertwined that he could not understand how anyone could claim to be one without the other. Certainly not if one was an Englishman. But today the flag was an aberration. Three times he'd told Joseph, the verger, to take it down; and there it still was, four days after Coronation Day, proclaiming heaven-knows-what to the parish. Soon it would have to go up again for the Duke of Edinburgh's birthday, but it made a mockery of his efforts if the two events ran together.

He put the car in its garage alongside the vicarage. He'd have to have a word with Joseph – be more firm with him. He hated any form of unpleasantness, though. And, of course, Joseph had worshipped here all his life, whereas he was a newcomer, relatively speaking.

No, he'd teach by example. Jesus washed His disciples' feet; he, Gerry Wilde, would strike the flag. Then he would leave it for Joseph to put away. Maybe that would impress upon the old man that he meant what he said. He took his tower key from its hook in the kitchen and set off across the graveyard to the church.

In the ringing chamber the six hemp ropes, with their coloured sallies, hung through the guides in the ceiling. The vicar noted that one rope was shorter than the others. That meant that the big tenor bell was in the vertical position, on the backstroke, ready to be set swinging with the minimum of effort at the next bell-ringing session. He locked the chamber door behind him and put the key in his pocket. If he was going up the tower he didn't want anybody touching the ropes.

One ton of bell was poised to fall – he didn't want it falling on him.

He was puffing like an asthmatic tuba player when he reached the belfry, and the pain in his chest had returned. Fortunately it was the wrong side for his heart. There was a walkway skirting the bells, with a handrail for extra safety. Nevertheless he kept a wary eye on the inverted tenor as he made his way to the bottom of the wooden ladder that led the last few feet up on to the roof.

The bolt in the trap door slid back easily, and a moment later the Reverend was outside, on the roof of his tower. He'd only been up here a couple of times before. The noise was deafening. What had been a moderate breeze at ground level was a gale at this height. The flag material was slapping and cracking with a ferocity that seemed as if it would rip to shreds, and the ropes were lashing against the mast. First of all he wanted to admire the view. He'd heard that you could see Lincoln Cathedral from up here. He peered in the right direction in vain. A few degrees to the left the columns of steam from the Trent Valley power stations were plainly visible.

'Twentieth-century cathedrals,' said the vicar with distaste, and started pulling on the rope.

He untied the flag and bundled it into his arms – it was impossible to fold in the swirling wind. As he was walking towards the trapdoor a wayward corner flapped up across his face. He pulled it away with his hand, but this allowed another fold of material to fall to the floor. The Reverend Wilde's right foot stepped on it and his left one became tangled in the beloved flag. He fell headlong into the open trap. His arms were enmeshed, so he could not use them to halt his progress, and he shot head first down the wooden steps, like a tobogganist down the Cresta run. Had there been anybody else in the church they would have heard the crack of his neck snapping as he hit the bottom, but there wasn't.

Chapter Four

Big Bernard Firth, captain of the team of bell-ringers at St Peter and St Paul's, was last to arrive for their weekly practice session of the Exercise, as they called it. He unlocked the door to the ringing chamber with his personal key and they went in. One of the others switched on the spotlights that were fixed to the ceiling, bathing the floor of the room in a dramatic glow.

'Right,' said Bernard, 'let's not mess about, I'm thirsty already. You lot pull off and I'll catch up.'

The other five began pulling on the ropes of the lighter bells, setting them swinging silently in the belfry. As they swung higher, almost reaching the vertical, the clappers struck the sides, causing them to sound. Soon they fell into the familiar rhythm. Bernard grasped the brightly coloured sally at the end of his rope and watched and listened for his cue to commence.

The vicar's body lay on the Union Jack, on the walkway that skirted the bells. The wind had teased and pulled at the flag until a large portion of it was enveloping the wheel and rope of the tenor bell. Bernard Firth tightened his grip, recognised his opening, and pulled.

'Bloody 'ell, it's stiff,' he cried, as the big bell came over the centre and started to fall, but without its usual urgency.

"Spect it's full of pigeon shit,' declared one of his colleagues.

'Ask Gerry to tell old Joe to oil the bearings,' suggested another.

'What's happened to Gerry? Nobody's seen him for two days,' stated a third.

At that moment the ceiling above them exploded.

For the briefest second they all saw the vicar hurtling out of the floodlights, Union Jack trailing behind, like a victorious Olympic skydiver on his lap of honour. Then he thudded, leadenly, on to the stone-flagged floor. They stood in a circle, open-mouthed and horrified, gazing at the broken heap at their centre, oblivious to the bells above them saying: *Dong-ding-dong... dong-a-dong... ding-dong... dong... dong... dong.*

The search for little Georgina was fruitless and depressing. We conferred with other forces who had missing kids on their books but it was a futile exercise. Usually there was a car or a stranger spotted near the scene of the disappearance, but we didn't even have that. Most had occurred in rural areas or on quiet council estates, but this one had happened in the middle of town during the rush hour. Only the grief was the same. You can only put all your resources into a job like this for so long. The world doesn't stand still while you look for a lost child. Slowly the urgency drains away as you run out of places to look, suspects to interview. Other crimes, some serious, demand attention, so you have to divert officers towards them. And every day that passes saps what little faith you had that you would find her alive.

Then the note came.

Dewhurst rang the office at eight in the morning to say that there was a ransom demand in his post. I told him not to touch it again and to wait. We were with him in ten minutes.

He'd opened the letter in the kitchen, standing at the worktop. It's not the way I would have expected a businessman to conduct his affairs, but he said the envelope had caught his eye. Normally one glance tells him what's inside, but he hadn't recognised this one,

so he'd opened it. It sounded reasonable. The address
on the white self-sealing envelope was typed on a
label. The note, lying alongside, had resumed its folded position. I smoothed it out, using my pen and a
fingernail. It was composed of letters cut from newspapers and glued to a sheet of white paper, like you see in
TV thrillers, except that all the letters were of different
sizes. It said:

> RAISE HALF A MILLION IN NEXT
> 7 DAYS TO SEE HER AGAIN. CASH

Our tame forensic boffins are at Wetherton, about fifty
miles away. I manoeuvred the letter and envelope into
a plastic bag and labelled it CP4, with the date, while
Sparky raised one of the Nigel Mansells in Traffic to
rush it there. Then I rang Professor Van Rees and asked
him to give it the full treatment.

Van Rees is a magician. Everywhere we go, everything we touch, we leave something behind and we
take something with us. It's called the Exchange
Principle. A hair, a flake of skin or a bead of sweat;
that's all he needs. Eighty per cent of the human race
are what's known as secretors. They leak blood cells
into their other body fluids. The letter was the first and
only contact we'd had with Georgina's kidnapper.
With just a little piece of luck the Professor would be
able to give us a genetic profile that would pick him
out of a trillion zillion others. All we'd have to do was
test them all.

'How much does a DNA analysis cost?' asked
Sparky, as we drove back to the station.

'Not much these days,' I replied.

'Could be just a nutter, jumping on the bandwagon,
you know.'

'Well, he's still lowlife. He deserves to be behind bars.'

Sparky was silent for a while, except for the noise he makes when he clucks his tongue against the roof of his mouth. He does it when he's deep in thought.

'What y'thinking?' I asked.

He pondered for a moment, then said: 'The note.'

'What about it?'

'It was odd. I want to see the photos when Traffic gets back to us.'

'Yeah. I would have liked to have studied it more. What was odd about it?'

'I'm not sure. I've seen one or two similar ones, but that one frightened the willies out of me. I think it was meant to.'

'You mean it was done for theatrical effect? Melodrama?'

'Mmm, something like that.'

We were approaching a pub where we occasionally ate and imbibed. 'Fancy an early lunch?' I asked.

'No thanks, Charlie. Wife's packed me some sandwiches.'

'Sugar! Looks like it's the canteen again.'

We'd asked the lab to rush us some copies of the ransom note. As soon as the Traffic officer brought them to me I distributed the prints to everyone concerned and sent the negative to our photographers to have some more made. Then I settled down to study it.

Sparky was right, and I could see why. A rational person wouldn't normally communicate by cutting letters out of a newspaper and sticking them together again. But if he did, if he was just, say, halfway rational, then he'd probably use letters that were all approximately the same size. There are plenty to choose from in any paper. If he wanted a Q he might have to look for a little one somewhere in the text, but he should have no problems finding a decent-sized E or S.

But our man wasn't even halfway rational. The note was comprised of letters that covered the full range of sizes available. Some out of the headlines, some from the smallest text. Four words – in, to, her and cash – were complete, cut directly from the little print. The overall effect was a sinister look that went far beyond the meaning of the message.

Or maybe I underestimated the author: maybe he was rational; maybe he knew exactly what he was doing.

I propped my copy of the note against the telephone and stared at it for several minutes, pencil hovering over a blank foolscap pad. The biggest letters were unusual. I'd studied lettering at art college, in my Age of Innocence, and could see that the proportions were wrong. They were in the style of the Roman, or Trajan, alphabet, but the vertical lines were much too broad when compared to the classical proportions of the original. It would be reasonably simple to find which newspaper used a typeface like that. I copied them on to the virgin pad:

E M O N Y

An anagram of MONEY. That wasn't too difficult.

Several other letters were in the same style, but slightly smaller. I wrote them down. They were:

R S E X S E

The X should be a giveaway. I said it to myself over and over again: X... X....X... How about EXPRESS? I wrote it on the pad.

It worked, but express had a surplus P. I carefully traced my pencil across the photo of the note. There was no P in it. The writer had no need for that letter. He'd obviously carved up the headings MONEY and EXPRESS before he'd set to work with the paste pot.

I looked through the window of my little room to see who was in the general office. Nigel was busy at his desk. I waved my arms above my head to attract his attention, but he stayed resolutely engrossed in whatever he was doing. Picking up the telephone to speak to someone fifteen feet away represented the triumph of technology over humanity, and I was damned if I was going to be a party to it. I hurled my pencil at the pane of glass that separated us and he looked up.

'You rang, boss?' he said as he came through the door.

'Yes. Does anyone in the office take the *Daily Express*, do you know?'

'Well, yes. Everyone, I expect.'

'Everyone?' I echoed.

'I'm not sure. Nearly everyone.'

'Jesus,' I sighed, sliding my notes and the photo across to him.

After he'd studied them for a few seconds, enlightenment flickered across his face. I said: 'It looks as if he carved up those two words to make his note. If we put them back together and see what's printed on the back, we should be able to pin down the edition he used.'

Nigel nodded his approval.

'Which information,' I continued, 'will be about as illuminating as a cement lightbulb.' It wasn't exactly a piece of the jigsaw; more like just one of the broken-off joining bits. Blue, out of the sky.

I rang Professor Van Rees and told him what we'd found. After he'd finished his other tests he would fax

the back of the words to the *Express* and see what they
came up with. He was pessimistic about his findings
so far. The envelope and address label were self-adhe-
sive; nobody had licked them. There were no fingerprints. It looked as if our man had worn a space suit
when he made the note. I mentally moved astronauts
further up the list of suspects.

Van Rees came back to me the next day, which was
quicker than I'd expected. He hadn't done any DNA
analyses because there was nothing to analyse. The
note was healthier than a bridegroom's armpit. The
only good news was that the *Express* had identified the
issue. The kidnapper had cut the letters from a *Sunday
Express* dated early April, six weeks before the kidnapping. The self-sealing envelope and the glue came
from Woolworth's, and there was nothing distinctive
about the scissors he'd used.

'I'm sorry I haven't more to tell you, Mr Priest,' Van
Rees said. 'The man you're looking for has been
painstakingly careful. I wish I could be more helpful.'

'I'm sure you've done all you can, Professor,' I
replied. 'And maybe you've told us more than you
realise.'

'I'm afraid I don't follow.'

'Well, maybe he's so cautious because he has to be.
He might be known to us. Perhaps he's right under our
noses.'

Some evidence would have been useful, though.

We didn't need the big conference room for our meetings any more. Four of us sat in the small incident
room we had been allocated, together with the civilian computer operator. The first team consisted of
myself, DS Newley, DC Mad Maggie Madison, Dave

Sparkington and Luke, our wizard of the keyboard. His terminal was linked to HOLMES, the national major enquiry computer. He had at his fingertips just about everything we knew about anyone. Ask him for information about, say, thefts of ladies' knickers from washing lines, in Dorset, in the last five years, and he'd have a print-out for you in minutes. We had a mountain of them to prove it.

'So he wrote the letter nearly three months before he posted it,' said Maggie.

'And two months before he did the kidnapping,' added Nigel.

'Yes. Unless he used an old newspaper from the pile under the sink. If you were making a note like this one, Dave, would you use any old paper or would you go out and buy one specially for the job?'

'He bought it specially, together with a packet of envelopes, some blank paper and a stick of glue. No doubt about it.'

'OK,' I said. 'In that case, did he have anyone specific in mind when he wrote the note?'

'Yes,' replied Sparky. The other two nodded in agreement.

'Because of the *her* in the note?'

More nods.

'And the half-million,' added Sparky. 'I'd guess that's about what Dewhurst could raise.'

'What's happening about the money, boss?' asked Maggie.

'Barclay's are holding it for us and it's being marked. It should be ready in good time.'

We'd had one reconstruction of Georgina's last walk across the bus station, and talked about the possibility of another. None of us was optimistic.

'C'mon, Luke,' I said, trying to inject some enthusiasm into the team. 'What does Sherlock say? Why not just ask it "Who did it?"'

He grinned. He was about half my age, and light years from all of us in style. When he first came to us Sparky asked him if he bought his clothes from a Punch and Judy man. He was good with the computer, though, and had a pleasant personality.

'Did any of you see the late film last night?' he asked. None of us had. 'It was brilliant,' he went on. 'There was this FBI agent who was descended from Sioux Indians. When he had this difficult murder to solve he went out and listened to the wind, and the answer came to him.'

'Thank you for that contribution, Luke,' said Sparky. 'It's about as useful as anything else we've got so far.'

'That's true, I'm afraid,' I agreed. 'So what are we all doing for the rest of the day?' I looked at Nigel first.

He had some files from other forces that he wanted to look at again. They were about kidnappings that had gone unsolved and kidnappers who were back on the streets. Not too many of them, though – it's not a British crime.

Maggie was our liaison with the family. Miles Dewhurst was burying himself in his work, but she tried to see him every day, or at least talk to him on the phone. She saw more of Mrs Eaglin, Georgina's grandma, and was giving her all the support she could. That was where she was going next.

DS Sparkington was doing some follow-up interviews – seeing people who hadn't been in when we called, or who couldn't remember where they were at the fateful time. Luke was putting Van Rees's report on file.

That left me. I went upstairs to see the Super.

'The bottom line, Gilbert,' I told him, 'is that he's clever, he's had it planned for a long time, and I'm confident that he's known to us.'

Gilbert pondered on what I'd said. 'So couldn't Forensic come up with anything at all with the note?' he asked.

I shook my head. 'Nope, nothing at all.'

'What about the typed address?'

'Done on a computer. Laser jet printer, impossible to trace. They're not like your old Remingtons, I'm afraid.'

'In that case, why didn't he print the whole bloody note on it?'

'Good point. Maybe he didn't know that it was untraceable. I wasn't sure myself until I asked. Sparky thinks the note was designed for theatrical effect.'

'You mean it's just someone making mischief?'

'Mmm.'

'Jesus Christ! Makes you wonder just who's out there. Do you need anybody else?'

'No, not at the moment, thanks.'

I was walking across to the door when Gilbert said: 'So what's your next move, Charlie?'

I paused with my hand on the handle. 'I'm trying a new technique this afternoon,' I replied.

'Oh, what's that?'

'I'm driving up on to the moors and I'm going to sit on a wall and listen to the wind.'

'Well, don't try pissing into it,' he called after me.

The idea appealed to me. Wildernesses have a way of helping you put things in perspective. The moors I live on the edge of have seen it all, heard it all. I love walking across them, the wind lashing my hair and the shadows of the clouds racing across the hillsides.

They speak to me, too, in their way. There are ghosts up there. They tell of hardship and cruelty; vast wealth for a few, and indescribable poverty and degradation for the rest. They don't come up with names, unfortunately.

For that I needed evidence. Van Rees's new fangled DNA tests and Luke's computer were more likely to produce the goods, than any half-baked voodoo. About four o'clock I swung the Cavalier into the drive of The Firs, Edgely Lane, and switched off the engine.

Dewhurst's big Nissan Patrol was standing on a paved area alongside his garage. That could mean he was using the Toyota. He'd told me that he saved it for 'best', such as when he was likely to be entertaining clients, or needed to cover large distances as swiftly as possible. The Nissan was his workhorse, handy for carrying samples or delivering rush orders. I did a rough calculation of their value. It came to about twice my annual salary.

The house looked quiet. It's hard to put a finger on the reason, but you can usually tell when a house is empty. I gave the doorbell a perfunctory stab with a finger and turned to survey the garden. It was about a hundred yards long, but only as wide as the house. A paved area, with rusting barbecue, gave way to lawns which stretched down to an orchard.

For late June the weather was bloody awful. Black clouds were piling up and the tops of the big fir trees gave a sudden shudder as the beginnings of a cold front caught them. The leylandii reminded me of a Van Gogh painting, done when the black dog of depression was at its most rabid. I shivered and turned up my jacket collar.

His grass was short and neat. There were even parallel lines up and down the lawn, left by the mower.

The ground was soft, so I walked flat-footed, trying not to leave too many prints behind. Dewhurst didn't spend enough time at home to do it himself, so he must have a gardener. I couldn't see any point in having it all dug up. Not yet.

At the front it was rose beds and an ornamental pool, with concrete cherub. Presumably, in more happy times, it peed into the pond. Then there was the Nissan. Dewhurst had used it on the Friday before Georgina disappeared, on the Sunday when they took Mrs Eaglin home, and also on the Monday morning.

I wandered round it, looking in through the windows. It didn't look anything special. There was a road atlas on the front seat and a pair of Ray-Bans above the dashboard. Otherwise it was neat and tidy. It was neat and tidy underneath, too. In fact, the whole thing was gleaming like a politician's smile. I ran my hand inside the wheel arches, like a motherin-law feeling the tops of the doors, and inspected my fingers. Spotless. I'd put some plastic bags in my boot, in case I collected a few specimens, but it looked as if I wouldn't need them.

The spare wheel on a Nissan Patrol is carried underneath, at the back, exposed to all the spray from the road. This one was wrapped in black plastic to keep it clean. It was a sensible precaution. I knelt down and reached through to feel the top of the wheel. My hand came back grimy. The front of the spare was probably caked in mud. I needed a sample of that mud, just for the records.

But first I needed the help of a mechanic. A single nut held the wheel in position, but I had nothing that would undo it. I went over to my carr and telephoned the station garage. Nobody was available. It was late and they'd all gone home. I rang Jimmy Hoyle.

Jimmy owns a little garage in Heckley. He services cars for a few regular customers and is an expert with a spray gun. My father left me an old Jaguar when he died and Jimmy helped me restore it. We've been pals since we played in the same football team. I'd just joined the force and I helped him steer his way out of some trouble. I took a risk, but he's never forgotten it.

'Sheepshagger! What do you want?' he greeted me.

'Hiya, baboon features. How did you know I wanted something?'

'You always want something. I haven't seen you since you hit the big time bustin' that drugs gang.'

'Ah, the ABC gang, Mr Cakebread and his pals. Those were the days. You know where I live, Jimmy; you're welcome to call in with a bottle any time. Bring a tin of salmon and I'll make you a sandwich.'

'I'll pass, if you don't mind, Charlie. I don't want to be around when someone puts a bomb under your car.'

'When I woke up this morning there was a horse's head in my bed.'

'I'm not surprised.'

'It was a right bugger trying to get the milk float back down the stairs. Listen, I didn't have to come to you. I've got other friends I haven't used yet.' I told him what the problem was and he was with me in fifteen minutes. After casting an expert eye under the Nissan he declared: 'It needs what we technicians call a twenty mil. socket. Won't be a mo.'

I collected a few plastic bags out of my boot and gave them to him. 'Put as much of the mud as you can in these, please. I'll stand at the gate and watch for the owner coming back.'

Jimmy looked at me in alarm. 'You mean he doesn't know you're doing this?'

'No.'

'Chuffin' 'eck. 'Ave you got a warrant?'

'No. Get on with it.'

'Chuffin' 'eck. Does this make me an accessory after the fact?'

'No, just an accessory.'

'What's the difference?'

'It's more serious.'

'Chuffin' 'eck.'

Jimmy sprawled on the ground at the back of the vehicle and I stood at the gate looking down towards the Penistone Road. A few big blobs of rain made dark spots on the pavement. Right on cue, the white shark-nose of the Toyota came into view, paused in the middle of the road for a moment while the traffic cleared, then swung into the lane.

'Jimmy! He's here,' I called. 'Pack up quick! Pretend you've been messing with my car.'

I walked into the road to stall Dewhurst. Fortunately Jimmy's van was blocking the entrance to the drive, so he'd have to wait until it was moved before he could go in.

The Supra came to a silent halt and the nearside window slid down. I squatted on my heels so that my face was level with it and Dewhurst leaned across.

'What's happened? Has something happened?' he asked. He sounded agitated.

'No, Mr Dewhurst, nothing's happened. I'm sorry to startle you like this. I just called in to see you, but when I tried to start the car again it wouldn't work. I sent for a mechanic and he's just fixing it. He won't be long. Have you heard anything?'

He hadn't. I asked him if Maggie had spoken to him today. I knew that she rang him early every morning and tried to see him in the evening. He was full of praise for her, and said he was grateful for the support she was giving Mrs Eaglin. After a few minutes Jimmy joined us. He did well.

'It's fixed, Mr Priest. Will there be anything else?'

'Not for now, Jimmy. Thanks a lot. Will you send me a bill, please?'

'It'll be in the post tomorrow. Will you, er, be needing a VAT receipt or will it be, er, cash?'

Cheeky sod. He moved his van and the Supra turned silently into the drive, as if driven by electricity. The garage door swung up and Dewhurst drove straight in. When he joined me again he was carrying a fat briefcase. After a few flashes and beeps the garage door closed itself and we went into the house.

Dewhurst hung his jacket on a hanger, filled the kettle and flopped into an easy chair, gesturing towards another for me.

I sat down and said: 'I thought I'd come to tell you that Barclay's bank are holding the money for us. As soon as you hear anything else we can have it over here.'

'The full half-million?' he asked.

'Yes.'

'Genuine money?'

'The real stuff. It's being secretly marked, but otherwise it's kosher.'

'Heavens. So if this money is handed over, who pays?'

'We do. The state.'

'But you'd expect to be able to follow it? You'd want to make the handover yourselves?'

I shook my head. 'Not because of the money. We'd want to handle it because we'd stand a better chance of getting Georgina back.' I stopped myself from saying 'alive'.

He was quiet for a while, then he said: 'I have to tell you, Inspector, that I'm making efforts myself to raise the money.'

I said: 'That's not necessary,' but he wasn't listening.

He went on: 'Six months ago I received an offer for Eagle. I turned it down, but I've just asked them if they're still interested. I'm trying to sell the house, too.'

'We already have the money, Mr Dewhurst. It's imperative that as soon as you hear anything you let us know. We can handle it best. You'll be involved every inch of the way. Understand?'

He nodded. Beyond him, through the window, I could see the Nissan, its shape distorted by the rain running down the glass. I wondered if Jimmy had managed to obtain a sample for me. I was painfully aware that I was floundering with this one. All we had to go on was the fact that we had nothing to go on.

'There is one other thing,' I said. He looked at me. 'The ransom note. The forensic people have found a spot of saliva or sweat on it. They can tell a person's blood group from something like that. Trouble is, it could be yours or mine. I've already given a sample. I wonder if you could make an appointment with Dr Evans – he's near Heckley nick – in the next couple of days. Just for elimination purposes. I'll give you his number.'

In the kitchen the kettle clicked off as it came to the boil. I didn't stay for a cuppa with him. I might be a bastard, but I've got my limits. I climbed straight into the car and drove home. If I hadn't been in so much of a hurry I'd have heard the wind, soughing in the tree-tops.

Chapter Five

It was the earliest I'd been home for months. First thing I did was ring Jimmy Hoyle. The rain was bouncing knee high off the garden, so I hadn't bothered to have a look in the boot to see if he'd collected anything for me.

'Hi, Catfish. Thanks for coming out. Did you manage to get me a sample.'

'A sample? I nearly donated one myself when you shouted,' he said. 'I scraped some mud into the bag you gave me, but when he came I just stuffed the whole lot in and put it in your boot. He'll notice that his spare wheel isn't wrapped up any more.'

I could tell from his voice that his adrenalin was still high. He'd enjoyed the whole thing.

'Never mind. He'll just assume the cover blew off when he was doing a ton on the motorway. I'll send it to the lab tomorrow. Well done. You'll have to let me know what I owe you.'

'It's OK. Buy me a pint sometime.'

I'd known he'd say that. I'd drop him a bottle of whisky when I got the chance.

I was sick of takeaways, so I cooked for a change. I had turkey, with stuffing, chipolata, sprouts, potatoes, carrots and gravy. It only took six minutes in the microwave.

For pudding I rang Annabelle.

'Hello, Charles,' she said warmly, 'this is a pleasant surprise.'

'I just thought I'd better ring now and again, before you forgot my name,' I told her.

'I don't think there is any chance of that,' she

replied, 'but it is still nice to talk to you. I know how busy you must be. Are you any nearer the end of it?'

'No, we're batting in the dark, swiping at shadows. Our luck will change, though, hopefully.'

'I saw the appeal on television. It was heart-rending listening to that poor man, her father. How can he ever recover from something like this?'

'He can't.' As soon as the conversation was back on a less traumatic level I said: 'I'm not eating too well, and I've been hungering for a nice, man-sized T-bone. Would you care to join me over the weekend? You could have a juicy tenderloin, grilled to your own taste and served on a bed of lettuce with half a tomato, two onion rings and seventeen sharply point-ed chips.'

'Mmmmmm,' she replied, 'sounds deeelicious. You really know the way to a girl's heart.'

'Is that an affirmative?' I chuckled.

'I'm sorry, Charles. Now it is my turn to back out. I've arranged to go to Northampton over the weekend. It's a long-standing arrangement and I don't really want to cancel it. You won't be too disappointed if I decline, will you?'

'Yes. Terribly. If we ever do meet again we'll have to compare diaries, but I wouldn't dream of expecting you to cancel. Never mind; the main thing is that you still remember me.'

'Of course I still remember you, dumbo. You are the short, bald one with the walking stick, aren't you? Aren't you?'

'That's me.'

'Listen, Charles, talking about food, I'm worried about how well you are eating. You will make yourself ill if you don't look after yourself. What have you had tonight?'

'I've done well tonight. I had turkey and vegetables and all the trimmings. Christmas dinner.'

'Frozen. That's awful! It's not good for you. What do you have for lunches?'

'Bacon sandwich in the canteen. Very streaky bacon. Followed by a cream bun and a quart of strong tea. Frugal but nourishing.'

'Just as I thought. Oh, Charles, what are we going to do with you? I'm busy the next couple of days, but I will be at home on Friday. Will you be able to make it here for lunch then?'

Try to stop me. It was nice being bossed about by a beautiful woman, although I knew I'd never understand them. I had a can of Newcastle Brown, showered and went to bed early. In the shower I did my Leonard Cohen sings Placido Domingo act. In bed I didn't dream about a little girl; not for a long while.

'I like the tie, boss,' Nigel told me as we congregated in my little office.

'Thank you. It is rather nice, isn't it?'

'Jumble sale?' suggested Sparky.

'Actually, it's a Hockney. Bought it at his exhibition in Saltaire. We'll hang on a bit because I've asked Mr Wood to join us. No point in repeating everything.'

'Did you go to college with him?' asked Maggie.

'Mr Wood? No, he was educated by the Jesuits. Or was it the Innuits?'

'I think Maggie meant David Hockney,' explained Nigel.

'Heck, no. He's six or seven years older than me. And our art schools were about two hundred miles apart. And severial light years.'

Severial was a local pronunciation, for Nigel's benefit.

'What sort of painting did you specialise in?' he enquired.

'Nudes,' Sparky chipped in. 'That was the only way he could get women to take their clothes off for him. Am I right?'

'As always, Dave,' I replied.

He warmed to his theme: 'He was a pubist. You might not know it, but Charlie founded a school called pubism. Spent his formative years painting hairy mots.'

Dave had rekindled some fond memories for me. I smiled and replied: 'Actually, in those days they were always shaven.'

The Super walked in and saved the conversation from further degeneration. 'What were always shaven? Good grief, where did you find that tie, Charlie?' he demanded as he sat down.

'It's a long story, boss. OK, Maggie, take it from the top.'

She coughed and flicked open her notebook. 'Right,' she began. 'I've spent much of the week talking to Mrs Eaglin and Mr Dewhurst. He's been busier than ever. I've spoken with him on the telephone twice a day, but only managed to catch him face to face once.'

'What's his excuse?' asked Gilbert.

'Just busy, sir; trying to catch up, throwing himself into his work, that sort of thing.'

'Mmm. And his attitude? To you, I mean?'

'Tolerant, but strained. When I meet him his face falls for a moment, then he smiles. He says he appreciates our concern, but it doesn't show. Except about his mother-in-law. He seems genuinely grateful for the time we're spending with her.'

'I see. Go on.'

'Well, the gist is, so far he hasn't heard anything

more from the kidnappers. That's up to eight o'clock this morning.' Maggie paused for a drink of coffee. She turned the page and went on: 'Charlie, er, Mr Priest, asked me to do some probing with Mrs Eaglin. It wasn't very pleasant. She's opened her heart to me over the last few weeks, regarded me as a friend, so it seemed dishonest to put the policewoman's hat back on, without telling her.'

'Yes, I can imagine,' said Gilbert. 'But it's kinder than inviting her to the station to answer a few questions. At least I hope it is.'

'Probably. Well, here's what I've found, for what it's worth. Eagle Electrical was founded by George Eaglin, Georgina's grandad. Miles Dewhurst was the chief sales engineer. After a whirlwind courtship he married Janet, their daughter. Mr and Mrs Eaglin weren't very pleased about it at the time, but when Janet gave birth to a daughter six months later they decided it had probably been for the best. And Dewhurst did well for the company. Built it up to what it is today – Mrs Eaglin gave him full credit for that. Old George Eaglin died of a brain tumour just after Georgina was born. In his will he left Eagle Electrical to Janet, his daughter, with a few provisions for Mrs Eaglin. That's about it.' She closed her book and had another drink of coffee.

Gilbert didn't have any questions, so I thanked Maggie and invited Nigel to speak.

'I've had a long conversation with Mr Wylie,' he told us. 'He's a partner at Dean and Mason, solicitors for the Eaglins and also the Dewhursts. I told him that it was off the record, but we believed that Dewhurst was trying to raise the ransom money himself. I told them what we were doing and that we were worried that he might try to act unilaterally.'

Gilbert winced. 'On his own?'

'Yes, sir. They were sympathetic. Apparently Dewhurst has asked them to arrange the sale of his house and the company. They're trying to resurrect the offer that was made a while back. Meanwhile they have heard, unofficially, that he's borrowed heavily against the properties from his business contacts.'

'How do you hear something like that unofficially?' asked Gilbert.

I shook my head.

'Talk at the golf club,' suggested Sparky. 'Or at the lodge. They all urinate in the same receptacle.'

'Oh, no,' groaned Gilbert. 'Not the Freemasons. Don't start Charlie off about them again.'

'That wasn't me. It was Wassock Willis,' I protested. Willis was one of my sergeants, now moved on.

Sparky leaned back in his chair, his face bearing a satisfied grin. He'd succeeded in goading Gilbert and myself into bickering. I kicked his shin under the table.

'Nigel.' I turned to him, scratching my ear with my pencil, to create a diversion. 'We need to find out what was in Janet Dewhurst's will; who she left the company to. Do you think your Mr Wylie will tell you?'

'Don't see why not. Shall I ring him?'

'Or would you rather see him in person?'

'No, I'll ring him. I'll use my own phone if you don't mind, the number's in my desk.'

When he'd gone I said: 'Nigel has a flair for dealing with people like solicitors. He gets more cooperation from them than I ever can.'

'It's called being polite,' said Gilbert. 'You let it be known that you don't like them because they're better off than you, so you get their backs up.'

'Thank you for putting me straight,' I replied.

'Any time. What's the shirt and tie for?'

'Er, I have a luncheon appointment.'

'Anywhere special?'

I was saved by a knock at the door and Geoff Caton poked his head in. "Scuse me, Mr Wood. It's Van Rees on the phone, boss. Shall I say you'll ring him back?'

'No, transfer him in here please.'

After a few seconds the phone rang. 'Hello, Professor, it's Charlie Priest here. Have you anything for me?'

'I'm not sure, Inspector. First of all, I've just received these dirt samples from you. We're having a quick look at them and cataloguing them for further reference. Is that all you wanted?'

'For the time being, Professor. It's just material that we might want to do a comparison with, one day. It's a long shot.'

'I see. Now, this blood sample. It's from a Miles Dewhurst.'

'Yes.'

'Presumably he's something to do with the little girl who vanished.'

'Yes, he's her father.'

'The SOCO brought us samples of hair from her hairbrush when she first went missing.'

'I know.'

'Was she adopted?'

'I don't think so. No, she wasn't. Definitely not.'

'Well, Inspector, statistically there's a chance that you are her biological father. There's even an extremely remote chance that I am her biological father, although I have to confess to having no recollection of the encounter. But this sample proves that Miles Dewhurst is no blood relation to her whatsoever.'

'Well, well,' pondered Gilbert when I relayed the message to the others. 'Mr Dewhurst becomes interestinger and interestinger.'

'If he's in the frame I've something to add,' stated Sparky. 'Go on.'

'He has a girlfriend.'

'A girlfriend? How do you know?' I queried.

'I've been keeping an eye on him. According to her car registration she's called Sarah Louise Parkinson. She's a dark, intense piece. Fashionable dresser. Glamorous, if you like that sort of thing. Her address is Oldfield, but they share a love nest in Todmorden. She's chief buyer at Clay's Manchester branch.'

'Thanks for keeping me informed, Dave,' I told him somewhat abruptly, throwing my pencil on the table.

'Sorry, boss. I was about to tell you.'

The door swung open and Nigel bounded in, like a puppy that's just learned to retrieve a stick.

'Guess what?' he challenged us.

'What?' I demanded, deflating him with a word.

'Er, Janet Dewhurst's will. She left most of it in trust for Georgina. Miles Dewhurst might call himself managing director, but he's still just a glorified employee.'

Maggie, Sparky, Gilbert and myself sat and stared at him, our jaws drooping at various degrees, like sea lions waiting for the keeper to toss a fish to us. Slowly Nigel's face sank, as if his master had taken the stick from him and used it to beat him.

'What did I say?' he wondered aloud.

Raymond Chedgrave could see Miss Jonas's cottage from where he stood. He wondered for a moment if the rumours about her and Father Harcourt were true, then turned back to his barley. He cast his expert eye over the expanse of it and smiled with satisfaction. This was the most widely grown crop in Britain. Some went for feed and some was destined for the brewing industry, but the best – the fattest, purest grain – was held back to use as seed for next year's crop. It fetched the highest price, and Raymond Chedgrave had over a thousand acres of it.

Before being accepted as seed it would be rigorously tested to verify that it was uncontaminated with wild oats or any other weed. Generations of what was regarded as good husbandry had banished the poppy and corn cockle from these fields, but the wild oat was a common intruder, brought in by impure seed. It was easy to detect, standing a foot taller than the barley, but the sterile brome was much more difficult to tackle. That was what Chedgrave was looking for this morning.

He'd started walking the fields as soon as the rising sun had burned off the dew, up and down the waving waist-high rows. The corn was as clean as a weasel's molars. He'd knock off now, he decided, and go back to Home Farm for a bite to eat. Maybe he'd have another couple of hours tomorrow; the weather looked like holding. He made a mental note of where he'd reached, then started working his way back to the Land Rover.

A covey of red-legged partridge suddenly whirred and clattered into the air from almost under his feet. Farmer Chedgrave was startled for a second, but he recovered immediately and raised his arms as if holding an imaginary gun and followed the path of the fleeing birds.

'*P-chow!*' he cried, and the pretend shotgun kicked upwards with the recoil. He didn't do much shooting, but the season had started and a brace of partridge would make a pleasant change of menu. He'd bring a proper gun tomorrow.

As he moved on, his foot tangled with something and he sprawled full-length into his barley. His ankle was held fast and hurting. For a second he thought he must have stepped into a gin trap. He rolled over on to his back to see.

It was a bicycle. His left ankle was jammed through the spokes of the front wheel of an old bike.

'Holy cow!' he muttered. 'I've found the Father's bike!'

The vanishing of Father Harcourt was the best piece of gossip to hit the village since the postmistress was prosecuted for growing marijuana. The police had walked all the drainage ditches looking to see if he'd ridden off the road, and a helicopter had scoured much of the local countryside. Then the momentum had waned and it was left to the passing of the seasons or the tides to reveal his whereabouts. PC Donald Watson was sent in response to Farmer Chedgrave's agitated phone call. He made a positive identification of the bicycle and radioed for further help.

Two hours later Sergeant Morgan Davis deployed his team of two constables in the road adjacent to the barley field.

'What exactly is it we're looking for, Sarge?' asked one of them.

Davis surveyed the antiseptic landscape with distaste. 'Anything suspicious, boyo,' he replied. 'That means that if it's not grass and it's not gravel, put it in a bag and label it. I'll be back at the station, directing operations, so to speak. Radio in if you find anything.'

He climbed into the panda car and drove off. A few seconds down the road his eyes made an habitual flick towards the rear-view mirror. Young Watson was standing in the road waving his arms, trying to attract his attention. The Sergeant stamped on the brakes, slammed into reverse and rocketed back towards him in a storm of tyre smoke and flying stones.

'What do you reckon to this, Sarge?' PC Watson asked.

Davis bent over to see where the constable was pointing. Lying in the grass at the edge of the road was a windscreen wiper arm. He carefully extricated it and held it between his fingertips. Stamped into the metal was the word: VOLVO.

'This, Donald, is what we more experienced police officers call a clue,' said the Sergeant.

'A clue, Sarge. I'll remember that. I've got two of them on my car.' His face glowed so brightly with pride, you could have marked roadworks with it.

'And will you be looking at this,' said Davis, pointing at the wiper with his little finger. Plainly visible along one edge were flakes of blue paint. 'Nearly as good as his name and address, that is.'

'So we're looking for the owner of a blue Volvo, eh, Sarge?'

Davis nodded. 'Carry on at this rate, Donald my boy, and you could be joining the detectives. Now, will you be handing me one of them plastic bags I know you're carrying.'

Next day the search party brought in from divisional HQ found Father Harcourt's body, or what the rats and maggots had left of it.

Chapter Six

I took Maggie to talk with Wylie, the solicitor, and we put our Mr and Mrs Nasty heads on. We'd let Nigel carry on being Mr Nice. Wylie told us that under the terms of the will left by Janet Dewhurst her husband drew a salary and a percentage of the profits until Georgina was eighteen. The rest was held in trust for her. Then, providing he had remained unmarried, they split the company fifty-fifty.

'Mrs Dewhurst was quite adamant about the marriage clause,' Wylie told us. 'She was determined that Georgina would not be brought up by a step-mother.'

He was not so forthcoming when I queried him about Dewhurst's efforts to raise the ransom money. I gave him the look that said I was thinking about pushing burning matchsticks under his fingernails and he opened up slightly. He confessed that, as trustees, his firm had given Dewhurst permission to look for a buyer or do some hefty borrowing.

'Can you do that?' I asked.

He looked embarrassed and fidgeted with a fountain pen. 'We consider we are acting in the best interests of our clients,' he said.

'Both of them?' I demanded.

'Yes, Inspector, both of them. If a life is at risk we feel that we would not be acting as responsible trustees if we did not act to save that life.'

'In that case I want you to withdraw the permission. We can supply the money.'

'I'm afraid it may be too late for that, Inspector,' he replied.

I asked him for a copy of the will and we drove back to the office.

Every morning the Superintendent holds what we call his morning prayer meeting. I informed the gathered brains of Heckley nick of the latest developments.

'Suddenly it's all falling into place,' said Gilbert. 'Do you think you've enough to bring him in? Maybe if we turned his love nest over, leaned on his girlfriend...'

'I'd rather not, if you don't mind,' I answered. 'He's been scrupulous so far, I doubt if he's left any muck in his own kennel. Plus he's got the press on his side. Arresting the distraught father wouldn't be good for my image if it didn't stick.'

'You could be right, Charlie. If he doesn't think he's a suspect, let's give him all the line he needs. Mind you, the Acting Chief Constable might not agree when I give him a progress report.'

'Trevor Partridge,' I replied. 'Leave him to me. I got him that job. If Dewhurst is convicted on circumstantial evidence he'll spend the rest of his life protesting his innocence, writing books and articles in his cell. Three-quarters of the population will believe him. And that's providing we'd convinced a jury first. Let's hang on and find some forensic. When he goes down, I want him to have lead in his shoes.'

I was about to add that I didn't think we'd have long to wait, but I was interrupted by a knock at the door. A uniformed constable poked his head round it.

'Excuse me, gentlemen,' he said. 'Mr Priest, Miles Dewhurst is downstairs, asking for you. He looks a wreck.'

Gilbert came with me. Dewhurst was unshaven and untidily dressed, displaying that careful indifference to personal appearance that takes years to cultivate. For a split second I wondered if that was why I disliked him so much. Not because I thought he'd murdered his daughter, but for his vanity. We sat him in an interview room and ordered tea.

'She wasn't there,' he sobbed. 'He promised she'd be there.'

'Georgina?'

He nodded.

'I think you'd better start at the beginning, Mr Dewhurst. I take it you've had another approach.' I glanced at the calendar on the wall behind him. It showed a picture of Fountains Abbey, and told me that this was the thirteenth day since the previous note.

His elbows were on the table, with his hands clenched together, and his thumbs pressed against his lips.

'Take your time, Mr Dewhurst, and tell us in your own words what happened,' said Gilbert, soothingly.

He lowered his hands. 'He rang me. Last night. Asked if I'd got the money. Not all of it, I told him. He asked me how much and I said three hundred and fifty thousand. He said that would do.'

'Did you have the money at home?' I asked.

He nodded.

'What did he say next?'

'He told me that if I did as I was told I'd have Georgina back by this morning.' He started sobbing, and apologised for doing so. We waited for him to start talking again. 'I had to immediately take the Nissan and drive east on the M62, at fifty miles per hour, until he contacted me again.'

'So he rang you on your mobile?'

'Yes.'

'What time, about?'

'About ten, ten fifteen. I never looked.'

'Go on.'

'He called me again, somewhere near the Bradford turnoff, I think. I had to go to the services at the junction with the A1 and park well away from everyone else. Then wait.'

He rambled on, pausing to blow his nose and gather his thoughts. It was a convincing performance.

'How do you feel about doing the journey again?' I asked.

He nodded. 'I expected you to suggest that.'

'OK. Have you had any breakfast?'

'No, I couldn't eat anything.'

'You've got to have something; a slice of toast at least. Come on, we'll go to the canteen. That all right with you, Mr Wood?'

'Yes, of course,' said Gilbert. 'I'll sort somebody out to go with you.'

Dave Sparkington was available, joining us in the canteen. We had a toasted teacake and set off in my car to follow the directions Dewhurst had been given over his mobile phone.

As we walked out through the yard, Dewhurst asked if the Nissan would be all right where he'd left it. It was in a space marked HMI.

We weren't expecting a visit from him, or even her, so I said: 'Sure, it'll be OK there,' quickly adding: 'Tell you what, let's leave your keys with the front desk, just in case.' Sometimes I think so fast I arrive back before I've started.

Dewhurst sat in the front of my car and Sparky in the back, taking notes. First stop was the Ferrybridge Services, where the A1 intersects the M62. We ignored the fifty miles per hour instruction and drove there as fast as I was able.

'Where did you park?' I asked.

'In that far corner,' Dewhurst said, pointing. I stopped in the same square he'd used.

'Was it very busy?'

'Fairly. There'd be about half as many vehicles as there are now, or maybe a few less.'

'You didn't notice anyone in particular?'

'No.'

'How long did you wait?'

'Nearly an hour.'

'And then he rang again.'

'Yes.'

If was like trying to extract the pips from a pebble. 'Would you care to tell us what the next instruction was, please, Mr Dewhurst?' I asked.

Eight miles down the A1, in a lay-by just past the Burghwallis turn-off, is a construction known as Little John's Well. It's very old, dating from when they made the Great North Road into a dual carriageway. About 1965. The voice on the phone had ordered Dewhurst to go there. We did the same.

'In the well was a flattened Coke tin with the end cut off. There was a message inside, with a diagram.'

'What happened to it?'

'I still have it.'

'Let's have a look, then.'

It had been done on a computer. It depicted the roundabout at the Blythe services, further down the Al, with precise instructions on where to leave the money.

I passed it back to Dave. 'Read 'em out, Dave,' I instructed.

Fifteen minutes later we were nearly there.

'First left and left again,' Sparky told me. 'And left again in a mile and a half.' We were in coal-mining country, or what remained of it. 'Left again in a quarter of a mile.'

It was a narrow lane, made of concrete. Probably an old British Coal access road. The remains of a gate marked the entrance. Now it bore signs of habitation by the less welcome members of the travelling fraternity, and several years' use as an illegal tip. It ended abruptly in a small wood after a few hundred yards.

'Is this where you came?'

'Yes.'

Before us stood a derelict building no bigger than a domestic garage. It was one of those mysterious, windowless places that have electricity poles bringing cables into them, and lightning conductors sticking towards the sky. Except that the copper fairies had already removed everything nonferrous from this one.

'It's an old Coal Board substation,' Sparky explained.

'Where did you leave the money?' I asked.

'Inside. There's a pit in the floor, with the old door across it. I had to leave the money in the pit.'

'OK. You two wait here; I'll have a look.'

I picked my way through the wet grass to the gaping doorway of the building. A pair of magpies flew up and crashed noisily through the branches of the surrounding silver birches. Inside was a rotting jumble of domestic garbage. Liberally strewn about were screwed-up pieces of pink toilet tissue.

Yuk! I thought, wishing I'd asked Sparky to do the dirty work.

The big door that had once protected the entrance now lay inside, on the floor. It was reinforced with a steel sheet, but fortunately had a large handle to grasp hold of.

I tugged at it. It was heavier than I'd expected. Slowly a hole underneath was revealed. I pulled some more and exposed the secret of the substation. There was a Nike sports bag down there. I lifted it out and wrenched back the zip. It's hard to judge these things, but at a rough guess I'd say it contained about three hundred and fifty thousand smackeroos.

We tipped the money into the boot of my car and put the bag, with a few stones inside, back down the hole.

'You didn't tell me it was a public convenience,' Sparky complained as he helped me push the door back over the hole.

'Just watch where you put your feet,' I told him. 'And wipe them before you get in the car.'

We phoned the local CID and a sergeant arrived a few minutes later. He was sceptical at first, but I lifted my boot lid and showed him some real money. It convinced him.

'Fuckinell! I wish I'd known that was in there. How long do you want us to watch for?' he said.

'A couple of days should be enough. I'll make it right with your super. Now, do you mind if we leave you and continue with our treasure hunt?'

He didn't mind. As we drove away he was radioing for assistance. 'Back to the roundabout and take the Blythe road,' instructed Sparky. I did as I was told.

'Quarter of a mile, left on a dirt road.'

It was marked Private, owned by the local council and leading to a storage area for their vehicles and various materials like lampposts and road grit. After a while a narrow bridge took us over the A1 and the road petered out. We were in a wood again.

'Next instructions, please,' I asked.

'I had to park here, leaving the car unlocked, then walk through the trees to the services. They're about a quarter of a mile away. After an hour I was to come back. Georgina should have been in the car.'

'I see. OK, you and DS Sparkington retrace your

steps to the services. I'll guard the money. See how long it takes you, Dave.'

'Right, boss.'

My bladder was complaining of neglect. As soon as they were out of sight I watered the grass beneath an oak tree. Then I telephoned Heckley CID.

'Heckley CID. DS Newley speaking. Can I help you?'

I had to admit it: Nigel would make a brilliant telephonist. 'Hi, Nigel. It's Charlie.'

'Hello, boss. Where are you?'

'Somewhere in deepest South Yorkshire. Listen, I want you to do a little job for me.'

'Fire away. I'm all ears.'

'In the car park is a Nissan Patrol. It belongs to Miles Dewhurst.'

'Yes, I've seen it.'

'Good. The keys are at the front desk. Raise a friendly SOCO and have him go over it with his sticky tape. Just take a few samples for the file.'

'Will do. Anything in particular?'

'Not really. A few fibres from a pink toilet roll might be interesting. Check his driving gloves, if he has any. Take some prints from them. You've got about... oh, two hours, no more.'

Villains assume they are safe if they wear gloves, not realising that we have a secret weapon. These days we can take gloveprints.

We had another cuppa at the services and returned to Heckley at a leisurely pace. Sparky and I could have eaten a mangy gnu between us, but Dewhurst said he wasn't hungry and it seemed unsympathetic to tuck into anything in his presence.

Gilbert gave Dewhurst a bollocking, or as close to one as I've ever heard him deliver. Gilbert's reprimands are normally of such well-honed subtlety that you come away thinking you've been praised until you reflect on it afterwards. I almost felt sorry for Dewhurst as he loaded the money into the Nissan and drove back to The Firs, Edgely Lane, via his bank. No, I didn't.

'So?' Gilbert said, after we'd settled down in his office with a coffee each.

'Got any biscuits?' I asked.

'Sorry, no. How'd it go?'

'Complete waste of time. It was a good scheme, could have worked. Don't believe a word of it, though.'

'It was a bit risky, leaving the money, don't you think?'

'A bit, but not much. The place was full of toilet paper. You didn't feel like doing much nosing around in there. I think it was a ploy to keep people away.'

'We could always send Scenes of Crime to give it a good going-over,' Gilbert suggested with a wicked smile. 'Why didn't he just steal the money and make it look as if it had been picked up?' he added.

'Then he'd have his own money, but illegally. And we'd be more suspicious.'

'Mmm '

'Let's keep playing him along, Gilbert. Things are building up – we'll get a breakthrough soon.'

Gilbert looked grave. 'I'm afraid you might not have the chance,' he said.

'Why not?'

'Acting Chief Constable Partridge has been on to me. He wants us to spin Dewhurst's premises. I let him know your feelings, so he said you can have a fort-night.'

I stared at Gilbert in disbelief. 'A fortnight?' I repeated. 'Why a fortnight? What difference does it make if it takes a month? Or a year?'

'That's what he said.'

'He's mad. We'll blow it. Everything we've got is circumstantial. You've seen Dewhurst perform; he'll twist a jury round his Filofax. We'll be the baddies; or I will be.'

I'd stood up to leave, but I sat down again. Dewhurst's story about how he was missing his little girl had been heavily featured in the tabloids. He was receiving letters of sympathy from all over the country, and prayers were regularly said for him in the local churches. If we went off half-cocked I'd be as popular as a turd in a jacuzzi.

'You're naive, Charlie,' Gilbert stated.

'So it appears. Go on.'

He sat back in his big chair and tapped the polished top of his desk with a pencil. He said: 'Acting Chief Constable Partridge's immediate, overriding ambition is not to apprehend little Georgina's abductor. No, it's to lose the *Acting* tag. It's the chief constables' conference in three weeks and he'll be there. Sometime after that there'll be the interviews for the vacancy. This is a high-profile case and he wants an arrest under his belt. The result, when it eventually comes to court, is secondary. If it goes wrong he'll be able to say that it was initiated before his appointment. In the interim he'll take all the credit.'

I shook my head slowly from side to side. 'You're right, Gilbert,' I said. 'Naive is hardly the word. I thought all we had to do was catch villains.'

'He's an ambitious man, Charlie.'

'Well, I refuse to feature in his plans. I want taking off the case.'

'I thought you might say that, so I've already given it some consideration. Your request is turned down. You've got two weeks, from the weekend. Come back after that and I'll think again.'

Chapter Seven

'Go on!' urged Lee Todd. 'Let's do it. We've plenty of time.'

'No,' pleaded his girlfriend, Vicky Smith. 'It's not right.'

'Not right? You've never said that before.'

'I mean now, before we see the vicar. You'll have to wait.' A shudder of delight ran through her. They were seated in his Mini, with its huge stereo speakers that blocked the view through the rear window blaring out rave music. Lee's hand was up her miniskirt and his fingers were exploring the crotch of her knickers.

'Stop it!' she demanded, half-heartedly. By sliding forward on the seat she could pull her pants so tight they dug into her puffy thighs and he couldn't get his blunt fingers under the elastic.

'Please!' he begged.

'No!' She snatched his hand away and sat up straight. 'Later, when we've seen the vicar about the banns. Then we'll do it, you know, how you like it.'

'Promise?'

'Yes, promise.'

'Oh, all right then.' He extricated himself from her and moved back to his side of the car. They sat smoking a rollyour-own cigarette, and Lee opened a can of Coke. 'Are you sure he won't ask if I've been christened?' he said.

"Course he won't. If he does, just say you 'ave.'

'But won't he check?'

'Nah. Anyway, things get lost. What difference does it make? Stop being such a wally.'

They sat without speaking for a while, bodies

jerking to the incessant beat of the electronic music, until Lee announced that he'd never been in a church before.

'It's not a church, it's a vicarage,' Vicky told him.

'Same thing,' pronounced Lee.

'You don't 'arf talk some rubbish!' declared Vicky. 'The vicarage is the 'ouse where the vicar lives. That's the bloody church, through the trees, with the clock on top.'

'Well, I'll have to go to church when we get married, won't I? Then it'll be the first time.'

'Come on,' she said, straightening her skirt and running her fingers through her variegated hair. 'It's time to go.'

'Wait a minute.' Lee fumbled with the pocket of his shirt and took a twist of silver paper from it. He unwrapped two small white pills and tossed one into his mouth, swallowing it with a swig of Coke.

'Hey! Where's mine?' protested Vicky.

'You've already had one.'

'So have you.' She snatched the last pill from him and gulped it down with a drink from the can. 'Come on!'

Bottle was something Lee prided himself in having in abundance, but walking up the drive to the vicarage door drew on all his reserves. Vicky pressed the bell push.

A dog barked, followed by a light coming on inside and a shadow falling on the frosted glass. The vicar's wife opened the door.

'We've come to see the vicar, about our banns,' announced Vicky. Lee stood a respectful yard behind her.

'Oh, how do you do? I'm Mary Conway. You must be Vicky and Lee.'

'That's right.'

'So pleased to meet you. Ronald said would you mind if he saw you in the church? He's in there now, if you'd care to pop along.'

'Oh, all right, then. G'night.'

'Just go straight in. Bye bye.'

They turned on their heels and walked back down the drive. Halfway up the path to the church Lee's power of speech returned. 'Hey, Vicky,' he whispered.

'What?'

'When we come out, when we've finished, we could always come back and have it in the graveyard. That'd be a laugh.'

'Lee Todd! You're obsessed. Sex! Sex! Sex! That's all you ever think about!'

'I know. That's why you love me, innit?'

Vicky embraced his arm in both hers and looked up at him. 'Probably,' she laughed.

The big door swung open and Lee entered a house of God for the first time in his eighteen years. He quietly closed the door behind them. It was not an example of ecclesiastical architecture likely to fill a young heathen with a sense of awe and wonder, being built during one of the Church's more austere periods. What did impress Lee was the power of the silence.

'What do we do?' he hissed.

'Dunno. Look for him, I suppose. Let's go down to the front.'

They walked down the aisle together for what was to be the only time in their lives, Lee's trainers padding noiselessly and Vicky's stilettos ringing out on the stone flags.

There was a door marked Vestry, with a glimmer of light visible under it. Lee, now confident that no bolt of lightning was about to smite him, knocked.

There was no answer. He turned the handle and they went in.

'Cor, it's a bit warmer in 'ere,' Vicky said.

'Yeah. Smells as if someone's been smoking Pashas.'

'Pashas? What's them?'

'Strongest cigs ever made, according to my dad. It's one of 'is catchphrases: "You smell as if you've been smoking Pashas," he sez,'

"Spect it's incense,' Vicky told him.

They wandered back into the nave and looked around them.

'How long do we wait?' asked Lee.

'Dunno.'

Down near the entrance was a notice board, with letters and schedules and various Third World appeals pinned to it. They studied the messages, and were unmoved by the pictures of pot-bellied children and weeping, wizened mothers.

Lee's bravado had returned by now. Or his animal desires had overcome his apprehension. 'Hello! Anybody there?' he shouted. Vicky laughed. Lee sprinted down to the front of the church and climbed into the pulpit. 'Today's hymn is "My Way",' he called out.

Vicky followed him. 'You're daft,' she giggled.

Lee put his arms around her and kissed her. He turned her around so that he was behind her and enclosed her breasts in his fingers.

'Don't,' Vicky moaned, as his tongue probed her ear.

'Hey! Who's that watching us?' he demanded.

'Where?' said an alarmed Vicky.

'Her up there.'

Vicky looked where he gestured. 'That's a statue of the Virgin Mary,' she explained.

'What, the vicar's wife?'

'No, idiot. Jesus's mum.'

'Blimey, bet they had to go a long way to find her.'

'Yeah. Specially with sex maniacs like you around.'

He resumed his fondling and Vicky rotated her buttocks against his loins. The Mother of God gazed serenely just above their heads as his fingers flicked open the buttons of Vicky's blouse and slid her bra up, revealing nipples as brown and hard as the carved acorns that decorated the oak lectern.

'Stay there,' he ordered, suddenly letting go of her. He sprinted to the church door, slid the big bolt across, and was back with her in seconds. Vicky stood pulling the front of her blouse together.

Lee grabbed her hand. 'C'mon,' he ordered.

'Where?' whimpered Vicky.

'In here,' he replied, dragging her towards the vestry. The only furniture in there was the vicar's ancient writing desk and a chair. On the floor in front of the desk was a thick woollen rug, woven in a pattern representing scarab beetles. It was from Morocco, and had been presented to the church by the local Bible-Koran Society, in a gesture of conciliation.

Lee closed the door behind them. The key was in the lock, so he turned it. He kissed Vicky roughly, fondling her and fumbling with her clothing, then forced her down on to the rug.

After the absolute minimum of preliminaries he hooked his fingers into her pants and pulled them off. This time she eased her buttocks off the ground to facilitate their passage.

Lee was kneeling between her legs. He undid his jeans and was on to and into her with a speed that would have impressed a Wensleydale sheep farmer.

Their lovemaking depended on enthusiasm and athleticism rather than tenderness and concern. The aim was to achieve a fleeting moment of intense pleasure as rapidly as possible, which would immediately be followed by a feeling of wondering what all the fuss had been about – until the urge to do it again slowly returned.

Sex in unusual places has its own eroticism, but it does sometimes fall down on practicality. Vicky was lying entirely within the borders of the woven pattern, but Lee's feet projected beyond it, on to the parquet floor, which the ladies of the congregation polished, with assiduity and Johnson's wax, every Tuesday morning.

He was wearing Reebok basketball boots, famed for their grip on slippery surfaces. Every thrust of his loins pushed Vicky and the rug across the floor, and every three or four thrusts his toes stuttered forwards to bring him back into the optimum position. Slowly they progressed across the vestry, like some Gothic, ratchet-propelled animal.

It was unsatisfactory for Vicky, too. She flailed her arms around, trying to find a fixture to cling to. There was nothing at all within the arc of her right arm, but the left was underneath the big wooden desk.

She groped about in vain for several seconds, then she thought her fingertips brushed something. The next thrust confirmed her thoughts and the one after that brought it within her grasp.

Vicky grabbed hold and braced herself. It wasn't the solid anchorage she was hoping for. It was soft and-yielding, as well as wet and sticky.

It was another hand.

Vicky gasped with terror and yanked her own hand back. She held it above her and blood dripped from it onto her face.

Her scream echoed around the high roof and set

the starlings flying from the tower. With a mighty convulsion she threw Lee off and jumped to her feet. The locked door delayed her progress slightly, but within seconds she was running barefoot out into the night, still screaming.

Lee had just reached the good bit. Vicky's first recoil action made him think that for once his timing was perfect. He was on the backstroke, on the verge of the big finale, when she shot out from under him. He impregnated a woven scarab beetle with half a billion of his healthy, if genetically undistinguished, spermatozoa.

Exhausted and frustrated, he collapsed on the rug. He was facing the underside of the desk, but his right arm was obscuring his vision. Beyond his arm, in the shadows under the desk, Lee could make out what looked like somebody's shoulder, wearing a tweed jacket. His hand was trembling uncontrollably as he drew it back, and he found himself staring into the sightless gaze of the late Reverend Ronald Conway.

Lee caught Vicky at the reproduction lich-gate. She was sobbing and screaming and cursing because she'd hurt her feet in her panic. He grabbed her arm and manhandled her into the car, before shaking her until her teeth rattled. It was an effective treatment for hysteria. When she quietened down they drove off. Parked in a farm gateway a couple of miles away, they reviewed the situation: they'd had an appointment with the vicar; his wife knew their names; Vicky had left her shoes and knickers behind and Lee had deposited a sample of his body fluids that would have provided for the nation's *in vitro* fertilisation programme into the next century.

'They'd find us,' Lee concluded.

So, for the second time that day, he voluntarily

walked into a building that he would normally have
avoided like a crocodile avoids sticky toffee. They
went to the police station and reported finding a body.

Detective Inspector 'Oscar' Peterson had seen it all
before. He didn't like churches and the last thing he'd
been hoping for was another murder. Especially one
like this. A nice juicy domestic would have been OK,
but the murder of a vicar didn't fall into the normal
pattern of crime. It jarred, like a satellite dish on a
Georgian terrace. Peterson could have retired on full
pension three months ago; so he was now working, as
he constantly reminded anyone who'd listen, for one-
third pay. He needed this like Salman Rushdie needs a
season ticket at Bradford Park Avenue.

He was standing in the doorway of the vestry, trying
to build a mental picture of what had happened. He'd
already set the wheels of a murder enquiry into motion,
and was waiting for the SOCO and the superintendent
from regional HQ to appear. At his elbow was the
young PC who had made the initial response to the
report.

'One thing I did notice, sir,' said the PC, eager to
please, 'was the smell. It was quite strong then, but you
can still smell it.' He sniffed audibly, as if to suggest
how.

DI Peterson inhaled through his nicotine-wrecked
nasal passages. What lingered of the heady mixture of
gun smoke, sex and Vicky's cheap perfume stirred his
few remaining receptors into life. He looked thoughtful.

The PC sniffed again. 'Mean anything to you, sir?'
he asked.

'Yes,' replied Peterson. 'Shithouse on a French
destroyer.'

It was nearly midnight when the coroner gave his permission for the body to be removed to the Princess Royal Hospital for a post-mortem. DI Peterson had done all he could at this late hour – organised his team, set up an incident room and taken steps to protect the scene of the offence – so he went home. He wanted to know the results of the PM as soon as they were available, but he'd no desire to witness the whole gory spectacle. He'd sat through plenty and knew he wouldn't faint or be sick, but didn't feel the need to prove it.

His wife, Dilys, was waiting up for him. The DI said he would be going out again and she made him a sandwich. He told her all about the murder at the vicarage.

They had a good marriage, based on love and, above all, an enduring friendship. Unlike most policemen he always told her about all his cases, especially the difficult or more spectacular ones. The job was the only thing he *could* talk about. That was what worried him. Could their happiness survive twenty-four hours per day of each other's company if he retired? Could he survive it? Three months was supposedly the average pension-drawing span of ex-police officers. He shuddered at the thought.

Professor Alan Tuke, the pathologist, raised his head from his grisly work as Peterson entered the mortuary lab. He winked at the DI and mischievously said: 'DI Peterson enters room at ...two ten a.m.' for the benefit of the video/sound recorder. Peterson picked up a swivel stool and took it to the furthest corner of the lab, where he could hear but not see. The Professor was nearing the end of his immediate investigation. He was removing various organs and putting them in glass jars for later analysis. Not that it would be necessary – the cause of death had been fairly obvious. Nobody poisons a victim, then cuts them in half with a shotgun to hide the evidence. The DI listened to him intoning his progress into the microphone and admired his thoroughness.

The final act was to stitch up the cadaver and make it reasonably presentable for the grieving widow to mourn over. Tuke allowed his assistant to do this. He peeled off his gloves, discarded his plastic apron and white overall and was immediately transformed from slaughterhouse worker into university professor. After he'd scrubbed his hands up to his elbows he walked over to Peterson and offered him something.

'Little present for your Black Museum, Oscar. Don't deny it; I know you have one somewhere in that desirable residence of yours.' He dropped a shotgun pellet into the DI's palm. 'I haven't recovered them all,' he went on, 'but I'd say it was one barrel from a twelve-bore, at a range of one metre to four feet.'

'Side by side, over and under, or single-barrelled?'

'Almost certainly. Ruptured his aorta, amongst other things. Must have pumped all his blood over the floor before he died. Bit like when the pipe comes off the washing machine.'

'Do you have to be so bloody graphic?' protested the DI.

'Sorry. Interesting case, though. His arteries were in a shocking state. Somebody wasted a shotgun cartridge on him; he was heading for a massive heart attack in the next few months.'

'Fascinating. Time of death?'

'Oh, between six and seven last night.'

'Thank you, Alan. Is there anything else you can tell me, or will it all be on my desk in your report by ten a.m.?'

'No chance,' replied the Professor. 'There was one odd thing though. Don't go away.'

He left the DI and went over to the trolley that stood alongside the operating table. He returned holding a small piece of paper.

'What's this?' asked Peterson, taking it.

'Found it when we went through his clothing. It was just stuffed into the breast pocket of his jacket. Does it mean anything?'

The DI held it by the corner between two fingers, as if holding a cigarette. 'It's just a picture of a mushroom,' he stated.

'Not necessarily,' replied Tuke. 'It could be a death cap, they're very similar. Odd thing to cut out and put in your pocket, though, don't you think?'

Peterson shrugged. 'Don't make it complicated, Alan, this is reality. Maybe he was a fungi... something-or-other.'

'Fortunately, that's your problem. Come on. I'll treat you to a bacon sandwich in the canteen.'

Peterson got to his feet and they walked out of the lab. He was as near to being shocked as he'd been for many years.

'A bacon sandwich!' he protested. 'After that!' He gestured with a nod of his head back to where the violated body lay.

'Got to look after the inner man, Oscar.'

'I'd have thought you'd seen enough of the inner man for an hour or two. And what about his stuffed-up arteries?' Peterson worried about arteries.

'I'm hungry. PMs are hard work. All that sawing and pulling gives you an appetite.'

They were approaching the big glass doors that led out on to the street.

'I'm worried about you, Alan. You're turning into a

bloody ghoul,' Peterson said. He went on: 'What moves you? When was the last time you had tears in your eyes? Watching a Lassie video on Christmas Day, I expect.'

'They're dead when I get them, Oscar. You have to deal with the living. I'd find that hard.'

They'd reached the doors. The Professor paused with his hand on the handle. 'Trent Bridge,' he said. 'About five years ago.'

'What was?'

'Last time I wept. You asked me, remember?'

'Cricket?' queried the DI.

'That's right. I'll never forget it.' A faraway look came over his face and his eyes fixed on a spot high on the wall. 'David Gower was batting. He'd been pinned down on ninety-eight for about fifteen minutes. It was the last over, and they brought on Curtly Ambrose to try to shift him. He was bowling out of the sun, and he unleashed one that went down like a ballistic missile. Gower stepped forward and drove it into the crowd for six. You could have heard the cheers at Headingley.'

When he was certain the Professor had stopped, Peterson said: 'So what did it? Gower's elegance? His courage? Or was it just his boyish good looks?'

'No, none of those,' replied the Professor, pulling the door open. 'It hit me on the kneecap. I was walking with a stick for a week. *Ciao*, Oscar.'

'S'long, pillock,' Peterson chuckled, and walked out into the night.

Chapter Eight

Denise Davison – wife of Reg, eager-beaver sales manager of Wimbles Agri – was watering the plants in the front bay window when the police car pulled into the street. She was filling the saucers under the cyclamen, being very careful not to wet the corms. As she watched the car go by she overflowed on to the windowsill, and as it turned round at the end of the cul-de-sac and began to creep back towards her she irrigated a Capo di Monte figurine of a shepherdess that Reg's parents had given them as a wedding present eighteen years earlier.

The police officer climbed out of the car, looked the front of the house up and down, and opened the gate. Mrs Davison wiped her hands on the front of her dress and waited for his knock. She opened the door instantly.

'Yes?' she quavered.

'Sorry to trouble you, ma'am. Are you Mrs Davison?'

'Yes.'

'Ah, good.' He introduced himself. 'Could you tell me if Mr Davison is at home?'

Her eyes opened wide in her pale face. 'No. I mean … you mean…'

'Mean what, Mrs Davison?'

'I thought… I thought you'd come to tell me… Perhaps you had better come in.'

She led the young PC into the obsessively tidy sitting room and gestured towards the settee. He sank into it while she sat on an upright chair opposite him.

'Now, Mrs Davison,' he intoned, 'what is it you want to tell me?'

'Nothing,' she whimpered. 'I thought you'd come to tell me about Reg... Mr Davison.'

'Tell you what about him?'

'I don't know... That you'd found him...'

'No, Mrs Davison. I'm just making routine enquiries of all owners of blue Volvos. You may have read about it in the papers. We're trying to trace one that was involved in a hit-and-run accident several weeks ago. I think you'd better start at the beginning. Why should we have found Mr Davison?'

She looked confused. 'He... he didn't come home last night,' she stammered.

'I see. Has this ever happened before?'

'No. He often works away; he's a sales manager and has to stay overnight sometimes, but he always lets me know.'

'Have you reported him missing?'

Mrs Davison shook her head. 'No. I thought he was doing it to hurt me. Things have been... strained between us these last few weeks.'

'Strained? In what way?'

She shrugged her shoulders. 'It's hard to say. He's seemed so touchy lately. It's his job; he has a lot of responsibility.'

'I see.' The PC was enjoying this. He was amazed how compassionate and responsible his own voice sounded, and Mrs Davison did have rather shapely legs. 'When did you last see your husband?' he continued.

'Yesterday morning. Tuesdays I have an evening class in word processing – I have a part-time secretarial job but I'd like to try for something a bit more permanent. I left Reg a meal ready to warm in the microwave, like I usually do, but he never came home for it.'

'What frame of mind was he in when you saw him last?'

'Annoyed. We were arguing. He stormed out in a mood.'

'Right. Well, my guess is that he's just cooling down somewhere and will come back when he's ready. You can formally report him as missing, but I have to tell you that the police will take little action. I'm afraid the law regards it as a person's privilege to go wandering off if they so wish. As there is no suspicion of a crime, our hands are tied.'

'I expect you're right,' she sniffed.

'I'm sure he'll be back soon,' he added comfortingly, as he watched her uncross her legs. 'Now, about the car. I presume your husband does still own a blue Volvo?'

'Yes, well, it's the company's.'

'I see. And he's taken it with him?'

'Yes. Of course.'

'Does he normally keep it in the garage?'

'No, out on the drive.'

'Right. In that case I will have to call back in a few days to see Mr Davison, presuming he returns home.' And if he hadn't? Well, in that case she'd need a sympathetic shoulder to cry on, wouldn't she? He'd always fancied older women.

The PC got to his feet and started towards the door. He was hoping that he would be offered a cup of tea, but perhaps the circumstances were too fraught for that. Next time, perhaps. He hesitated, trying to second-guess the sergeant he would have to answer to when he returned to the station after a fruitless mission.

'Have you checked to see if the car is in the garage, Mrs Davison?' he asked, after a rare burst of inspiration.

'Why, no.'

'In that case, do you mind if I have a look now?'

'If you insist, but I can't imagine Reg putting it away and then going off somewhere – he drives every-where.' She took a key from a hook just inside the kitchen door and handed it to him. 'This fits the side door. Just leave it in the lock when you've finished.'

The side door to the garage evidently wasn't used much. It was seized with paint, and some gardening tools were leaning on the inside of it. He pushed and the tools fell over as the door creaked open and the evening sunlight spilled in.

The blue Volvo was there. So too was Reg Davison. He was hanging from a roof joist by a length of electric flex. It had bitten so deep into his flabby neck that the skin had met around it. There could be no doubting his determination when he'd kicked the buffet from under himself, but he'd soon changed his mind as the wire cut into his throat. The boot of the Volvo bore the scratches his flailing feet had made as he desperately tried to get them back on something solid.

Our valiant PC looked at the grotesque face, like a fermenting pumpkin, and was promptly sick in the corner. It would come to visit him many times in the next few months. He relocked the garage door and walked slowly to his car, wiping his mouth. After radio-ing for assistance he sat quietly for a few moments, com-posing himself and a short speech to the long-legged Mrs Davison, informing her that she was now eligible for a widow's pension.

Inspector Peterson's parents, May and Joe, had been desperate to give their first born a name to remember. Something with style. A few days before the birth they saw *Citizen Kane* at the Tivoli and decided on Orson. He grew up hating the name. Throughout his school

years he was known to children and teachers alike as
Orson Cart. In 1962 the musical genius he shared a sur-
name with came to town and someone accidentally
called him Oscar. He made no attempt to correct them
and it just grew from there. His wife, Dilys, had
thought this was his name until two days before their
wedding, when he realised that a before-the-altar reve-
lation might be his undoing. Even so, he distinctly
heard gasps of surprise from his friends in the pews
behind as the vicar addressed him.

None of the detectives he was now deep in a brain-
storming session with knew his secret. The warbling
of the internal phone interrupted them and a DC
answered it.

'Yes, sir.' He pulled a face, pointed upwards with
his index finger and passed the instrument to Peterson.

'Yes, sir, right now.' Peterson put the phone back in
its cradle. 'Excuse me, gentlemen, but the Screaming
Skull wants me to go up and check if his parting's
straight.'

A minute later he knocked on the door of Chief
Superintendent Tollis's office and went in.

'Come in, Peterson, and sit down. This won't take a
minute. First of all, any new developments in the
Reverend Conway case?'

'No sir, not since our morning meeting.'

The morning meeting had concluded less than an
hour earlier, so the chances of further revelations were
slim.

'Quite. Right then, let me show you what I received
in today's mail.'

The Superintendent picked up a large manila envelope and drew its contents out on to the top of his desk.
There were three large cuttings from newspapers. One
described the death of the Reverend Gerry Wilde, who

had fallen down his church tower; the next told of the brutal murder of Father Harcourt; and the third was a front-page splash from a tabloid describing the last moments of the Reverend Conway.

'Obviously some crank, cashing in on other people's misfortunes,' stated the Superintendent. 'Can't think why he's sent them to me, though.'

Maybe it's because you've let all the press know that you're the officer in charge, thought Peterson. He didn't dwell on the thought. He would have been delighted to hand over this investigation to anybody who wanted it. He could see his retirement date slipping away, like a pair of tail lights receding into the motorway fog. This was going to be a big one, and he needed it like the Super needed a comb.

He sat there, transfixed by the three cuttings. Neatly pinned in the top left-hand corner of each was a picture of a mushroom, similar to the one found in the Reverend Conway's top pocket.

'No, sir,' he said eventually. 'It's not a crank. We've got a fuckin' loony on the loose.'

Up to then the investigation into the murder of Ronald Conway had been a parochial affair. Everybody who'd known him was in the process of being interviewed. Detectives were knocking on doors, working outwards from the vicarage in an ever-widening circle. Questions were being asked and people encouraged to gossip. There was plenty of gossip about Reverend Conway.

Enquiries with Criminal Records showed that he'd received a caution for an unspecified sexual assault when he was seventeen.

'I don't believe any of the dirt that's coming up about him,' asserted DI Peterson in one of the morning meetings. 'It's all hearsay. OK, so maybe he flashed in the park when he was a kid. That doesn't mean anything. From then on it's been handed down, following him around like a starving dog. If he'd been a member of some paedophile group, or into SM, we'd have found out about it by now. All the evidence is that he was a decent, devout, happily married bloke. It's not the angle we're looking for.'

'I'm not so sure, Peterson,' stated the Superintendent. 'The leopard can't change its spots. That sexual offence must show what type of man he is.'

'With respect, sir, there are only two types of men.'

Eight pairs of eyebrows shot up. The Super's went so high they'd have vanished into his hairline, if he'd had one.

'Wankers and liars,' the DI explained.

Now the murder was linked with the other deaths the scope of the enquiry widened. Peterson visited Norfolk and obtained the relevant files. The evidence that Father Harcourt was knocked off his bike by Reg Davison was fairly conclusive. The jack in his car boot had almost certainly been used to finish the priest off. To Reg, the archetypal salesman, appearance was everything. He'd topped himself because the hopelessness of his situation, and the disgrace that would follow, were more than he could bear. Gerry Wilde could have fallen down his tower accidentally, but he could have been pushed. It didn't make sense, but murder often doesn't.

There was still a mood of discontent in certain branches of the Church of England over the ordination of women priests, but they hadn't resorted to terrorism yet. And investigations showed that Conway was in favour of them, Wilde almost certainly against. Any Roman Catholic movements in that direction were invariably aborted immediately after conception.

Possible unification of the C of E and RC churches raised emotions to a level that were completely beyond Peterson's grasp. He sent a lone officer down this avenue, as he did with the sexual and anti-women theories. The bulk of his team were dedicated to following the hypothesis dictated by the feeling in his bile ducts: that they were looking for a loony; a loony with a mission.

'Take a look at this, guv,' said one of the DCs when Peterson arrived back in his office. He placed a large but slim hardback book in front of the Inspector. It was called *Mushrooms and Toadstools*, by Jacqueline Seymour. When Peterson had read the title the constable flicked the book open to page five. In a corner was a colour picture identical to one of those sent to Superintendent Tollis.

'See what it's called.' He ran his finger down the text until it was under the name.

'Good God,' muttered Peterson. He riffled through the pages of the book and said: 'Is this yours, Trevor?'

'Yes, guv. Well, my daughter's.'

'Are any of the other pictures in here?'

'No. I've had another look at them and reckon they're three different pictures of the same type of mushroom. Or toadstool, to be precise – it's poisonous.'

'Mmm. I'm not surprised, with a name like that. So he must have cut the pictures from three different books.'

'It looks like it.'

'And where would be the best place to do that?'

'The library?'

'Just what I'm thinking. Get your coat; let's educate ourselves in matters fungoid.'

They intended walking the quarter of a mile to the library, as they knew it would be difficult to park nearby, but it had started to rain. Fortunately a police car came into the yard at the opportune moment, so Peterson hijacked it and had the driver take them there.

The library was a purpose-designed building, constructed when the town centre was redesigned about fifteen years previously. It was airy and pleasant, and well used by all sections of the community. The Inspector was surprised to see shelves and racks filled with videos and CDs, as well as books. It was a long time since he'd had the time to visit a library.

'First,' he said to DC Trevor Wilson, 'let's just see how many books we can find on fungi.'

They located one each, in the section marked Natural History. A short while later DC Wilson found another on a shelf for books that were oversize – the ones filled with glossy photographs and normally described as Coffee Table, because they cost about as much as one. All three were intact – no pictures had been cut from them. They asked an assistant if they could see the chief librarian.

She disappeared through a door marked Staff and came back a few seconds later with a tubby little man wearing rimless spectacles and a blue suit.

The two detectives produced their ID cards. 'This is Detective Constable Wilson and I'm Detective Inspector Peterson. You are...?'

'Oh, goodness me. I'm Mr Treadwell. This is most unusual. Er, what exactly can I do for you, gentlemen?'

'First of all, could we sit down somewhere, sir?'

'Oh, yes, of course. You'd better come through into my office.'

Treadwell's office was small but surprisingly lacking in clutter. There were two desks: one obviously for a typist, who wasn't there, and the other presumably his. On it were two silver frames containing family portraits. Peterson noted that Treadwell was the proud husband of Khrushchev's widow and father of two gnomes.

Maybe he just has the pictures there to warn him to keep his hands off the typist, he thought, sitting in her chair and swivelling it to face inwards. DC Wilson perched on a corner of her desk and wondered what she looked like.

'We won't keep you long, Mr Treadwell,' Peterson began. 'First of all, do we call you chief librarian?'

'Oh, no. I'm a group librarian. I'm head of this group. That's this library and seven branches.' He listed several local small towns.

'I see. Now, we have a problem, and we're wondering if you will be able to help us with it.'

'Oh, well, if I possibly can, Inspector.' He relaxed, now that he knew that they were here to call on his expertise, and not to relay some trouble at home or with the staff. 'What exactly is it you want to know?'

The Inspector spread the three books on the desk. 'Somebody,' he stated, 'is going round cutting photos of mushrooms from books like these, presumably borrowed from libraries. We need to catch that person, fast. Is there any way we can circulate a message to all librarians?'

'Goodness gracious, this is good news!' Treadwell said. 'You'd never believe the amount of malicious damage that people do to them. I sometimes wonder what the world is coming to. And it's not just the youngsters, you know. Why, sometimes –'

'Ah!' interrupted Peterson. 'I think I may have misled you. Serious as the vandalising of books might be, that's not our principal interest in this character. He also has a nice sideline in murdering people. That's why we'd like to meet him, but you can have him after us.'

'M-m-murdering people!' stammered Treadwell, immediately assuming that 'people' meant group librarians.

'Well, just one person that we're certain of, and so far it's just a theory we're exploring.' Peterson thought that perhaps he had been too blunt with the nervous Mr Treadwell, but then he glimpsed the family photos and decided that the man was made of sterner stuff. He went on: 'So, is there any way in which I can circulate every library in the country and ask them if they can check their books on fungi for missing pages?'

Treadwell looked perplexed. 'No, not from here,' he replied. 'I could only circulate my group. You'd have to contact every group individually.'

'What about head office, sir? There must be a libraries HQ somewhere.'

'Well, yes. There's the Library Association.'

'The Library Association? Where do they hang out?'

'London, Ridgmount Street.'

'Who's in charge there?'

'Er, the chief executive.'

'That sounds rather grand. Is he a figurehead or does he work for a living?'

'Oh no,' asserted Treadwell. 'He's a librarian, come up through the ranks.'

'He'll do then. Have you his number, please?'

Treadwell, having a tidy mind, knew exactly where to find it.

'Do you mind if I use your phone, Mr Treadwell?' asked the Inspector, adding: 'You can always invoice us for the charge, if you wish.'

Treadwell, fascinated, gave his gushing consent. He didn't mind if they conducted the entire enquiry from his office. What a story he'd have to tell Edwina and the boys when he arrived home.

After several transfers, the Inspector found himself addressing Olga Friedland, Chief Executive of the Library Association. He introduced himself, confessing to being called Oscar, and made a daring joke about their names. Treadwell listened open-mouthed as this coarse copper flirted with someone he'd never spoken to in thirty years of service and regarded as remote as royalty.

Peterson told her how helpful Mr Treadwell had been, but how, unfortunately, his powers were limited. He outlined what he would like to do. Ms Friedland informed him that each of the one hundred and sixty-seven local authorities ran its library service independently. She could provide him with address labels for all their chief librarians. Alternatively he could have access to the full list of twenty-five thousand members.

Peterson thought for a moment. 'This is an enquiry into a very serious crime, Olga,' he told her. 'I want to act as quickly as possible. If I get a letter to you, would it be possible for you to circulate it to the hundred-and-sixty-odd head librarians and then invoice the police for your costs?' This time he meant it about the charges.

Treadwell attracted his attention. 'You can fax it in from here,' he hissed.

'Mr Treadwell has kindly suggested we fax a letter to you from here,' Peterson said. He listened for a few seconds, then added: 'That's very obliging of you, Olga. We'll have it with you as soon as possible.'

'What a pleasant woman,' he declared, replacing the receiver.

'Er, yes, er, Olga is, er, very pleasant,' replied Treadwell, who had never realised that O. Friedland, his chief executive, was, in fact, a woman.

'Right, Mr Treadwell,' said the Inspector. 'If you

could possibly loan us a pad and put up with us for a few more minutes, we'll draft a letter.'

'Yes, yes, right away, be my guests,' he replied, producing a brand-new A4 pad from a drawer and handing it to Peterson. The Inspector passed it straight over to DC Wilson and stood up.

'Sit here, Trevor, and earn your keep,' he said.

Treadwell realised that he was no longer wanted. 'Well, gentlemen,' he said. 'I've got things to do, so I'll leave you to it, if you don't mind.'

'Thanks for your help, sir. We'll only be five minutes,' Peterson told him. He was a great believer in charm when he didn't have the authority to kick butts. He sat quietly in the chair vacated by Treadwell while the DC exercised his literary skills, and resisted the temptation to turn the two photographs to the wall.

'How about that, guv?' asked Wilson, after a while, handing the pad back. After the introductions the message read:

> Will all librarians check, as soon as possible, any books they hold on the subject of fungi (i.e. mushrooms and toadstools) to see if any pages or photographs have been removed. If you find any such books will you please report this information to Detective Inspector Oscar Peterson at...

It finished with the words:

> This is an enquiry into a serious crime, so will you therefore treat this and any other information with the utmost confidentiality.

'It'll do,' said Peterson, after crossing out the Oscar. He didn't want anybody thinking it was a practical joke.

DC Wilson smiled with satisfaction – that was the deliberate mistake he'd included.

Treadwell came back and agreed to type it and fax it to Olga. He smiled at the thought of adding a conspiratorial covering note of his own. Peterson said he'd call in tomorrow to pick up a copy, but really he just wanted to make sure it had been forwarded.

When they'd gone, the Group Librarian set to work on the word processor, secretly pleased that the typist had taken the day off. He wasn't happy with the letter, and felt that the Inspector should have written it himself, instead of delegating it to a junior officer. That was something he would never have done. He studied the finished document on the screen, but couldn't quite put his finger on what was wrong with it.

He ran off a copy and studied it some more. Then he realised where the error was. He tore the sheet into shreds and dropped them into the bin. Turning back to the screen he rattled his fingers expertly over the keyboard for a few seconds and examined the result. After Peterson's address and telephone number he'd added the words: 'or your nearest police station'.

That was better. Now it looked professional. He tapped the keys again and the printer zipped away at another copy.

Chapter Nine

I awarded myself a weekend off. I'd worked nonstop for nine weeks, averaging over twelve hours per day with no paid overtime. The car had clocked up five thousand miles in that time, for which I would be reimbursed. I called in at the office on the Saturday morning, but I was determined not to stay long.

There were reports to read from the few officers I didn't see regularly. We had people floating about the country, interviewing suspects, informers and the mother-in-law's first cousin, twice removed. We also had search parties out when we could borrow the manpower. Plenty of local groups offered their help, but they needed organisation to do the job properly. Sometimes I caught myself wishing that they'd find a body, and a feeling of revulsion came over me, but I couldn't imagine a plausible alternative.

The house was a dump. A lady came and cleaned it for a while, but her husband needed a lot of attention and she'd had to give me notice. I pleaded with her not to desert me, but to no avail. Eventually she agreed to iron my shirts if I took them round, once a week. I filled the washing machine and set to work with the Hoover.

I made a big impression on the mess, but it left me feeling knackered. Pub grub is not my first choice, but I couldn't face cooking so that was where I went. The chicken Kiev tasted as if it had walked from there, and the landlady's home-made apple pie was made from tinned apple that she'd opened all by herself. The company was about as interesting as the food, so I downed a couple of pints and went home.

Sunday breakfast was cornflakes and toast. Then I mowed the grass in the front garden. The borders were overgrown and neglected but a couple of hours with the hoe and secateurs made them respectable again. Well, I thought so, although the Best Village judges might disagree. Lunch was a roast beef ready-meal for one. I remembered what Annabelle had said about my eating habits and felt guilty. Happy, but guilty. When I'd cleared up I rang her.

'It's Charlie,' I said. 'I've done my chores, washed the car, wallpapered the coalhouse and had my dinner. I'm fed up, so I was thinking about having a drive up on to the moors; blow away a few cobwebs. Any chance of you putting your tapestry down and coming along?'

'Goodness! You mean you are having a day off?' she replied.

'That's right.'

'What about the crime wave?'

'Anarchy will break out all over the nation, but I don't *care*. Are you free?'

'I'd love to come, but I have a PCC meeting at seven. I'll have to be back about six-ish. Is that all right?'

'No problem. I'll see you in about forty minutes. And put your walking boots on.'

We went to Blackstone Edge, a rocky outcrop at the scrag end of the Peak District, where the high moors fade into the Aire and Calder valley. I parked in a lay-by, where the local water authority kindly still allow their subjects access to the land, and we followed a track into the moor. The path quickly became narrow and muddy, so I led the way, making diversions at intervals to avoid the worst of it. Soon we were on rocky ground, with no distinct trail, just marker poles at irregular intervals. You clambered across the boulders as best you could.

We were both wearing hiking boots and jeans, but Annabelle's jeans seemed to go on for ever. Her navy coat would have been a donkey jacket on anybody else, but on her it looked straight from a Paris fashion house. Walking on rough ground is an art, but she had obviously mastered it. She moved effortlessly, her long legs never hesitating or stumbling.

A gang of sheep, about ten of them, raised their sullen heads and watched us pass, like the honest folk in a western town contemplating a couple of outlaws riding down Mainstreet. A bird with pointed wings and down-curved beak flew leisurely by.

'Curlew,' I said, pointing. We followed it till it was a speck against the sky.

'What's that one then?' Annabelle asked, as something flew from under our feet, showing a flash of white as it sped away.

'Er, SBB,' I told her.

'SBB?'

'Small Brown Bird,' I explained.

'It was a meadow pipit.'

'Oh.'

After about twenty minutes we reached the ancient cobbled road. I stood in the middle of it, arms outstretched, and said, '*Voilà!*'

Annabelle looked amazed and delighted. 'I never knew this was here,' she said. 'It's Roman, isn't it?'

I nodded.

She knelt on the cobbles and ran her hand along the groove that runs down the centre. 'I've seen pictures of it in books, but never knew where it was. Does anybody know what this is for?'

'No,' I replied. 'Lots of crackpot theories, like it was

made by the keels of Viking ships as they were
dragged overland; or maybe by charioteers as they
trailed a foot along the ground to try to slow down.
Must've ruined their sandals. It's anybody's guess.'

'What do you think?'

I shook my head. 'The truth,' I replied, 'would probably be mundane and obvious, once we knew it. It
usually is. Far better for it to remain concealed.'

Annabelle stood up, and slowly turned in a full circle, studying the view. I watched the wind ruffle her
hair. When she was facing me again she said: 'You love
the moors, don't you, Charles.'

It was a statement rather than a question, but I
replied to it. 'Yes, I suppose I must.'

'Why? What is it about them that draws you?'

I'd never tried to put it into words before. 'I don't
know. They're beautiful. And mysterious. They have
stories to tell that we can only try to imagine. They're
never the same for two days together, or even for ten
minutes. They reveal themselves to you in brief
glimpses, like a curtain blowing open and then closing
again. But all the time there is a constancy about them.' I
shrugged, struggling for the right words. 'I don't know,
I suppose I just feel at peace when I'm near them.'

Even as I spoke I was wondering if it was my feelings for the moors I was describing, or for the woman
who'd asked the question.

Above us, ragged clouds, the colour of wet slate,
were scurrying eastwards. Thirty thousand feet higher,
the pale sky was patterned with pink fish-scales,
through which an invisible jetliner etched its trail,
straight as a laser beam. We walked, hand in hand,
back up the hill to the outcrop of millstone grit that is
Blackstone Edge.

'Are we in Lancashire or Yorkshire?' Annabelle asked.

'Neither,' I asserted. 'We're just about on the border, but history has been rewritten. The Wars of the Roses were now fought between Calderdale and Greater Manchester. It was a close-run thing until Kirklees joined in and tipped the balance.'

When we reached the piled-up boulders of the Edge, I pointed to a smooth one and told Annabelle to sit there. We were both puffing with the exertion. I sat on the ground, leaning back against a rock and facing her, with my legs splayed out in front of me.

'I want to tell you something,' I said. 'About me.'

Her smile was replaced by a look of concern. She sensed from my tone I was being serious, and she was uncertain and possibly worried about what I was about to say. 'What is it, Charles?'

I picked up a small stone and tossed it at my left boot. It bounced off the toe and rolled into the grass. I followed it with my gaze, as if it were some juju that might tell me the right words to use.

'Just over a year ago,' I began, 'not long after I first met you, I... I... killed a man.' There, I'd said it. 'We were on a raid, and –'

'Yes, I know.'

'– he came at me with a... You know?' I looked up at her face, into those eyes the colour of a bluebell wood in spring.

'Yes,' she replied, very softly.

'How do you know?'

'I read in the papers that a drug dealer had been shot. It said he fired a shotgun at a policeman, who fired back and killed him. I wondered if you were involved, and when I didn't hear from you for a long time... Then, one day, I bumped into Gilbert – Superintendent Wood. So I asked him.'

'You've known all the time?'

'Yes. Do you want to talk about it?'

'No, I don't think so. I just wanted to tell you.'

She slid down off her rock and reached out for my hand. Hauling me to my feet she said: 'Come on, then. Get me to my PCC meeting.'

High above, the vapour trail was breaking up and drifting away. The jet that had made it would be heading out over the Atlantic by now. I was glad I wasn't on it. I wouldn't have traded places with the Emperor of China.

We threw our coats on the back seat of the car and I pushed the heater controls to maximum and started the engine. Annabelle clicked her seatbelt fastened and looked across at me.

'Thank you for showing me the Roman road,' she said.

I winked at her and said: 'You're welcome, ma'am.'

'Does it have a name?'

'A name?'

'Yes, like Watling Street, or the Fosse Way.'

'Oh, didn't I tell you?' I replied, thinking fast.

'No, you haven't mentioned it.'

'Sorry about that. It's called the M... let me see... the M... LXII.'

She chuckled and smiled. It was an indulgent smile, tolerant, and, I thought, affectionate. We arrived at her gate well before six. I politely declined the offer of a quick cup of tea and drove home.

The Peak District is chopped off the bottom of the Pennines by what Yorkshire geography teachers call the Aire Gap, although their Lancastrian colleagues may have a different name for it. The Gap acts as a funnel for migrating birds, working their way from one coast to the other. It's also a major transport route between the conurbations of Manchester and Leeds, especially since the coming of the motorway.

It's a good area for a young, ambitious policeman to work in. The wool and cotton barons left a legacy of fine houses, mills and remote farms, built like castles from the local stone. Property prices are low, and the attractions for today's highly mobile criminals are tempting.

There's a lot more to the area than that, though. Something in the water, or the air, reacts with the genes of a few susceptible people to produce villains who break all the rules of the game.

This valley spawns serial killers.

Everybody knows their names. They were splashed over the front pages of the tabloids, feeding the egos that created them. Even Haigh and Christie, who did their foul work in London, were born near here.

Then there are the ones who worked within the law – brutish, inarticulate men who were driven by something within to write misspelt letters to the Home Office, volunteering to become the Public Executioner. And the Government, glad to find the final cog in the mechanism that started in Westminster and ended in the lime pit, accepted them. Six hangmen, including three Pierrepoints, were born in the valley. Between them they despatched, with varying degrees of incompetence, over a thousand of their fellow men and women.

I was having a restless night. All of these things, plus a few faces from the past, came to disturb my sleep. Twelve years ago I caught a double killer. In the heat of the moment I could cheerfully have pulled the trap myself; but now, and in the quiet of the night, I'm glad he didn't hang. He's still inside, and will be for a long time. That's good enough for me. I can live with knowing I put him there. The memory of those two kids in that blood-splattered room easily dispels any doubts that may arise.

Once the birds started singing I knew that any chance of sleep was gone. I rose ridiculously early, shaved and showered, and drove to work; pausing only to put on some clothes, of course.

We always made a point of having a full team conference on a Monday morning, although 'conference' was putting it a bit grandly, these days. Due to my change in routine I hadn't seen a Sunday paper, but I was quickly brought up to date. Georgina's disappearance had attracted the attention of a good number of cranks. Unsolved crimes, especially murders or potential murders, always do. Some were sincere, some were mischievous, all were time-wasters. Now one of them had hit the headlines.

Madame Julia LeStrang, medium and psychic healer, said she could find Georgina. The *Sunday News* believed her, and the police's reluctance to cooperate amounted to sheer incompetence.

I tossed the paper I'd been given to read straight into the bin. 'You had finished with that, hadn't you?' I asked Sparky, who'd brought it in.

'Yes, boss. Texture's no good for me.'

'Mmm, it is a bit coarse. Jeff, you've handled most of the crank calls. How many times has Madame LeStrang been in?'

'I've seen her three times in the last month. She wants access to something personal from Georgina. Then she claims she can find her using a pendulum. She's already receiving messages from the ether, or somewhere.'

'More like her bank manager. What did you tell her?'

'Er, well, I suggested she pissed off, with varying degrees of emphasis.'

'Good,' I said. 'So let's get down to work.'

I broke the news about the deadline that the Acting Chief Constable had given us. It didn't go down well. The three main types of evidence are Witnesses, Confessional and Forensic. We had none of these. Motive and Opportunity are worth less in a court of law than a dipsomaniac's vows of abstinence, and they were all we could offer. The entire investigation would rely on us discovering something damning if we searched Dewhurst's premises. Short of finding a body under the floorboards, it was hard to imagine what that might be.

We reviewed the current situation, pooled our findings and shared out the various lines of enquiry to be followed. I sensed that morale was waning, so before the team dispersed I suggested that we all have a jar or three in the pub that evening. The proposal was received with enthusiasm. After much argument a decision was made that we'd meet at the Golden Lion. Monday was karaoke night. I wished I'd kept my mouth shut.

'Somebody remember to invite Luke along,' were my parting words.

One of the best parts of being a detective is that you work with a partner. When you are the boss you can choose your own. I had suppressed all personal or emotional signals and worked with DC Dave 'Sparky' Sparkington. It was the most objective decision I ever made.

We joined the force within a year of each other, but Sparky had never chased promotion. Thief-taker was the only recognition he ever aspired to. Many policemen say that sergeant is the most satisfying rank, but all Sparky ever wanted to be was a DC, and he was the best I'd known. We went down to the canteen for some breakfast.

Nigel and Mad Maggie joined us for a mug of tea and a toasted currant teacake.

'I have the impression that you're not a believer in the supernatural, boss,' stated Maggie.

'Correct,' I replied through a mouthful of toast.

'There's a woman in Heckley who has a terrific reputation for fortune-telling,' she said. 'I've spoken to several people who've visited her, and they've been told things about themselves that have really shaken them. I don't believe in it, but she's very clever.'

'You've said it all there, Maggie,' Sparky confirmed. 'They're clever. Shirley once went to a spiritualist with a neighbour. She came home full of it. This chap had the audience hanging on his every word. Claimed he was receiving messages from some poor woman's dead husband. I had to put my foot down to stop her from going again.'

'You?' I said. 'Put your foot down with Shirley? Pull the other one.'

'My grandmother held regular conversations with my grandfather,' Nigel added. 'Went on for years. Mother said it used to drive her potty.'

'Through a spiritualist?' asked Maggie.

'No. Across the dinner table. He wasn't dead.'

We all laughed far too much, but it was a special event – Nigel had never made a joke before. He blushed with pride.

The boss always has the last word. 'Listen,' I told them. 'There's a simple proof that telepathy is bunkum. Think of all those poor page-three girls and big-bosomed film stars. If thoughts could be transmitted they'd never have a moment's peace. They'd constantly be imagining they were being ravished, by building-site workers and third-formers and little men in big rain-coats.'

'And policemen?' asked Maggie.

'And policemen.'

'It could work the other way round, too, boss,' she insisted.

'Well, it's never happened to me,' I declared; modestly adding, before anyone else did: 'Not that that proves much.

'C'mon, let's check the streets.'

I knew what karaoke was, but I'd never seen how it worked. I was fascinated by the technology. The list of songs available contained hundreds that I hadn't heard of, but there were still plenty of golden oldies from the sixties. Nothing that I felt like singing in public, though.

The pub was crowded, but we managed to get the last two tables, and pushed them together. I bought the first round. When I reached the bar I discovered that the landlady was an old friend. She used to work in the canteen at Heckley nick. It was not long after my divorce, and she was attractive, in a flashy sort of way. Sexy. The restrictions on having affairs with colleagues didn't extend to the civilian staff, and the possibilities offered by coordinating my flexible hours with her afternoons off made my hormone levels run berserk. We'd almost reached the your-place-or-mine stage when someone tipped me off that her husband played in the scrum for Wigan. It worked better than a cold shower.

'Hello, Charlie,' she said warmly. 'Don't see you in here very often.'

'Hello, Karen,' I replied, with equal delight. 'No,

I've not been in for years. Still married to that rugby-playing gorilla?'

'Ted? Yes, he's here, somewhere. What about you? Still on your own?'

I'd met Ted and liked him, dammit. It was a struggle to prevent my eyes flicking down towards her cleavage as she wrestled with the pumps. "Fraid so. If he ever leaves you, let me know.' I didn't mean it, but might have done, a few years ago.

She smiled at me as she pushed the last pint across and took the money. 'Want a tray?' she asked.

'No, I've enough here to carry,' I replied.

A Tom Jones lookalike was at the microphone. Unfortunately the similarity didn't extend to the voice. His hips swung in unison with his medallion as he asked Delilah to forgive him because he just couldn't take Kenny More, whoever he was.

'Is he serious?' I asked.

'Deadly,' was the answer from the others. Then I joined in with the enthusiastic calls for an encore.

We had a pneumatic Dolly Parton with a slow-punctured voice, and a passable Kenny Rogers, although his Yorkshire accent didn't do anything for the red-necked lyrics. Then it was Luke's turn.

He grabbed the mike, turned up the corner of his lip as he waited for his cue, then launched into 'Jailhouse Rock'. The place was instantly on its feet, dancing along with him. He uh-uh'd and gyrated like he'd invented the style. A final pelvic thrust had everybody cheering, but this time they meant it.

'I think we just found Elvis,' said Sparky.

'We're not looking for him,' I stated, draining my glass. 'Get the beer in.'

Luke was waylaid by a girl with the face of a Disney princess and hocks like a Derby contender. We watched him dismiss her with unmitigated hatred seething inside us.

'Charlie?' said Sparky, reaching for my glass.

'What?' I replied, passing it to him.

'If you had your life to live over again, would you do it all the same?'

I watched the girl retreating, her bum pushing the properties of lycra beyond its design limits. 'Yeah, probably,' I said.

Luke sat down and I gave him a brothers handshake. 'You should practise that lip-curl,' I told him. 'You could be good.'

'I do,' he admitted.

Sparky and Jeff returned laden with replenished glasses. 'There's an old friend of yours behind the bar, Charlie,' Sparky told me.

I feigned ignorance. 'Oh, who's that?'

'Karen. Used to work in the canteen. We all thought you had something going with her.'

'Karen? Karen?'

'You know. Has a divine right and a heavenly left.'

'Ah! That Karen!'

'Yes, that Karen. Rumour was that you and her were having it away.'

I shook my head. 'Sadly, we were just good friends,' I confessed.

'She's looking her age now,' he went on. 'Bags under her eyes. Looks tired.'

'I'm not surprised, running a place like this,' said Jeff. 'It must be an eighteen-hour day, seven days a week. It'd give anyone bags under the eyes.'

I licked the froth off my top lip. 'There could be another reason for them,' I said, brightly. 'Maybe there is something in this telepathy, after all...'

* * *

It looked suspicious, the way he stood up and followed me into the gents' toilet. If he'd been over five foot four and under sixty-five I'd have been worried. He was just a little old man, though. Definitely not my type. Probably one of the old regulars who still came into the pub even though it had been overtaken by the youth boom. He hovered behind me as I did what I'd come in to do. I was drying my hands under the blower when he spoke:

'Er, it's Inspector Priest, isn't it?'

I didn't answer, waiting for him to continue.

'You're, er, in charge of looking for that little girl, aren't you? Can I have a word?'

I cast a glance at the cubicles. Both doors were closed. I nodded and pointed at the exit.

Instead of returning to the big room where the music was, I turned left, into the old-fashioned taproom. This was where the men did the serious drinking while their wives, one night per week, sipped a milk stout or a port and lemon.

The room was almost empty on a Monday evening, hence the karaoke. I led the little man to a quiet table in a corner and we sat down.

'I saw your picture in the paper, and on the telly. I, er, hope you don't mind me talking to you in here; when you're, er, trying to relax, like.'

Not so far, I thought, but I'm getting close. He shuffled nervously and fidgeted with a beer mat.

'My daughter,' he continued. 'She said I should have a word with you. I don't want to waste your time, though. You've plenty on your plate already.'

Well, it didn't sound as if he wanted my autograph. He fumbled with the beer mat and it fell from his fingers. I reached across and placed my hand over it.

'What's your name?' I asked.

'Er, my name? It's Toft, Norman Toft.'

'Right, Norman. Start at the beginning and tell it in your own words. First of all, where do you live?'

'Er, Crowfields Road. Number twenty-six.'

'Go on.'

'Well, I first noticed it two weeks ago...' He licked his lips and glanced towards the bar, but I ignored the gesture. 'Saturday night. I'd been in 'ere for a couple of pints, like I usually do. I was looking out of the back window, just before I went to bed. I have a back garden, then there's a dirt road, and then there's the gardens of the 'ouses on Crowfields Street. They're a rum lot live on the street. Problem families, gipsies, that sort. It used to be a good neighbourhood before they started bringing them in from...'

Now *I* was beginning to feel thirsty. He'd get a drink out of me by attrition if he didn't come to the point soon. 'Just tell me what you saw, Norman,' I interrupted.

'Right. Flashes.'

Oh no! Not Unidentified Flashing Objects!

'Flashes?' I echoed.

'Yes, well, not at first. There was a car parked in the lane. I turned the light out and watched it for a while, er, through my binoculars.'

He must have noticed my change of expression, and looked embarrassed. 'I wasn't pimping!' he protested. 'We get all sorts of carrying-on in that lane. Last year I had a row of cabbages stolen. And all next door's runner beans went.'

'That's OK, Norman. You were being a good citizen. So what did you see?'

'Well, I've worked it out. If I'm number twenty-six, the 'ouse behind me is probably number twenty-five, so next door to him will be twenty-seven. That's where I saw the flashes. Number twenty-seven, Crowfield Street.'

'Where were these flashes?'

'In a bedroom window. The curtains were closed but I could still see 'em.'

'And what were they like?'

'Like from a photographer.'

You work on a case for months, sometimes years, searching for evidence, sifting meaningless facts and observations, waiting for the breakthrough to come. And you pray that when it does come you will recognise it, because it is never quite what you expected. I thought about it until I realised my teeth were nearly meeting through my bottom lip. 'Maybe he's a keen amateur photographer,' I suggested.

Norman shook his head. 'Not on Crowfield Street. Dog fighting and pigeons is the only 'obbies they 'ave.'

'So how many flashes were there?'

'Dozens. 'Undreds. Went on for best part of an hour.'

'OK. Anything else?'

'Yes. I saw them leave. They got in the car and drove away.'

'Can you describe them?'

'Yes. There was a man, a woman, and a little girl.'

I had a salty taste in my mouth. I wiped my lower lip with my finger. It was bleeding. 'Let me get this straight,' I said. 'You told me it started two weeks ago. So when did you see what you've just described?'

'Two Saturdays ago. And then again this Saturday.'

'What time?'

'Oh, about... just before midnight to one o'clock.'

'Same thing? Same people?'

'Yes.'

'And now you're reporting it to me?'

'Er, yes.'

I thought: You stupid, doddering old fool! You idiot-ic apology of a human being! I didn't say it, though. Instead I stood up and nodded towards the bar. 'What'll it be, Norman? Pint of bitter?'

Chapter Ten

The girl on the switchboard told me that my contact had been made redundant at the last reorganisation, so I needed to cultivate a new one. I explained who I was and the nature of the investigation I was involved in, and they were very cooperative. People usually are. That was how, nine o'clock Tuesday morning, Sparky and I came to be dressed in green overalls and driving a gas board van towards Crowfield Street.

Paedophilia and child pornography must be at the sick end of the league table of offences. It's all around us all the time, but mostly it is spread so thinly it remains unnoticed and undetected. It's kept within the family, and the victims suffer in silence, repressed by fear, guilt and an ignorance of what is normality. Nobody ever complains, and without a complainant we have no crime.

We stumble across the evidence, and prosecute for possession of indecent material. In the various raids during the Georgina investigation we'd found more than we expected. All the owners claimed they had bought it mail-order from abroad, but our vice people were confident it was being produced locally.

There is a mythology around the subject, created in the dreams of the evil genie who lives inside all of us. For some, the genie takes over, and when we catch them we judge and vilify, then whisper a little prayer of thanks that it didn't happen to us. We hear the horror stories and dismiss them as fantasy. But we can't be sure.

Sparky parked the van and we walked along Crowfield Road, noting the house numbers. I was armed with a clipboard and the relevant page from the electoral roll.

'This looks like one of ours,' he said, standing over a manhole cover.

I read the legend cast into the metal. 'That's the water board,' I told him. 'We're gas.'

'Are we?' He looked back at the van. 'Oh aye.'

Number twenty-six had the neatest garden in the street. Norman was mainly a roses man, and the borders round the shaven lawn were a blaze of colour. It was like finding a smiling face at a disciplinary hearing. A gorgeous Nelly Moser was climbing up the wall round his front door.

'That looks gorgeous,' I said.

'It's a Nelly Moser,' Sparky replied. That's how I know. I wrote it on my board as he rang the bell.

Mr Toft looked surprisingly dapper for the hour. We flashed our IDs and I made the introductions. Eventually recognition dawned on him like the sun rising out of Filey Bay on a balmy bank holiday and he invited us in.

'Cup of tea, lads?'

'No thanks.'

'Yes please.'

'Go on, then.'

I followed him into the kitchen. 'The garden looks a treat, Norman,' I said. 'It's a credit to you.' Through the back window I could see rows of vegetables stretching down to the lane he'd told me about. Now I could understand his concern about thieves and vandals.

'Aye. It's all I've got to do, these days. Biscuits?'

I shook my head. 'No thanks, a cuppa will be fine. How long have you been on your own?'

'Fifteen months. Do you both take milk?'

'I don't. It must be hard for you.'

'I get by. Can you carry them through?'

I picked up the mugs and sugar bowl and we went back into the front room. A wizened little terrier was curled in a basket near the fireplace.

I sipped my tea and stared at the dog. The problem with drinking it black is that it comes boiling. I was still blowing and sipping when Sparky put his empty mug down and said: 'Could you show us where you were when you saw the flashing, Mr Toft?'

We trooped upstairs to the spare bedroom at the back of the house. It was as neat as expected, used to store a few spare pieces of furniture. The wallpaper pattern looked like a huge dissected kidney, repeated in great diagonals across all four walls.

Through the window we could see the backs of the houses on Crowfield Street, about a hundred and twenty yards away. I picked up the pair of ten-by-fifty binoculars that were lying on the windowsill and looked through them. I was transported straight into the bedroom of the house opposite. The alarm clock was ten minutes fast and something black and lacy was dangling across the bedside cabinet. I could almost smell the bodies. You dirty old sod, I thought, as I fumbled with the focus control.

I handed the binocs to Sparky. 'Which house was it?' I asked Norman.

He pointed. 'That one, to the left, with the curtains closed.'

'Are the bedroom curtains ever open?'

'No.'

They didn't look like curtains. There were no folds or drapes. My guess was it was just a piece of material pinned over the window.

In my mind I was juggling with the various ways of handling this. First intention had been to set up twenty-four hour surveillance of the house opposite, but now I was having second thoughts. It would have been satisfying to catch them in the act, but we had the welfare of the kid to consider.

I was satisfied that the little girl that Norman had seen leaving the house wasn't Georgina. He'd said she had long fair hair, whereas Georgina's was dark and short. There was probably no connection, but we couldn't be sure. We'd heard stories about the evils that these people perpetrated, and what one person is capable of imagining, another might be motivated to act out.

I turned to the old man. 'Norman, would you mind leaving us alone for a few minutes?' I asked.

He looked crestfallen. 'Oh, er, OK. I'll be downstairs if you want me.'

When I'd heard him reach the bottom of the stairs I asked Sparky what he thought of things.

He lowered the binoculars and examined them. 'He'd be better off with a pair of eight-by-thirties,' he replied.

'Or a tripod,' I suggested.

'Mmm, a tripod. Definitely.'

'Is the dog stuffed?'

'No, I saw it flick an ear.'

'Thank God for that. We've got four options,' I said. 'One – we move in soon as pos.; two – we wait till the flashing starts and move in; three – we wait till the flashing finishes and move in.'

'Number two, the little girl will be in the middle of things,' said Sparky. 'For three, we'll have put her through it all again, while we sit outside. I couldn't go along with that.'

'I agree. And today's only Tuesday. They might not come back until Saturday, if then.'

'What about option four?'

'I haven't thought of it yet.'

'Me neither.'

'There's bound to be one.'

'Quite. And there might be a simple explanation.'

'Quite.'

'Shall we have a ride round and read his meter, then?'

'No,' I said. 'Let's not bother. We can do it in the morning, nice and early. C'mon, let's get back and arrange the paperwork.'

We drove slowly round the block in the gas board's van and had a good look at number twenty-seven. A naked lightbulb glowed in the kitchen. We were both itching to knock at the door, but resisted the temptation. The garden was converted into a dog compound, and a smart caravan stood in it. A two-year-old Mitsubishi Shogun was parked in the road, registered to one Paul Darryl Lally, which was also the name shown on the electoral roll. The other name on the list was Fenella Smith.

As we reached the gas board depot, CRO were coming back to me with Lally's criminal record. It was longer and more depressing than a Moscow bread queue. Mainly petty theft and receiving. Nothing heroic.

'He drives a better car than me,' stated Sparky.

'And me,' I replied.

'Well, we can't have that, can we?'

'No way,' I concurred.

I didn't really have time for lunch, but the night before's excesses were growing more apparent as the day wore on. I fetched a cheese sandwich from the canteen and ate it in the office, with a couple of aspirin for dessert. Tea is always in plentiful supply. If any of the team were ever suffering from overindulgence I'd lean on them all the more, so I wasn't pleased with myself.

Sparky went to find a magistrate, preferably female, to sign a search warrant; I filled the Superintendent in on the story so far. Gilbert agreed with how we'd decided to play it, but suggested we ask for expert help from the Regional Pornography Squad. They immediately attempted to take over the enquiry. I made it clear that they were only invited along to assist. Six thirty a.m., our place. Take it or leave it.

It's fair to say that when the front desk rang to say that Julia LeStrang and a journalist were downstairs demanding an audience, I wasn't in a receptive mood.

'Where's Caton?' I growled.

'They insist on seeing you, sir.'

'We decide who they see. Where is he?'

'Bentley Prison, talking to Section forty-three offenders. Won't be back today.'

'Oh aye. OK, stick 'em in an interview room and tell them I'll be ten minutes.'

I drank my tea and finished bringing the daily reports up to date, managing to spin the time out to nearly twenty minutes. Then I went downstairs.

Madame LeStrang was a riot of colour, dressed in chiffon and leopard-skin from the Oxfam rejects box. Her hair looked like it was crafted from fibreglass. The wind tunnel at Farnborough wouldn't have ruffled it. The man could have stepped straight out of Home's window. They both jumped to their feet as I entered, but it wasn't out of politeness.

'Inspector Priest! We've been waiting –'

'I'm sorry. I'm very busy. What can I do for you?'

She opened her mouth, but he spoke first. 'Madame

LeStrang is convinced she can be of use to you in the Georgina Dewhurst enquiry. She believes –'

'I'm sorry, sir, I didn't catch your name,' I interrupted.

'Er, Bond, Quentin Bond. Madame Le –'

'And what is your involvement in this, sir?'

He gave me a look that could warp a formica table. She stood there puffing and glowering like ridiculous old bags do. 'I'm acting on behalf of Madame LeStrang,' he stated.

'As her agent?'

'I suppose you could say that.'

'But you're a journalist.'

'Yes.'

'Freelance?'

'I don't see the relevance of these questions,' he spluttered.

'OK.' I turned to her. 'Right. Mrs LeStrang, what do you have to tell me?'

She was lost for words for a moment, but the fluency soon came back. 'When little Georgina disappeared the stars were propitious for a monumental event in her short life. She was born with the Moon in the third –'

I cut her short. 'I'm not interested in the stars just facts. How can you help us?'

'I'm trying to help you, Inspector. I need something of Georgina's. A lock of –'

'No. We'll be grateful for any practical help you or anybody else has to offer. We are not interested in mumbo jumbo or witchcraft. If you've nothing else –'

Bond made a desperate attempt to rescue his investment. 'Inspector Priest,' he began, with forced moderation, 'Madame LeStrang is a well-respected expert in the art of dowsing. There is overwhelming evidence from similar cases on the Continent and in America that –'

I shook my head and opened the door. 'Good afternoon,' I said.

Her face reddened, like high-speed photography of a ripening tomato. 'I've never been treated like this in my life!' she spluttered, clutching a huge handbag to her bosom.

I pointed the way with my forefinger.

'You'll regret this, Inspector,' she promised. 'I would remind you that the root of the word divine is from the –'

'No, Mrs LeStrang, let me remind you of something.' I pulled the door shut and shepherded them down the corridor. 'Let me remind you of just how good we are. If you as much as blink, sweat or break wind we can tell if you have been there, so don't dream of planting or tampering with any evidence. I won't ask you for any samples just yet, but I might do in the near future. Mind you, looking at the trail of dandruff your pet leech is leaving behind we probably have enough already.'

'Well, I've never –' she protested.

'No, you don't look as if you have,' I continued. 'Listen carefully, because I'll say this once, and once only: we are conducting an investigation into a very serious offence. If I ever have any reason to suspect that you have interfered with this enquiry, or with any evidence, we'll drop on you so hard you won't know if the Moon is in Jupiter or protruding from one of your more intimate bodily orifices. I hope I make myself clear.'

I yanked open the outer door to let them out. If looks could kill, the RSPCA would now be able to afford a new flea collar with my modest bequest.

'They didn't stay long,' observed the sergeant as I walked past the front desk.

'No,' I said. 'Something cropped up.'

I took the stairs two at a time and hummed the kids' tune that was currently driving everyone crazy: 'Ramty tamty diddle, ramty di de doo. If I could play this fiddle would you take me to the zoo?'

It wasn't often I gave anybody a bollocking. I hated unpleasantness, unless it was with someone really unpleasant. If a member of the team made a mistake, I was content that they knew it. If I didn't trust them, they didn't make the team. I deluded myself that it was good management, but maybe it was just cowardice. Slagging off a defenceless old lady had proved surprisingly enjoyable. I'd have to do it more often.

The kettle had hardly boiled when the front desk was back on the phone. 'It's a lady, sir, with some information. Do you mind seeing her?'

'What does this one do? Read entrails?' I asked.

'No, boss. Books.'

'Books?'

'That's right, books. Mrs Chadwick is a librarian. She's come in in response to a letter sent out by Trent Division. Doesn't mean anything to me. Something about mushrooms.'

'Mushrooms?' I was beginning to sound like an echo. 'Are you having me on, Arthur?'

'No, boss. Shall I send her up?'

'If you're not sending me up then you'd better. I'll look out for her.'

I stood at the office door as Mrs Carol Chadwick came round the top of the stairs. She was the type of woman who makes me think that growing older is not too bad after all. Perhaps just a touch wide at the hips, but lately I've revised my standards in that area. Her hair was grey, but she had a warm, slightly bemused smile, probably engendered by a lifetime surrounded by fine literature. Unless she sniffed coke.

One of those big organiser bags hung over her shoulder. I ushered her into my little office and pulled out a chair for her. It was time to stop being Mr Nasty and let Mr Nice come out.

'Sit down, Mrs Chadwick. I'm just making some tea; would you like a cup?'

'No, thank you.'

'Right. Well, I'm DI Priest. What can we do for you?'

She held out a letter. 'I've come in response to this. It says... contact your nearest police station, so here I am.'

I read the letter twice. 'Mmm,' I said, several times, adding, when I'd digested the contents: 'And what have you found at the library?'

She produced two books from the bag, with pictures of gaudy fungi on the covers. 'These,' she replied, fumbling with the pages. 'In this one, page five is missing.' She slid it in front of me. 'And in this one, page eleven is gone.'

I riffled through the sheets. All the rest were there. The missing ones had been neatly sliced with a sharp blade.

'These are from Heckley library, just down the road?' I asked, pointing vaguely out of the window.

'Yes, Inspector.'

'Are you chief librarian there?'

'Yes.'

I'd have to renew my membership. 'Well, Mrs Chadwick, I haven't a clue what it's all about,' I confessed. 'But I know a good way of finding out.'

I picked up the telephone and dialled the number given for Inspector Peterson.

* * *

Father Declan Birr was the nearest that most of his flock would ever come to meeting a saint. All his waking hours were spent in worship of the Lord and the proclamation of His message. He did this in a way the most ardent sceptic would have had difficulty faulting.

Father Birr had come up the tough way. The youngest of ten children, he overcame hardship and many tribulations to work his way through theological college. And he never forgot his humble beginnings. After stints in rural Ireland he worked in Calcutta, Mexico City and the East End of London. Always he believed in feeding the hungry body first; a full belly made for a receptive mind. He preached by example, and only tried to answer questions after they had been asked.

The phone call, received in the middle of that Tuesday afternoon, was nothing unusual. The problems of the people in the inner-city area of Sheffield where the Father now held office were little different from anywhere else in the world. Poverty, with the attendant bad housing and crime, knew no national boundaries. Another poor soul, he thought, reaching the end of its tether.

'Of course you can come and see me, my child. As soon as possible, you say. Well, let me see. I can be in the church, that's St Patrick's, any time this afternoon. Shall we say... four o'clock? Will that be all right?'

He didn't ask if the caller wanted to make a confession, or even if they were a Catholic. It wasn't important. At this stage all that mattered was that another human being had made a cry for help. The Father glanced up at his kitchen clock and slipped his shoes back on. As he left the house the electric kettle, with which he had intended making a cup of instant soup, came to the boil and clicked off.

The door to St Patrick's had a character all its own. When it was ajar some freak of architecture caused an outrush of air, which would snatch the door from the hand of the hapless person who had just entered and slam it shut. The resultant reverberations would set the candle flames shimmering at the other end of the church, and columns of black smoke would spiral from them towards the roof.

Deep as he often was in supplication or meditation, Father Birr could never pray undisturbed through a door slam. It was a source of amusement to him, and he privately regarded it as God's early-warning system.

He was half expecting it, this time, for he was certain that the voice on the phone was a stranger. When it came he continued his devotions with practised serenity. The visitor would pause, then walk slowly through the nave towards the altar. The picture he would find there was all part of the healing process.

Father Birr said a final prayer asking for God's guidance in the immediate task, kissed the altar cloth and rose to his feet. He took three steps backwards and genuflected. Then he turned to meet his mystery caller.

Never shocked or surprised, he was not disturbed by the slightly built figure before him. It wore a trilby hat pulled down over the eyes, leaving the face in shadow. Slung diagonally across the shoulders was the strap of a large sports bag, with the name Adidas emblazoned on the end. The right arm disappeared into the bag. The hand was resting on the mechanism of the twelve-bore shotgun it contained, but the priest could not see that.

Father Birr smiled just enough to convey empathy

but not pleasure. 'Hello,' he said. 'So glad you made it. I'm Father Birr, but most people call me Declan. Do you want to tell me your name?'

'Yes,' said the figure, almost apologetically. 'I'm... the Destroying Angel,' and a forefinger tightened around the trigger.

Declan Birr died instantly, the flash and the roar of the shotgun frozen in his mind for eternity. Behind him the candle flames shivered as the shock wave passed through them, and plumes of pollution streamed heavenwards.

Chapter Eleven

Warning bells were clanging in the head of the detective superintendent who launched the enquiry into the death of Father Birr. 'See if you can raise someone in the HOLMES unit,' he told his sergeant as soon as he had the opportunity. 'Ask them to input church, vicar, shotgun; that sort of stuff. There was another of these about three weeks ago, somewhere near Nottingham.'

The Home Office's purpose-designed major enquiry computer software flicked silently through the millions of bits and bytes that represented the thousands of crimes, mainly murders, that were stored in its implacable brain. It recognised the key words quicker than a man could blow his nose and spewed out the case of Ronald Conway; investigating officer in charge: Chief Superintendent Raymond Tollis.

Fifteen minutes and four phone calls later Tollis was speaking to Oscar Peterson, asking to be picked up.

Eighty per cent of murder victims know their assailant, and the majority of cases are solved in the first forty-eight hours. After that time the odds grow longer. Unsolved murders are never taken off the books, they are just pushed to the back of the file, to be forgotten by everyone except the people closest to them. DI Peterson was coming to terms with knowing that he might retire with the killer of Ronald Conway still free. He had decided that he could live with it.

Tollis's phone call displeased him at first. He did not like the man and wanted to play no part in furthering his ambitions. Then his policeman's instincts took over and his initial dismay was replaced by the familiar urge to be in the thick of the action.

A few minutes earlier he had donned a pair of old trousers, with the intention of doing an hour's gardening before the light faded. It was part of his self-imposed Training for Retirement programme. Dilys noted the eagerness with which he changed back into his work suit and shoes. She pecked his cheek and told him not to wake her when he returned.

They went to the church first, having to ask directions from a woman at a bus stop. Peterson abandoned the car about fifty yards from the gate and followed in the Chief Superintendent's wake. Over the wall, in the graveyard, a search party was methodically working its way over the ground in the gathering gloom.

Tollis ignored the lone reporter from the local radio station as they showed their IDs to the constable at the gate who was logging all visitors. Maybe there would be more when they came out. He'd better prepare some sort of statement, he thought. A short assertion that they were following certain lines of enquiry, combined with an appeal for witnesses. That should do it.

The young PC at the door glanced at their cards before holding it open for them. Every time it had slammed he felt that some vital clue was destroyed and he was responsible. Tollis strode straight through, but Peterson gave the youth a wink. At the front of the church three heads turned to examine the intruders from another force who might take the enquiry away from them.

Peterson hung back and let the chief do the talking. He was better at it. He heard himself described as 'my righthand man', followed by confirmation that Tollis and Andrew, the Sheffield super, had been at Staff College together. No, Andrew hadn't applied to do the Senior Command Course this time. Everybody agreed that the killing was a 'nasty job'.

'Any minute now they'll arrange a round of golf,' the DI muttered to himself.

The body had gone, but the photographer was still there, in case the SOCOs needed him. Peterson wandered to where they were working. A pool of blood, shaped like Australia with a smudged Gulf of Carpentaria, marked the spot where the priest had fallen. He looked in vain for Lake Eyre, but then remembered seeing a TV programme about it drying up.

Peterson turned to the photographer and jerked a thumb at the red stain. 'What was he wearing?' he asked.

'His long black frock, sir, over a shirt and trousers.'

'It's called a cassock. Did you notice if it had any pockets in it?'

'Pockets? No, I don't think so, sir. Just slits in the side.'

'Mmm, that's what I'd have thought.'

The DI ran his expert gaze over the vicinity of the murder, for there was no doubt that it was murder, and he was certain that this was at least the second in the series. He scanned the altar – the holy of holies; the pulpit from which Father Birr would never again dispense his gentle wisdom; and the notice boards with the numbers of last week's hymns.

It looked so innocuous, another person might have missed it. Lying on the front right-hand pew – where the bridegroom usually sits – was a piece of paper, with a prayer book resting on top so it could not blow away. Peterson walked across and bent over it. Without moving the book he could recognise the coloured illustration of a toadstool.

'Over here, please,' he said, catching the SOCO's attention. He stood well back, with his hands in his pockets, so as not to contaminate the evidence. 'That's his trademark,' he told the officer, 'so give it everything you've got. I want to know his blood group, his skin, hair and eye colour' – he counted them off on his fingers – 'his DNA profile, his sperm count, fingerprints, chromosomes, what he had for breakfast, oh, and his telephone number.' He stepped back in modest triumph to let them do their work.

'What is it?' asked the local super as the little group joined him.

'Picture of a toadstool, sir,' explained Peterson.

'A toadstool?'

'Actually, Andrew,' interjected Chief Superintendent Tollis, anxious to assert his authority, 'it's called a destroying angel. *Amonita virosa*. Well spotted, Oscar.'

Get stuffed, Baldy! thought Peterson.

'A destroying angel? Does that have any significance?' asked Andrew.

'Well, yes,' expanded Tollis. 'Our culprit uses that as his *nom de plume*. It would appear that the man we are looking for is some sort of religious fanatic.'

'Holy Moses!' exclaimed Andrew.

'Quite possibly, sir,' said Peterson.

They were all back at Don Valley nick when DC Trevor Wilson finally made telephone contact with Peterson.

'Hi, guv, how's it going?'

'OK. What do you want?' the DI asked.

'Is it another one?'

'Looks like it.'

'Why didn't you send for me?'

Peterson glanced up to see who was in earshot. 'Because I'm just the bloody chauffeur,' he hissed. 'Did you want something, or is this all part of your campaign to drive me out of office?'

'We've had a reply,' stated the DC.

'To what?'

'The mailshot to libraries. A DI in Heckley left a message this afternoon saying his local librarian has found two books with pictures cut out.'

'Brilliant! Where's Heckley?'

'Yorkshire, not far from Halifax. Do you want me to go there?'

'When?'

'Now.'

'Is it an all-night library?'

'Er, no, I don't suppose it is.'

'Then the morning will do. Big meeting first, seven o'clock. Then we'll drive up to Eeh-By-Heckley together. And Trevor...'

'What, guv?'

'Just think of all those sheep!'

We hit Paul Darryl Lally's house at seven a.m. on Wednesday morning. The seven o'clock knock on the door doesn't have the same police-state overtones that the two o'clock one does, but it catches the suspect in the same degree of unawareness. He's usually snug beneath his smelly sheets, and expecting to be there for at least another five hours. The criminal classes have no timetable imposed on them, so they invent their own. Their day starts at nightfall – daylight is for sleeping through.

I didn't go in with the raiding party, but Nigel is still talking about the expressions on Mr and Mrs Lally's faces when he shook them out of their sleep and cautioned them. They hadn't heard the front door being sledgehammered, having indulged themselves in an evening of bondage and supermarket red wine, plus an odd snort of sherbet. First I saw of them was when they were led, bewildered and bleary-eyed, to the waiting police car. She was wearing an anorak over her nightdress, fluffy slippers and an air of disbelief. They looked as if they'd just escaped a direct hit on their home by a Scud missile.

Nigel watched them leave as if he were seeing his parents off on their holidays, then gestured me inside. He was grinning like a eunuch in a hurdle race.

'Come and see the bed, boss,' he said, leading me upstairs. Best offer I'd had in years. He opened a door and stood back. 'How about that!' he declared.

In another room I could see Jeff Caton and the others. He saw me pass and said: 'Come and look at this, boss.'

'In a moment, Jeff.'

I walked past Nigel into the master bedroom. The bed was a magnificent brass job, all gleaming black enamel and gold. It nearly filled the room. The duvet cover was black satin, as were the pillows. The ceiling was mirrored and fitted with several spotlights. Nigel flicked them on and off. Dangling from each corner of the bed was a silken rope, made from red, black and white strands plaited together. A video camera stood on a tripod at the foot of the bed.

I looked across at Nigel with my best attempt at a bored expression on my face. 'So what's special?' I asked.

We hadn't gone in heavy-handed, but we'd taken a few experts with us – someone to take care of the dog; a sergeant, Frank Marriot, from the Porn Squad, and a photographer to make sure we didn't muck up any unprocessed material. Jeff was in a room converted into a studio, with the photographer.

'Cartier-Bresson, I presume,' I said as I joined him. All the walls were painted white and there was a white sheepskin rug on the floor. A thirty-five-millimetre Minolta fixed to another tripod was pointing down at it.

'Forensic,' I said, indicating the rug. The photographer was inspecting the camera. 'Any good?' I asked.

'Nothing special. Good enough, though.'

A voice in another room shouted, 'Tell Charlie to come and look at this lot.' I followed the sound into the third bedroom.

A loft ladder was in the lowered position and a pair of legs were visible at the top. 'What lot?' I asked.

Sparky withdrew from the aperture and looked down at me. 'Hi, boss. It's his dark room. There's a light switch, but maybe we'd better let Lord Lichfield have the first look. Don't want to spoil anything.'

Nigel wandered in to join us. 'It's a water bed!' he announced.

'I'm going back to the office,' I told them. 'You know what to do. And Dave...'

'What, boss?'

'Lock up when you've finished, but don't let Nigel have the key. We don't want him bringing that red-haired WPC from Halifax round and showing her the evidence. She might get seasick.'

Colour rose up Nigel's neck like beetroot juice spreading across a napkin. 'Who... how... who told you about her?' he stammered.

I winked at him and tapped the side of my nose with a forefinger.

'Is she a genuine redhead?' asked Sparky.

'Er, I'm not sure. I suppose so,' he replied.

'Yes, she is,' I surmised, and fled down the stairs.

The custody officer had put Lally and his wife in separate cells. His face lit up when I walked in and asked him where they were. 'Did they really have straps on the bed?' he asked.

'Not straps – silken ropes. I'll talk to them later – let them stew for a few hours. Have they asked for a phone call?'

'Didn't want one. She claims her name is Fenella. Did you get a look at her?'

'No, not really,' I told him.

'If I were guessing, I'd say she *had* to tie him to the bed.'

I went upstairs. As I walked into the office two voices cried: 'Boss wants you.' I did a stiff U-turn and walked straight out again. Superintendent Wood's office is up another floor. I knocked and walked in. Two strangers were sitting opposite him, sipping coffee, and the two books from the library were on the desk.

'Come in, Charlie, come in,' Gilbert said. Flapping his hand between us he went on: 'This is DI Oscar Peterson and DC Trevor Wilson, from Trent Division. DI Charlie Priest.'

I shook their hands. I have a bad habit when I shake hands. A few years ago one of my sergeants was convinced that the Freemasons were behind all the major crime in the world. According to him they made the Mafia look like a netball team at a garden party. In the course of his research he learned the secret handshake.

While shaking hands in the normal manner you place your thumb in the middle of the back of the other person's hand and wriggle it about. If they respond you say something really mundane, like 'It's a nice day.'

They reply: 'Yes, and it will get nicer before it gets worse.'

Peterson's thumb wriggled back and he said: 'Not very warm out, is it?'

I replied: 'No, and it will get cooler before it gets as warm as it is now, again.'

Gilbert gave me a funny look. 'Oscar's come about those photographs, Charlie. Can you look after him? I've a meeting at Division in an hour.' Turning to Peterson he said: 'Will you excuse me if I leave you with Charlie?' They shook hands again and Gilbert put on his coat and left us in his office.

The DI from Nottinghamshire wore a bemused expression on his face. 'You wouldn't like to swap your super for that bald-headed bastard of ours, would you?' he asked, quickly adding: 'You didn't hear that, Trevor.'

'Hear what, guv?'

'No thanks,' I told him. 'Gilbert's one of the best. Mind you, the secret is to treat them right. Can I ask you a personal question?'

'Fire away.'

'Is Oscar your real name?' From Trevor's reaction I knew that nobody had ever dared ask this before.

'Yes. My mother was a sucker for clarinet players.'

'I thought he played the trumpet.'

'Who?'

'Oscar Peterson.'

'Did he?'

I made myself a cup of Gilbert's coffee and rejoined them. 'Coming down a bit heavy on book vandals, aren't we?' I asked. 'Or is there something else at the back of it?'

'Books are expensive,' Peterson told me. 'And it leads to other things. Now he's killed a couple of people as well.'

I sat up. 'Really?'

'Yes, he's bagged a brace of vicars. With a shotgun. He left a picture of a toadstool cut from your books at the scenes. He's also claiming two others, but we think they were accidents.'

'Crikey. Any theories about the motive?'

''Fraid not. All contributions welcome. The interesting thing is that the first one, which may have been an accident, was in East Anglia. Gradually they are working this way, to where the pictures originated. It's as if he's growing tired of driving so far.'

'Or can't afford the petrol,' I added.

'Possibly.'

'So you want to concentrate your efforts up here?'

'That's right. We need an office, telephones, a fax, a HOLMES terminal, all the manpower you can spare. You name it, we want it.'

'You'll want Eric's address, too,' I said.

'Who's Eric?'

'He's the local vicar-killer. It sounds as if Gilbert didn't tell you about our own little investigation. We've an eight-year-old been kidnapped. I can give you a couple of offices and a DC to be going on with. We'll make him Acting DS. He'll organise the rest for you.'

Peterson didn't look pleased. 'A rooky DS!' he protested. 'We need a bit more weight than that.'

'He's got it,' I told him. 'What about the librarian?'

'We want to see her next.'

'OK. C'mon, I'll show you your offices and introduce you to John Rose. Then he can take you to the library.'

I stood up and held the door open for them. Peterson paused in the doorway and said: 'Can I ask you a personal question, Charlie?'

'Er, yes. Fire away,' I replied.

'Thanks. Tell me this: have you ever shagged a sheep?'

'No,' I answered. 'But I'm in a long-term relationship with a Swaledale ram who has.'

* * *

Nigel and most of the others arrived back about two o'clock. I asked him what they'd found.

'About twenty rolls of negatives, plus a part-used one in the camera,' he informed me.

'Where are they now?'

'The photographer has taken them to Foto Finish to be printed. He said it would take him a week to do them himself, but they'll put them through this afternoon. He has an arrangement with them. It'll cost us, though.'

'Who's with him?' I asked.

'Sparky's gone along to make sure nobody runs off a spare set.'

'Well done. You had me worried for a while. What about the video?'

'I replayed the one in the camera. It's just him and her. She's double-jointed. We found another six tapes, though.'

'Has that pervert Marriot from the Porn Squad taken them?'

'Yes, boss. They have the set-up to watch them all at the same time. What a way to spend an afternoon.'

'Mmm. Did you look at any of the negatives?'

'Yep. Plenty of arms and legs and writhing bodies. Couldn't tell who was who, though.'

'That'll do to be going on with. Let's see what the Lallys have to say for themselves.'

We went downstairs. As we walked past the front desk the sergeant called out to me: 'Mr Priest!'

I spun to face him: 'Mr Jenks!'

'Er, Charlie. You wouldn't happen to have a radio, would you?'

'Er, yes, I would just happen to have,' I replied.

'Good. Where is it, please?'

'It's next to the sideboard, under the CD player.'

'C'mon, Charlie, you know what I mean.' He looked exasperated.

'Oh! *That* radio,' I said. 'It's in the car. Why?'

'Thank Christ for that. One of the new ones is missing and someone's calling this afternoon to take them back. They're faulty. The buttons aren't waterproof and they stick in if they get wet. You wouldn't like to fetch it, would you?'

'No, I wouldn't. I'll leave you my keys, though.' I fished them out of my pocket and dropped them on the desk. 'It looks new and shiny; that's why I chose it.'

'The car?'

'No, the radio.'

We dragged Lally out of his cell and installed him in an interview room. He didn't kick and scream, fortunately. These days we have to treat people like him as if they were Fabergé eggs. I hovered over the twin tape recorders for a few seconds, then switched them on. I droned the words with studied indifference: 'Taped interview with Paul Darryl Lally. Also present DS Newley and DI Priest. Mr Lally, you have been informed that you are entitled to have a solicitor present during any interview. We can arrange a duty solicitor or send for one of your choice. Do you understand?'

He wasn't much of a specimen. Easy to dislike; that's how I prefer them. He was skinny, but with big, bony shoulders. His hair was long and lank, and a row of tattooed dots ran round his neck. A similar row were visible on his wrist, with a big letter A that was looped at the top. His fingers were decorated with the inevitable LOVE and HATE.

'Do you understand, Mr Lally?'

He stared at me.

'I take it, Mr Lally, that you are forgoing your right to have a solicitor present.'

Silence. I felt like a man who was trying to teach a parrot to talk, but didn't realise it was a sparrowhawk in the cage. He just sat there unmoved and unblinking.

'For the tape, please,' I said. He didn't stir, so I added: 'Mr Lally nods.'

'I'm saying nowt!' he blurted out.

'Ah! So you *can* use your tongue for speaking,' I said. 'After watching the video we weren't sure if you knew its proper use. Now, let's see how good it is at names, eh?'

He lounged back in his chair and folded his arms, to demonstrate that he was bored and had no desire to continue.

I leaned forward, two-thirds of the way across the table. 'Names, Lally, of all your customers. But most of all the procurers of the kids. I don't care if you get one year or twenty, but I want those names. Understand?' I paused for a second, before adding: 'Mr Lally nods.'

'I said fuck all!' he yelled into my face.

Now I sat back. 'Look, Lally,' I told him. 'At the moment you are charged with allowing your premises to be used for immoral purposes. At the best you're going to cop for taking photographs of under-age children in sexual acts. If I'm feeling benevolent you might get away with having taken part in those acts yourself. Do you follow?'

'I'm saying nowt!' he said.

'Let's see, then: there's assault, procuring children of tender age for sexual purposes, unlawful sexual intercourse... the possibilities are endless. But no doubt you know more about it than me.'

He scowled at me as if I'd just popped out of a boil he'd squeezed.

'OK,' I went on, 'play it your way. We'll have the photos printed in a couple of hours. Let's see what they tell us. Meanwhile you might like to know that our forensic people have been having a look at the sheepskin rug from your studio. So far they've found enough sperm on it for a trout farm. I wonder if any of it is yours? Interview terminated. Take him to his cell, Sergeant.' I stopped the tapes.

Nigel came back and paced up and down the interview room, clenching and unclenching his fists.

'For Christ's sake, sit down,' I told him. 'This is the cheapest carpet known to mankind. It wears out quicker than a Rottweiler's patience.'

'Grrr!' he said, holding his fists up.

'Sit down!' I ordered.

'Didn't you... don't you... didn't you want to smash his fucking head in?' he growled, dragging the chair away from the table and flopping into it.

'No,' I replied.

'No!'

'No. He'd probably enjoy it. All you can do is not let him know he's got through to you. Sometimes it's impossible. Do you think he'll talk?'

Nigel shook his head. 'He's rehearsed the situation. Or he's been brainwashed. Say nothing and let them try to prove otherwise, that's the code.'

'Yes, you're right; he's been on the course. It's going to get tougher, y'know. We've all the photos to look at, for a start. Once we've ascertained that little Georgina isn't involved, we could hand the whole thing over to the Porn Squad, if we wanted.'

'No, boss. Let's go through with it. It's just that...

well... I wonder how everybody else handles something like this?'

'Not very well, Nigel. Mainly through booze and taking it out on the wife.'

'What if you haven't a wife?' he asked, looking straight at me. He obviously didn't want the ten cents answer.

I twisted my chair sideways away from the table and stretched my legs out. 'Various ways,' I said. 'We all find our own. We even run seminars on it, I believe. Maybe we should all go on one. That won't help today, though.'

'What do you do, Charlie?'

Nigel, the paragon of politeness, had never called me Charlie before.

'What do I do? Oh, I make a joke of it; look on the bright side. I try not to see victims; just people who are involved. Maybe I pretend that some are even willing victims. It just happens that someone has done something that is against the law, and that's where I come in. We employ social workers to pick up the debris. It's not so much handling the situation as ignoring it. Maybe I'm storing trouble for the future, but it seems to work for me.'

It was a lie. It had worked for me in the past, but last year's future is today. 'It's a depressing job, Nigel, but what would happen if we didn't do it? Go fetch the other one; let's see what she has to say for herself.'

To hell with political correctness – Fenella Smith, common-law wife of Paul Lally, was a slag. I wouldn't have shagged her with the ragman's trumpet. Her skin was the colour of curdled milk, and in spite of being dragged out of bed at seven in the morning she had more black around her eyes than a steam tug has around its funnel, except that most of it was no longer around her eyes.

'Right, so how do we get to them?'

'Circulate descriptions.'

'Yep. So we need decent mugshots of them all. To start with maybe we should sort the pictures according to the adults on them, then do some cross-referencing. Jeff, could you have a think about that, please?'

'Will do, boss.'

'Then what?' I asked.

'See what Forensic come up with.'

'Yes. A few sets of dabs would help cut some corners. We can't afford to sit around waiting, though.'

'How about trying to identify the children, Charlie,' Sparky suggested. 'CPU might have them on their at-risk file. And we know where they all are between nine and four, most days.'

CPU was the Child Protection Unit. We'd have to call them in as soon as any kids were involved. I told Jeff to give them pictures of the girls. Sparky wandered over to the big map on the wall and started attacking it with a highlighter pen.

'What are they, Dave?' I asked.

'Schools.'

'What are you thinking?'

'School photographs, Charlie. We can't rely on just rolling up and flashing pictures before the head-mistress's eyes; but if we could obtain pictures of all the kids we could do a practical comparison.'

'They won't keep a spare set,' said Jeff Caton, 'but we could chop the best of what we have, to show just the kids' faces. Then ask all the teaching staff if they recognise them.'

'Bang goes confidentiality,' I stated. 'They'd soon guess or invent what we were doing.'

'There's another objection to that,' Sparky told us. 'About three years ago a teacher at the primary school was fined and sacked for dealing in computer porn. Others no doubt escaped.'

'That's right, I remember. So what are you saying?'

'That we'd have to take our own photographs: identify the kids ourselves,' Sparky replied.

'You're assuming the kids are local,' I stated.

'We've got to start somewhere.'

'Right!' I decided. 'We'll do it Dave's way. This one needs hitting with all we've got while Lally is still inside. How many schools have you found, Dave?'

'Four. The two big middle schools and a couple of medium-sized ones. What's that ... oh, about, say, fifteen hundred pupils.'

'Half boys, though,' said Nigel. 'And we might be able to disregard some who are too old or too young.'

'Mmm. These in the photos might look younger than they are. Let's try to do them all,' I replied. Turning to DS Newley I went on: 'Nigel, round up four photographers, if possible, and four WPCs to act as their assistants. Then we want photos of all the girls, with the WPCs cataloguing their names and any other characteristics we can come up with. Let's have a look at the children again.'

Jeff rummaged through the collection of pictures and spread samples on the desk, looking for any that gave good views of the faces. Not many did.

Sparky pointed with a forefinger. 'They're both wearing earrings, for a start,' he said.

One girl had small gold rings in her ears, and a pair of shiny stones glinted in the other girl's. 'Would they be allowed to wear those at school?' I asked. This was foreign territory to me.

'Probably,' Sparky told me. 'Things are different to your day. They're allowed to write left-handed now. So we want to know which kids have pierced ears.'

'And look where it's brought us. Make a note of that, Nigel: pierced ears.'

'Done, boss.'

'What else?'

'This one's wearing a chain around her neck.'

'Yep. Look, let's call them child A and child B and make a list.'

It didn't take long. Child A had pierced ears, a neck chain and rings on two fingers. B had pierced ears, a neck chain, two bracelets and one ring. We added various facial characteristics and estimates of height and weight. Jeff found photographs that showed some of the jewellery better and distinguishing marks on the girls' features.

'Match that lot and it will be better than finger-prints,' he declared.

You always feel more cheerful when you are doing something positive. Although Georgina wasn't involved we all had the feeling that something worthwhile was happening: villains were about to be put behind bars, and kids rescued from a life of hell. If being taken into care could be called rescued.

I told the three of them to visit the four schools first thing in the morning. They would have to stress the seriousness of the offences to the heads and arrange for the photographers to visit in the afternoon, if possible. It would disrupt the school day, and a couple of bol-shie teachers could wreck the whole thing. Tact and diplomacy were called for.

'That's it for today, then. I've had enough. We'll go home at a reasonable hour for once,' I said. It was about six thirty.

'I'll sort out these pictures first,' said Jeff.

'No you won't,' I told him. 'They can wait. Let's lock them in my drawers and have a full day tomorrow. Are you all right, Dave?'

Sparky was the only one of us with children. He had three. Jeff had one on the way.

'Yeah, nothing that fourteen pints and kicking the dog won't cure,' he replied.

'C'mon, then. Let's go.'

It was still drizzling outside and I didn't have a coat, but it felt pleasant and cleansing after the oppressiveness of the office. Walking across the car park with Nigel, he asked: 'What will you do tonight, Charlie?'

'Tonight? Oh, I don't know. Something to eat, have a shower. Listen to some decent music with a can of beer. Try to get some quality into my life after the daily grime of this job.' I gathered my thoughts and continued with the theme. 'I try to shed it, like a miner washing off the coal dust and appearing as a new person. We can't live two separate lives, one as a policeman and one as a civilian, and none of us would want to, but you've got to learn to cultivate a space for yourself. End of sermon. G'night, Nigel.'

'Er, Angela's coming round tonight, to cook a Chinese meal. It'd be no problem to put an extra portion in. You're welcome to join us, if you want.'

It sounded a cosy arrangement. I wondered if it ought to be me asking advice from him. 'Angela? The WPC from Halifax?'

He blushed and nodded.

'It's good of you to ask,' I told him, 'but I'd be in the way.' I'd reached my car and fumbled in my pockets for the keys. 'Enjoy your meal,' I said, adding with a stab of the finger: 'And treat her properly. That's an order.'

I'd lost my keys. Then I remembered that I'd left them at the front desk. It would have been easier, and drier, to have fetched the duff radio myself. So much for being assertive.

Chapter Twelve

Acting DS John Rose took DI Peterson and DC Wilson to Heckley Town Library, where they interviewed Mrs Chadwick, the chief librarian. John was pleased at the sideways move into this new investigation. The Georgina case had given him a taste for high-profile work, but it was bogged down now that most avenues of enquiry had petered out.

Mrs Chadwick went through her story again and demonstrated the library's computer to them. They came away with the names and addresses of the last twenty people to withdraw the mutilated books. Peterson fell for the chief librarian's charms and twice managed to boast of his friendship with Olga Friedland, Chief Executive of the Library Association. He added 'library' to his list of retirement activities.

'Be nice if he took the books home before he cut the pages out,' DC Wilson stated, in the car on their way back to Heckley nick.

'True, but sadly, he didn't,' Peterson told him, passing the printout across. 'Nobody appears on both lists, but maybe he took just one of them home. He must know something about fungi, he can't have dreamed it all up.'

'We have plenty of Travellers and New Agers around these parts,' ADS Rose said. 'They know all about mushrooms: which ones are good to eat, which are poisonous and which give a good trip. I'd be looking for a connection there, for a start.'

'Do many of them carry library cards?' Peterson asked with undisguised sarcasm.

'No, but they could still go in. Plenty of them are educated – university dropouts and such,' John answered.

'Fine. So tomorrow you two can ask Mrs Chadwick about any traveller types coming in for a read and a warm, then start going through the list of names.'

At the station Peterson sniffed round his allotted accommodation and gave John a list of requirements to organise, before starting back to Trent Division. In the car, driving down the M1, DC Wilson said: 'They seem a friendly bunch, don't you think?'

Peterson looked sourly across at him. 'Think so?' he growled.

'Yes, guv. Don't you?'

'Set of complacent sheepshaggers. Inbred, I wouldn't be surprised. Need a bloody good kick up the arse.'

Wilson smiled as he remembered the look on his boss's face when he'd been asked if Oscar was his real name. 'That Inspector Priest is a decent bloke,' he announced.

'For a bleeding Freemason,' Peterson snarled.

Chief Superintendent Tollis had left early, intending to have a previously arranged round of golf before being joined by Mrs Tollis for dinner in the clubhouse. Peterson knocked on his door and entered the empty office. As always he was amazed how tidy the desk was. He glanced round, decided there was nothing he wanted to steal or read, and turned to leave. The phone rang.

Peterson put it to the side of his head and said: 'Carapace Bonce.'

A male voice asked if he was speaking to Chief Superintendent Tollis. The DI uttered a silent prayer of thanks that it was nobody who knew him and said: 'No, sir, I'm afraid Mr Tollis is unavailable. Who's speaking, please?'

'My name is Alistair McLeod, editor of the *UK*

News. Could you put me through to whoever is in charge of the Ronald Conway murder investigation in his absence.'

Peterson cursed at having been caught by the press, and all the familiar platitudes ran through his mind. 'This is DI Peterson speaking. I am the investigating officer in the Ronald Conway case. How can I help you?'

'Ah, good evening, Mr Peterson. I presume from that that you are the one who does all the work.'

'Very astute of you, sir. I can see how you got to where you are today. Did you ring about anything in particular?'

'Well, yes. I've just come across a letter in my mail from someone confessing to killing him, along with a trio of other clerics. I thought you might be interested.'

'Ah! A confession, you said?'

'Yes.'

'Well, that is good news. Confessions can be a very important part of any investigation, sir. Sometimes they are what we in the business call a Breakthrough. The first question that comes to my razor-sharp detective's mind is... er... is it signed?'

'Yes, it is.'

'Good. And the second one is, if I can trouble you to look at the end of the aforementioned document, by whom?'

'It's from someone who calls himself... let me see... the Destroying Angel. Do you know him?'

Peterson manoeuvred himself round Tollis's desk until he was able to sit in the Super's big leather chair. 'Alistair McLeod, of the *News*, I believe you said, sir.'

'That's right. Is there anything in this I can print, or is it just some crank making mischief? I've looked in the files and the first two deaths were passed off as accidents. There seems to be a link between Conway and the priest called Birr, though.'

'Yes. I think you and I had better have a little talk, Alistair.'

Half an hour later he left the station to interrupt Chief Superintendent Tollis's round of golf and tell him what he had arranged, or most of it.

From home he rang Trevor Wilson to update him and tell him to do the same with John Rose, before settling down to a relatively early meal of lamb chops, new potatoes and garden peas; with home-made cherry crumble to follow. Over it he discussed the day's developments with Dilys. After two small whiskies and a cup of cocoa he slept like a carved figure on the lid of a tomb, the night unbroken by any more news of death. But only just.

The Reverend Gordon Ibbotson was in a confused, mixed-up, fed-up, wish-I-were-dead mood as he swung his middle-of-the-range Audi into the vicarage drive. He reached out with his left hand to prevent the Pyrex container on the passenger seat from sliding away and spilling its cargo of home-made samosas on to the carpet.

'Very nice, Gordon,' Mrs Sharmini had told him. 'But perhaps just a little more generous with the turmeric next time.'

It had been the final night of his Indian cookery class, and had not gone as expected. They had all prepared their specialities and enjoyed a boisterous evening sampling each other's fare and entertaining members of the other classes. The rather informal plan was that they would then all repair to the pub and continue the convivialities; after which the Reverend

Ibbotson intended offering one of his classmates, whom he knew only as Pauline, a lift home.

When the subject of the pub was raised, however, heads were shaken. 'Sorry, I can't make it,' was the common cry. A mysterious person called Ray was coming to collect Pauline from the class, no doubt attracted by the thought of sampling her shakooti rassa. The Reverend placed the lid over his sad-looking samosas and came home.

As the car jerked to a standstill on the drive the five-hundred-watt security light flicked on, dazzling the vicar with its glare and triggering off photosynthesis in his herbaceous borders. In the shadows, darker than a sea-cave, between the garage and a *Pyracantha watereri*, a claw-like hand tightened its grip on the shotgun.

The figure in the shadows watched the clergyman climb from the car, fumbling with keys and casserole, and unlock his front door. The intention was to wait until he was inside, then gain admittance by ringing the bell for the side entrance.

The vicar reappeared almost immediately. He'd come out again to put the car in the garage. The figure, high on the adrenalin that the role of Destroying Angel generated, withdrew into the darkness, breath held and heart pounding like a desperate prisoner hammering on a cell door.

When the Audi was safely tucked up for the night, the clergyman pulled the garage door down and locked it. He cast a brief glance across his lawn to see if any hedgehogs were foraging for worms or moths that had been scorched flightless by the security light, then pushed his front door open again. The Destroying Angel relaxed and stretched upright.

'Reverend Ibbotson! Gordon!'

A middle-aged woman was coming up the drive

and calling his name, trotting from the knees down in the way that some women do.

'Mrs McFadden!' said the vicar, with undisguised enthusiasm.

She was slightly out of breath as she stopped before him. 'Oh!' she puffed. 'I saw your light come on so I thought I'd bring you your typing. You did say it was urgent.' She passed him a pink folder.

'I didn't expect you to do it tonight, Brenda. Tomorrow would have been soon enough, but it's very good of you. Did you have much trouble with my terrible spelling?'

She gave a little giggle. 'There were one or two bits that I couldn't understand, but I can soon correct them if I did it wrong.'

'I'm sure it will be all right. Well, this is really kind of you. I'm, er, just about to make a coffee. Would you, er, like to join me in a cup?'

'Ooh, that would be nice. Just a quick one, then.'

'Lovely. After you. I can offer you a samosa, too. Do you like...' The door clicked shut, restricting her tastes in oriental cookery to the ears of the Reverend Gordon Ibbotson only.

One and a half hours later, cold and stiff and deep in the depression that often follows euphoria, the Destroying Angel skulked away. A decision had been made. Frustration was dangerous – it led to mistakes. One more would have been perfect, but the risk of discovery was growing every day. The time had come to conclude the preliminaries – the next move must be the *coup de grâce*.

DI Peterson found Chief Superintendent Tollis's office not quite as pristine as it had been the evening before. His jacket, neatly draped on a hanger, was behind the door, and a sheet of paper, held down by a monogrammed Sheaffer fountain pen, broke the symmetry of his desk top. The man himself was absent.

Peterson sat down in the hard visitor's chair and placed a copy of the *UK News* on his boss's desk. Gurgling noises told him that Tollis was in the adjoining bathroom. Probably polishing his pate, he thought.

There were a few words written on the sheet of paper. The DI leaned forward to read them. They were upside down to him, but bus conductors and detectives are trained to read upside-down writing. They said:

> THE DESTROYING ANGEL
> REVELATIONS
> ABADDON a.k.a. APOLLYON
> THE SATANIC ANGEL OF THE BOTTOMLESS PIT

They were the Chief Superintendent's notes for the little talk he thought he was about to give. Stone the bleeding crows, thought Peterson, whistling through his teeth at the same time. Over my dead body, he added, as an afterthought.

From the bathroom came the sound of a toilet being flushed. Peterson grabbed the newspaper again and jumped towards the door that led in from the corridor. He stood with it ajar, firmly grasping the handle, and counted to five. As the Chief Superintendent emerged from his ablutions he saw his DI apparently just entering.

'Ah, good morning, sir! Timed to perfection,' said Peterson, closing the door for the second time.

Tollis, after sitting down, carefully folded the sheet of paper and placed it in his inside pocket. 'Er, yes, good morning, Peterson. Is that the, er, the *UK News*, did you say?'

'Yes, sir. A later edition.' He passed it across the desk, headline uppermost. 'Hope you managed to salvage the rest of your golf last night, sir.'

'Yes, thank you. You did the right thing, bringing me news of a development like this.' Actually he'd rather enjoyed the interruption, in front of several of the club worthies, and it had given him a suitable excuse to explain his collapse over the last fifteen holes. He turned the page. 'They don't get much on a sheet, do they?'

Peterson practised his upside-down reading skills on the naked bimbo his chief had exposed. 'No, sir. They do tend to come to a point rather quickly. I've arranged the press conference for nine o'clock, and the hand-out should be ready before it ends.'

'Oh! I was hoping to see it first. Any chance of an advance copy?'

'Sorry about that, Mr Tollis. Problems with the photocopier. I'll see what I can do.'

'Nine o'clock. Right. Well, I suggest you make the introductions and hand over to me. That fine by you, Peterson?'

'No problem, sir. Just what I'd planned myself.'

The press conference was deliberately convened in the smaller of the conference rooms, which was Tollis's first disappointment of the morning. No television was invited, which was his second. The room rapidly filled with representatives from all the local papers, many of whom doubled for the nationals, local radio, and people from the agencies. Peterson hid himself in the toilet, with the handouts he had carefully composed, and smoked several cigarettes.

At five past the hour he called the meeting to order.

'Good morning, ladies and gentlemen. Thank you for being here so promptly. First of all I have to say that you are in a non-smoking area. Violators will be drenched by the automatic sprinkler system.' Individuals in his audience groaned their disapproval. 'Filthy habit,' he told them. 'Do you good to be without for half an hour.' To his left he sensed Chief Superintendent Tollis throwing him a get-on-with-it look. 'But we didn't bring you here to lecture you on the evils of the weed. No doubt you have all read today's *UK News*. It's probably your compulsive reading as you devour your morning muesli. And no doubt you also noticed that they are claiming an exclusive story, concerning the murders of two men of the Church, namely the Reverend Ronald Conway and Father Declan Birr.'

He briefly outlined the two cases, stressing the similarities and the discoveries of the pictures of fungi. He also told them about the deaths of the other two priests. From the corner of his eye he could see Tollis impatiently smoothing his notes.

'Last night,' he went on, 'there was a development; and this is where we are asking for your cooperation. Mr Alistair McLeod, editor of the *UK News*, received a confession from someone claiming to be the murderer of all four deceased. This person called himself... wait for it, the Destroying Angel.'

A murmur ran round the room. Tollis threw himself back against his chair. Peterson continued: 'We are certain that he was responsible for the last two murders, but the first two are very doubtful. At my request, Mr McLeod kindly agreed to print the story without using the name Destroying Angel, although it did reduce the impact somewhat. I would like to take this opportunity to publicly thank him for his responsible attitude. The purpose of this meeting is to put the facts before the rest of you and to ask you not to describe the killer in the way he describes himself.'

'Why?' someone cried.

'Why? I'll tell you why. First of all, we don't want him glamorised. I realise that in this aspect we differ, but glamorisation leads to copycats, and the last thing I want is deranged individuals all over the place bumping off the clergy. To you, no news is bad news, but I prefer the quiet life. Secondly, we want to catch him. The letter he sent to the *News* is being given every test known to the forensic scientist, but unfortunately it was handled by a hundred people before it reached them. We'd like to frustrate him into writing again, but this time we'll be ready for it. Sadly, our best chances of apprehending him are when he tries to kill again. With your cooperation, maybe we can goad him into doing something foolish before then. I have a hand-out here which gives details of the deaths and what we would like you to print and not print. Any questions, before I hand you over to Chief Superintendent Tollis?'

Several hands were raised. Peterson gestured to an elderly man whom he knew worked for an agency. He stood up to speak. 'Thank you,' he began. 'Inspector, can I get this clear: there is a serial killer on the loose who describes himself as the Destroying Angel, and you are seriously asking the press not to use it?'

'Yes, that's right. You can print the story, but not the name. That's what I'm asking.'

'So what do you want us to call him?'

'Well, the killer, I suppose. You're the wizards with words.'

'But he has to have a name. All serial killers have names.'

Peterson looked thoughtful. 'I don't know. Call him... how about... call him...' He was floundering, but inspiration came from nowhere, welcome as an empty taxi in a blizzard. Call him... the Mushroom Man,' he said.

A buzz of approval ran through the room; the Mushroom Man it was. He noticed Tollis screwing up his notes, his knuckles standing out like a row of snowy mountain peaks against his suntanned hands. 'And now,' Peterson told them, 'I'd like to introduce Chief Superintendent Tollis, who is the officer in charge of the enquiry. I'm sure he will be more than ready to answer your questions, and far more ably than me. Mr Tollis...'

Tollis got to his feet. 'No, no,' he told them. 'I think Inspector Peterson has covered everything. I'll just remind you how much we value your cooperation and bid you good morning.'

He turned and left. Peterson was alarmed to see a blood vessel on his chief's head pulsing like a neon sign with a loose connection, and briefly wondered if he'd really done it this time. 'Thank you... sir,' he called after him.

Chapter Thirteen

Sparky had a problem with the headmistress of the Moorside middle school. 'Dismissed the idea out of hand, boss,' he told me on the telephone. 'Says she can't possibly authorise us to take the pictures without the say-so of the governors.'

'Did you tell her that the photos would be destroyed as soon as we'd finished with them?'

'Yeah. It made no difference. More than her job's worth, plus a deep distrust of the police. I tried to ring Nigel – thought he might have a better chance of sweet-talking her than me – but he's not answering.'

It was the first time ever that Sparky had acknowledged Nigel's talents, so I was pleased with that. He also had a habit of bypassing Nigel whenever possible and coming straight to me. I'd been wondering what to do about it, but now it looked as if the problem had gone away. It meant the team was still a strong one.

'I'll go see her,' I said. 'Any ideas how I should play it?'

'Mmm... branding irons and thumbscrews. If they fail you'll just have to fall back on your speciality – seduction.'

'You really know how to hurt a friend,' I told him.

Electrical impulses were queuing inside the telephone wires, waiting for me to replace the handset and make the connection. It rang again before I'd relaxed my grip. 'Priest,' I said.

'Detective Inspector Priest?'

I didn't recognise the voice at first. 'Yes, can I help you?'

'It's Frank Marriot, Charlie. I've some bad news, I'm afraid.'

DS Marriot was the Pornography Squad sergeant. He sounded out of breath. Lally and his woman friend were appearing at the magistrates' court this morning, from where they would hopefully be committed for trial at the crown court. Frank was there to oppose any application for bail. We desperately needed them out of circulation for the next few days.

'Why? What's happened?' I asked.

'I blew it. Lally's been remanded in custody, but the woman, Fenella Smith, was released on bail. Claimed she was just visiting and knew nothing about his activities.'

'But her name's on the electoral roll for that address.'

'I know, but I wasn't given the chance to tell the court. Afterwards she was whisked away in a taxi. I had some crazy idea about arresting her again for perjury and went charging out, but I was too slow. I saw the bloke she went with, but didn't recognise him.'

'Damn!' With her on the loose we were wasting our time – we'd only get the small fry. 'OK. Don't worry about it, Frank. I'm sure you did your best.' I brought him up to date with our morning's activities.

In the corridor I met DI Peterson. 'Morning, Oscar,' I said. 'Settled into your new accommodation yet?'

He had a worried look on his face. 'Yes, you've done all right for us, eventually, but I'd like a word about something else.'

'Will it wait? I'm in a bit of a hurry.'

'Aren't we all? That big DC of yours – I want to complain about him.'

'Dave Sparkington?'

'That's him. He was downright insubordinate to me earlier today; offensive even.'

I sighed inwardly. 'What's he done?' I asked, stopping

myself before I added 'now'. Sparky regarded it as his
duty to play the blunt Yorkshireman with anyone from
south of Doncaster, especially if they were from another force, moving in on his patch. Rank was no protection.

'I passed him in the car park, about eight o'clock.
"Good morning," I said, as you do. He said: "You'll get
your share of it." Ignorant sod. I warn you, Charlie, I
won't tolerate that attitude from anyone, never mind a
DC.'

I tried not to smile but I must have done. Peterson
said: 'It's not funny, Charlie. If we were in Trent I'd
have him on a fizzer.'

'Sorry, Oscar, I'm not laughing. I think you misun-
derstood him.' I was struggling for an explanation.
'What he, er, really meant was, er, God willing. That's
it. God willing you'll get your share of the good morning.'

'Bollocks!'

I was warming to my theme. 'No, it's true. It's just a
cultural thing. It's like... well... if you said to an
Englishman: "Look, no hands," he'd assume you were
showing off. But if you said it to a Saudi Arabian he'd
come to an entirely different conclusion. Wouldn't he?'

'You're a bullshitter, Charlie.'

'Maybe you're right. Leave it with me, Oscar. I'll
have a word with him.'

Moorside school was one of the smaller ones on our
list, but the nearest to Lally's address. It comprises a
flat-roofed building, not very old, and a couple of por-
takabin classrooms to cater for some unforeseen demo-
graphic blip. I tried to remember if we'd done well in
the World Cup about ten years ago. We hadn't – it
must have been a power cut.

Everybody was at lunch. I wandered down the corridors looking for the school office and pausing to admire the kids' paintings that brightened all the walls. Some of them were terrific. I was less enthusiastic about the smell of the place. I hadn't enjoyed my own schooldays, and the cocktail of sour milk, sweaty bodies and furniture polish brought the memories back.

Mrs Quigley would be back in her office at one thirty, the school secretary told me. I went outside and sat in the car, listening to the news. A cabinet minister had been sacked for having a happy marriage; otherwise it was all depressing. At one thirty-one I rat-tatted on Mrs Quigley's door with my right hand. In the other I carried a large manila envelope.

What profession makes policemen feel old? Headmistresses who look about twenty-two certainly do. She was brusque and efficient, though, and wore these qualities like armour.

'Inspector, I have nothing further to add to what I said to your constable this morning. I really don't see how I can help unless the board of governors sanction it. I'm afraid I cannot allow photographs of my children to be used in a criminal enquiry.'

'We are talking about very serious offences, Mrs Quigley, and with your cooperation we could bring the perpetrators to court. All the photographs will be destroyed as soon as –'

'Yes, yes,' she interrupted. 'The constable went through all that.'

I gestured to a spare chair. 'May I sit down, please?' I didn't wait for the answer. 'Mrs Quigley,' I went on, 'yesterday we raided a house and found evidence of a paedophile ring, operating from Heckley. To put it bluntly, someone is having sex with what the law terms children of a tender age. These children must go to school somewhere, and we'd like to find them, protect them from further abuse. I'd have thought that you would, too.'

'My concern is completely for the children, Inspector. If the school governors give their approval I will cooperate fully, but meanwhile my answer has to be no.'

'And while we wait for that approval the birds will fly. Right at this moment they are probably destroying the evidence, until they can set up in business again somewhere else. I want to save those kids, even if you aren't so concerned.'

This wasn't the way I'd intended to handle it. She turned on me: 'Save them from what, Inspector?' she shrieked. 'At least they have parents. What do you think will happen to them if they go into care? Do you believe they won't be abused there? Have you asked the children if they want their families destroyed? I'll give you the name and address of the chairman of the governors; you can take it from there.'

That was meant to be her last word. I unfolded the flap of the manila envelope, extracted two of the ten-by-eight prints and slid them across to the head-mistress. She looked at the confusion of arms and legs, turned a print round because she thought it was upside down and turned it back when she realised it wasn't.

'That's what I want to save them from,' I said very quietly.

Mrs Quigley's eyes scanned rapidly from one picture to the other and her hands began to shake. 'Oh my God!' she gasped, and was sick into the wastepaper bin at the side of her desk. Unfortunately it was at the end where I was sitting. School dinners haven't changed much since my day. They'd had shepherd's pie, broccoli, and jam sponge pudding.

I grabbed her coffee cup and nipped out to the cloakroom I'd noticed earlier. After giving her a moment to compose herself I went back in with a cup of water. She accepted it gratefully.

'Mrs Quigley,' I said. She looked at me. Her face was the colour of an old man's legs. 'Please may I send a photographer and a lady police officer round to photograph your children?'

'I think you'd better,' she whispered between sips.

It wasn't as difficult as we'd expected. On some jobs you learn as you go along. When we briefed the WPCs who would be acting as secretaries to the photographers we realised that they would be able to eliminate most of the kids there and then. With luck they might be able to make a positive identification.

I was with Gilbert. 'Your fortnight's up, Charlie,' he told me. 'Partridge travels to the conference at Bramshill on Monday and wants his moment of glory on Tuesday. Where's this pornography job taking us?'

'It's taking us to court with a bunch of paedophiles, Gilbert, but it's nothing to do with the Georgina case.'

'Mmm, pity. So do you think we should spin Dewhurst?'

'You know I don't.'

'Right. Do you still want taking off the case?'

'You couldn't manage without me.'

'Once I couldn't manage without sugar in my coffee, but I do now. Tell you what, let's have a cup.'

Gilbert has a secretary, but he brews his own tea and coffee in the office. He doesn't make a political song and dance about it, just gets on with it. It's one of the little touches that makes him popular.

He turned round, coffee jar in one hand, spoon in the other. 'Well, if you're staying I suppose we'd better

play it your way. The ACC will just have to make do
with a smashed paedophile ring to impress the conference. Now then; if I put all the sugar in yours and all
the milk in mine they should be somewhere near.'

The phone and the kettle started making the appropriate noises at the same instant. I grabbed the phone.
'Superintendent Wood's office.'

'Is that Mr Priest?'

'Yes.' It was me they wanted. I listened. And listened.

Gilbert appeared at my elbow with two steaming
mugs. 'They've positively identified one of the little
girls in the photographs,' I whispered to him. I pulled
his writing pad towards me. 'Give me the address
again.' It was a block of flats, but one of the more
respectable ones. They are not all disaster areas. 'What
time does school finish?'

'A quarter to four.'

'OK, that gives us... just over an hour. That's enough.
You carry on there, I'll organise a posse and see if her
dad is at home. Well done.'

I put the phone down and told Gilbert the details.
'A little girl called Anne-Marie Briggs matches the fair
girl in the photographs. She has pierced ears and identical jewellery, plus a mole over her eye in exactly the
right place. The WPC says she appears shy and with-
drawn. She'd have picked her out as a contender without a description. Sorry about the coffee, Gilbert, but I
have promises to keep, and miles to go before I sleep;
and miles to go before I sleep.'

'Stuff the coffee, I'm coming with you.'

We rang the Child Protection Unit at Divisional HQ
and arranged to meet one of their specialists near the
flats. I also alerted Social Services.

* * *

The flats were not as tidy as I remembered them. The downward spiral that started with general neglect and went through graffiti to vandalism and ultimately abandonment was well underway. Gilbert knocked so hard he nearly broke the window.

The door was answered by a woman wearing tiger-striped leggings and a top that said Armani across the front, although I think Georgio would have sued for defamation had he seen the state it was in. Her hair was the colour of dead cabbage leaves, and a look of fear flashed across her face as she surveyed us.

'Superintendent Wood,' said Gilbert, 'and this is Acting DCI Priest and WPC Rawcliffe. May we come in?'

I'd forgotten I was supposed to be an Acting Chief! We didn't wait for an answer and marched straight past her.

"Ere, what's going on?' said a voice in the dismal recesses of the flat, and a skinny figure appeared from one of the rooms.

'It's the police,' the woman told him.

'What the 'ell do you want?' His T-shirt advertised the Dallas Cowboys and the gold chain round his neck could have anchored a respectable liner. His hair was cropped short on top but was long at the back.

'Mr Briggs?' I asked.

'What of it?'

'We'd like to ask you a few questions, and have a look around.'

'You got a warrant?'

'No, but I could have one in fifteen minutes. I'd prefer not to wait until Anne-Marie comes home from school, though.'

Mrs Briggs sank on to the sofa and her putty complexion moved several little squares towards the pale end of the colour chart.

'Questions about what?' she murmured, dreading the answer.

'Child abuse,' I said, confirming her fears.

We didn't find anything. The flat was cheaply furnished but clean and tidy. It was nearly four o'clock and our search had not been particularly thorough, but the little girl would be coming in through the door any moment. Gilbert and WPC Rawcliffe were uncertain, but I wasn't.

'Paul Briggs, I'm arresting you on suspicion of being involved in paedophilia. You are not obliged to say anything unless you wish to do so, but anything you do say may be put in writing and given in evidence against you. Do you understand?'

He didn't reply. Back at the station he wasn't any more talkative. We tried an interview but it was a waste of time. It was like talking to a donkey with ear muffs on. I told him that we'd keep him in police custody overnight and have him in front of a nice, upstanding lady magistrate next morning, to be remanded. All we had, though, was a collection of photos, some bearing a likeness to him, others to his daughter. It wasn't an impressive case.

'Put him in number four,' the custody officer told me when all the paperwork was completed and Briggs had been informed of his rights.

I grabbed him under the arm and lifted him off his chair. 'This way,' I said, propelling him forwards. He tried to shrug off my grip but I didn't let him. WPC Rawcliffe was hovering nearby, about to go back to Division, or, more likely, her husband and kids. I caught her eye and signalled for her to follow me.

In the cell I said: 'Shoelaces, please.'

'Shoelaces?'

'That's right. We don't want you making a rope ladder and escaping, do we? Or, heaven forbid, doing yourself a mischief.'

He removed the laces and thrust them towards me. 'Right, on your feet and face the wall,' I ordered. I went through the motions of frisking him. 'Better take your belt, too,' I said. I extended my arms around his waist, skinny as a girl's but not a zillionth as alluring, and undid his belt buckle. Before he knew what was happening I'd flicked open the top button of his jeans, hooked both thumbs over the top and yanked the lot down.

He yelled a curse and tried to turn on me, but it's difficult with your pants round your knees. I grabbed his shoulders and pinned him against the wall.

On his arse was the distinctive tattoo with the Union flag and the number 18.

'Seen one of those before?' I asked the WPC.

'No. Not since the video of the royal wedding,' she replied.

Chapter Fourteen

Gilbert was a lot happier when I told him about the tattoo on Briggs's backside, although he'd have preferred to have authorised my inspection before I committed the deed. We found several photographs of Briggs, some with little Anne-Marie. More than one officer asked me if they could have five minutes alone with him in his cell.

'How much further do you want to take it?' Gilbert asked. He'd called to collect me on his way out of the station. It was nearly seven o'clock.

I pulled my jacket on and made sure the drawer containing the photographs was locked. 'I think it's the end of the road for us,' I replied. 'It was important that we act fast, but now we might as well hand it over to the Porn Squad. Unfortunately we haven't found any mailing lists or other names. Maybe they'll have better luck.' I'd turned off the light and was pulling the door closed when the phone rang. Gilbert didn't put it into words, but his look suggested that I ignore it. I couldn't, though.

'Inspector Priest,' I intoned wearily.

'Oh, thank God,' said the voice. 'It's Miles Dewhurst here. I've just had another message.'

I waved a frantic hand at Gilbert. 'A message from the kidnapper?' I asked.

'Yes.'

'Another letter?'

'No, a phone call.'

'When?'

'Just now.'

'Ok, Mr Dewhurst, now please tell me exactly what the message was.'

'He said – it was a man – he said: "Go to Little John's Well. There'll be a note for you. Don't tell the police."'

'And that's all?'

'Yes.'

'I take it you are at home?'

'That's right.'

'Well, stay put and I'll be with you in about ten minutes. We'll go together.'

'No, he might be watching. I'm going now.'

And he hung up.

'Bugger!' I exclaimed, and repeated the bits that Gilbert hadn't heard. After a few moments' thought I said: 'How's this sound, Gilbert? I'll try to beat him to the note. If you radio Traffic they might be able to hold him up while allowing me a few liberties with the speed limit.'

'Yes, no problem. Then I'll raise Sparky and Nigel and have them standing by. Once you find the note we can take it from there.'

I grabbed my book of numbers and wrote out a couple for Gilbert. After stuffing a few plastic bags into my pockets I was down the stairs faster than a lighthouse keeper with diarrhoea and an outside toilet. Twenty minutes later, cruising at a cool hundred and ten near the Castleford turn-off of the M62, I passed a Traffic BMW and a white Toyota Supra parked on the hard shoulder. So far, so good.

There were five assorted drinks cans in the well, but only one had an end cut off with a tin opener. I didn't pick it up immediately. No tyre marks or imprints of obscure trainers announced themselves. Only crisp packets, fast food containers and a disposable nappy. I put my usual curse on my fellow men and their habits and retrieved the Coke can.

The note, printed by computer, said:

A1 NORTH. 69 MILES. LAY-BY BEFORE B6275.

I had a book of maps in the car but I happened to know the B6275. It starts just past Scotch Corner, and was an interesting route to Scotland before the motorways were built. On the map it looks as straight as a centurion's backbone, but the map is flat. The B6275 is the biggest switchback in the country.

Nigel was in the office when I rang on the mobile, and he said Sparky was hovering by the phone at home. I relayed the contents of the note and told them to follow me. 'And fetch the Almanac, please. We might need it.'

Traffic was heavy, so it took me well over an hour to find the lay-by, and the light was fading fast. An elderly couple were having a picnic in a Maestro. They watched me walk to and fro as they masticated their ham sandwiches, faces devoid of expression. A miniature television was perched on the dashboard of their car – they were having a night out. Maybe they have obnoxious neighbours, I decided, struggling to justify their behaviour.

The Coke can was wedged in the branches of a hawthorn bush, five yards in front of the Maestro. I pulled an exhibit bag over my hand and retrieved it. The couple's jaws moved up and down in unison, as implacable as a steam engine. I wrote down their registration number.

The note in the can read:

CAPSTICK COLLIERY. BLACKSMITHS. 35 MILES

Now I had to consult the book of maps. There'd been a big fuss about a pit closing somewhere about six months ago. Last coal mine in the area. They'd held marches and meetings, and a couple of MPs had staged an underground sit-in; but it had closed just the same. I had a feeling it had been Capstick.

I needed longer arms. Either that or a pair of spectacles. The thought dismayed me – soon it'd be the teeth. By holding the book directly under the light and squinting I could just read the index. Then I found Capstick on the map. I made a note of the road numbers, rang the other two and set off. It was right where the map said it should be. A sign at the entrance to the town told me they were twinned with a place that sounded like a bad hand at Scrabble.

The weekend starts on Thursday amongst the young. The narrow main street was alive with youths dressed in jeans and T-shirts, in spite of the drizzle, and girls in the shortest minis I'd seen in years. They were in single-sex groups of three or four. Presumably some sort of pairing-off process would be enacted throughout the evening, after the ritualistic consumption of large quantities of lager. Ah, those were the days.

I drove slowly past the curry houses and the taxi drivers dozing in their Ladas, waiting for the evening's trade to begin. Many businesses were boarded up and there was the usual smattering of charity shops. Prosperity was reluctant to come back to the area. A level crossing marked the end of downtown Capstick. I paused in the middle and looked both ways. The rails didn't exactly shine like silver threads in the gloom. Probably disused. Must have run near the pit, though, once upon a time. Quarter of a mile further on I found the sign.

I turned right down a concrete road for another half a mile. The night was blacker than a mole's armpit, the only illumination coming from the car's headlights. Eventually they shone on a British Coal notice board at the entrance, with the manager's name proudly displayed. Someone had scrawled an obscenity next to it. I crawled along in first gear, the tyres squelching in the thin mud that covered the road.

I reached a cluster of buildings. Away to the right a glow in the sky marked the town centre, where people would be drinking and swearing and lusting for each other's bodies. For a lucky few their dreams would come true. The rest would find consolation in a skinful or booze, until tomorrow night brought another chance.

I wished I was with them. A feeling had come over me that I didn't immediately recognise. I did my deep breathing exercises; always a good stop-gap when you're lost for ideas. It was fear. Not for myself, but for what I might find.

At the side of the road was a big board, listing the various facilities at the mine, with arrows pointing in the appropriate directions. Lorries dashing backwards and forwards had showered it with mud, but now the rain was washing it clean again, revealing enough for me to understand. I silently read them off: Manager's Office, No. 1 Winder, No. 2 Winder, Stores, Stockyard, Surveyors, Weighbridge, Pithead Baths, Canteen, Electricians, Fitters, and, right at the bottom, barely visible through the streaming mud, Blacksmiths.

The arrow was still covered. I got out and wiped the mud away with my hand. It pointed straight ahead.

Most of the buildings had been reduced to piles of rubble. There was no sign of the once-proud headgears, but half of one of the giant wheels was propped against a wall. It would have been as tall as a house when it was whole. No more would its spinning be an indicator of the prosperity of the community. It had been cut down to size.

The headlights shone on a long, low building with three big sliding doors evenly spaced along the front. It was red brick, dark with age, with a slate roof and small windows, all broken. I swung the wheel slightly to the left and crept towards the first door. Outside were piles of discarded cables, some as thick as a man's arm, heaped up like writhing serpents. As if to confirm my deduction a sign on the door read: Electricians.

The middle door was the fitters' workshop. Pieces of rusting machinery stood outside, like dinosaurs bristling with teeth and chains and cogs. I swung the lights across until they illuminated the third door. There was no painted notice on this one, but the language was universal. In the middle of the door, nailed to it, was a single horseshoe. The ends were pointing upwards; the way, they say, that provides a seat for the devil.

I switched off the engine and headlights and the darkness enveloped me like a magician's cloak. It would have been easy to sit waiting for the others to catch up with me, but I didn't. The rain had almost stopped, and the car made soft clicking and hissing noises as I found my flashlight in the boot. Picking my way through the mud and the puddles, I approached the blacksmiths' workshop. There was a small door let into the large one, fastened with a sneck – one of those old-fashioned catches operated by your thumb. I pressed and pushed, and the door swung inwards.

Everything inside was the same colour – a greyish-red amalgam of a hundred years of oxidised iron and carbon. I swung the torch round. Along the far wall were four big hearths, where the blacksmiths had heated the metal, and next to each was an anvil. I remembered something I'd read somewhere. The gist of it was that to the man who can work steel, it can become anything he wants; to the man who can't, it will become everything except what he wants.

I found some ancient light switches, but the cables were chopped off just above them. The beam from the torch was feeble, and a thick layer of dust over everything softened the outlines, blurring shadows and making shapes indistinct. The door slammed shut and something inside me did a five-point-nine somersault.

I steered a course gingerly across the floor, which was littered with bits of metal, heavy pieces of chain and a variety of blacksmiths' tongs that looked like instruments of torture. Once the place would have rung with the sound of hammers on iron, illuminated by dancing fires and showers of sparks. Now it smelt of corruption.

The workshop was alive with ghosts, but there was nothing there to interest the policeman in me. Except the door in the end wall. I walked towards it and shone the torch. Stencilled neatly in the middle was the word Office. Someone with a black felt-tip had added a few additional comments. He'd also had a go at the page-three girls who adorned the wall. He wasn't very good at spelling. Or anatomy. Well, I hope he wasn't.

The door pushed open against a spring. The office was about six feet wide and ten feet long. A high desk that looked as if it belonged in a Dickensian orphanage ran the full length of the long wall, with a bench beside it for sitting on. I let the door close behind me and shone the torch around.

More big-busted ladies adorned the walls. Underneath the bench were four plastic bin-liners, fastened round the tops with string. I pulled the bench out of the way and dragged the first bag into the open.

There was a movement and a rustle near my feet. I pointed the torch down and saw a rat run over my shoe. I let out a yell and jumped on to the bench, like a woman in a cartoon. Two rats were scurrying round the bottom of the, wall I'd heard people say they could be dangerous when cornered, but it was me that felt cornered. I reached down and pulled the door handle. It would only open a few inches, because the bench was now in the way, but it was enough. The rats ran out to terrorise someone else. This time the gymnast inside me scored straight sixes, right across the board.

When the door was firmly closed again I stepped down and repeated my deep-breathing exercises for a few seconds. There were no stabbing pains in my chest or pins and needles in my left arm, so I decided I'd survive. I shone the torch back on the bag.

The small blade on my Swiss army knife is the one I don't use much, to keep it nice and sharp. I placed the torch on the bench so I had two free hands to work with, and sliced through the plastic.

The bag was full of books. I pulled one out. It was softbacked and damp; with a characteristic musty smell, but more powerful than I'd ever experienced before. The title on the cover read: Mines and Quarries Form no. 277; Reports of Examinations of Winding Ropes. Each page was a separate certificate, filled in at about monthly intervals in an immaculate script, saying that everything was in safe working order. They were done with a fountain pen and proudly signed. A lesser penman had countersigned each page. All the books were the same, and must have represented countless years of conscientious endeavour. I pulled the bag to one side and dragged the next one out.

It contained more books. So did the third one. I grabbed the final bag and immediately knew it was different. For a start it was made from much less substantial plastic than the other three – household grade rather than industrial – and the contents were less angular. I held the top with my left hand, the knife poised and the shadow of the blade dancing from side to side in the torchlight. As soon as the blade was steady for a second I plunged it through the thin plastic and drew it downwards.

Chapter Fifteen

To this day I thank God that she was facing the other way. I widened the slit with my fingers and a mop of dull black hair tumbled out. I'd found Georgina.

Holding the torch again I could see the curve of her cheek, as lifeless as alabaster. I stretched out my reluctant hand and touched it. The skin yielded under my fingers, but didn't spring back when I removed them. I let my hand fall on to her bony little shoulder and squeezed it. It was like holding a paper bag with a few dry twigs inside. I wanted her to know that not all hands were as evil as the last ones that had held her. Or as callous as the next ones would seem.

Outside, I retraced my steps to the car as best I could and reversed it about fifty yards back down the lane. I leaned on the car boot, waiting for Nigel and Sparky to arrive. The water on it soaked through the seat of my pants and the drizzle ran off my face and down my neck, but I hardly noticed it. I wanted to curse the moon and the heavens and any so-called omnipotent being who lived up there, but I didn't have the energy. It's just another body, I told myself. Another kid whose luck ran out. Just another job. And you're a bloody liar, Charlie Priest, I thought.

For the next day or so only the experts would be allowed anywhere near. We'd hit the scene with every scientific aid known to us. Photographs, plaster casts and samples would be taken, followed by a fingertip search of the blacksmiths' shop and the approaches to it. Everything found would be labelled, catalogued, analysed, dissected and turned inside out. Then we'd have the results of the post-mortem on little Georgina. Somewhere amongst all this there would be, hopefully, a tiny atom of evidence that would lead us to her killer.

The headlights came creeping unsurely down the lane. As they swung round the last turn and shone on me, Nigel switched them to dipped beam and then off. He's very considerate about things like that. They drew right up to me, stopped and got out.

'Hi, boss. Find anything?' Sparky asked.

I gestured behind me with a jerk of the head. 'She's in there,' I told them. They were both stunned to silence.

'Georgina?' Nigel asked, very quietly.

I nodded.

'Poor kid. What's happened to her?'

'She's in a bin-liner. Probably been there since May.'

'Jesus.'

'You're soaked to the skin, Charlie,' Sparky declared. 'Go sit in our car with the heater on. We'll do the necessary.'

'I'm OK. Did you bring the Almanac?'

The Almanac is the Who's Who of the police force, listing everybody down to the rank of inspector. Strictly speaking we should have let someone know that we were coming into their area. Apologies were due.

'Right here, boss,' Nigel replied.

'Good. Then let's ruin the Regional DCS's lodge meeting – tell him we've found a body on his patch and he's going to be on telly in the morning, explaining it to the nation.'

Thirty minutes later the clouds above the colliery were pulsing like the intestines of a living creature, reflecting the blue lights of the police vehicles lined up in the lane. The whole area was cordoned off except for a path leading to the position of the body, and a constable was appointed to log all visitors. When the local detective superintendent was convinced that we weren't a trio of loonies, he sent for the police surgeon. The doc confirmed what we already knew and told his favourite pathologist to scrub-up for a rush job.

We were drinking tea at Divisional HQ when the message came that the coroner had given permission for Georgina to be removed to the mortuary at the local teaching hospital, where the PM would take place. I rang Gilbert to bring him up to date, and suggested that Miles Dewhurst be organised to identify his daughter's body. It was broad daylight outside and the rain had stopped. Looked as if it might be sunny, later.

Nigel agreed to stay behind for the post-mortem, and I let Sparky drive the two of us back in my car. We'd done about fifty miles before I broke the silence.

'Oh, I nearly forgot. Consider yourself bollocked,' I said.

'Thanks,' Sparky replied, preoccupied with the driving and his own thoughts. Six miles later he looked across and said: 'What for.'

'Insubordination.'

'Oh.' Another long silence, then he said: 'Sorry if I go too far now and again, Charlie. What did I call you this time?'

'Not me, prat. Oscar Peterson. He's complained to me about you. Threatened to report you to the Rubber Heel boys.'

'Oh, 'im. Now he is a prat. The old school. Nobody does things as well as they used to. Modem methods are a load of hocus-pocus. Do you know, he thinks a DNA test is what you have to pass to get into the National Association for Dyslexia?'

I looked out of the side window, pretending I hadn't heard. The barley in the fields was ripening well. I said: 'Just leave him alone, Dave. He's a lot on his plate.'

'We've a lot on our plates.'

We were turning off the Al on to the M62 when Dave said: 'I'll have a little bet with you, Charlie.'

'What on?'

'This Mushroom Man that Peterson's after.'

'You mean the Destroying Angel. Did you know that the Book of Revelations has inspired more serial killers than Michael Winner has had free dinners?'

'Gerraway. OK, you know this Destroying Angel?'

'What about him?'

'I bet you a tenner we get him before Peterson does.'

'A tenner. A tenner we catch the Angel?'

'Yes.'

'Heckley CID? We're not even on the case.'

'Take the bet, then.'

'OK, it's a deal.'

It's been said a million times but it's true: the waiting is the hardest part. We had a fruitless chat with Gilbert at the station, just so he didn't feel neglected, then went home to bed. The news that Georgina's body had been found was broadcast on the morning radio and TV news. Saturday it would adorn the tabloids. They'd be annoyed that the story had broken on their slowest day, but no doubt some creative journalism would stretch it through to Monday.

Slowly, bits of information came filtering through to us. If you could call it information. Nigel reported that the preliminary examination found no apparent cause of death; we'd have to wait for analysis of internal organs. There was no sign of sexual interference.

Capstick is in North-East Division. They had agreed that all the forensic stuff could go to the lab at Wetherton, which was more convenient for us. I had a word with Professor Van Rees who is in charge there and told him what we might be looking for – in short, anything. We were grasping at dandelion clocks.

Saturday morning we held a big meeting. We now had, in theory, a couple of reports to work on. The first one told us that Georgina had been given a massive dose of a barbiturate compound prior to her death. According to the pathologist this could possibly have suppressed her respiration sufficiently to kill her on its own, but he'd added a note saying that he suspected a little manual assistance had been applied. No alien fibres were found in her respiratory passages, so a plastic bag was the likeliest culprit.

The other one was a very preliminary report listing the various samples that had gone to Wetherton. The mud that so generously coated the area was a mixture or clay, coal and industrial lubricants, all stirred together for a hundred years. It was as unique as an English summer, but we had nothing to match it against. The fingertip search had failed to reveal any broken bracelets bearing the owner's name, or dropped credit cards.

'In short, gentlemen,' said Gilbert, 'we still haven't a bloody lot to go on. Sod chuffin' all, in fact.'

I'd been listening with my arms folded and my chair rocked back so I was leaning on the wall. Nobody wanted to speak, so I said: 'In all my years –'

'Which is quite a few,' Sparky interrupted.

I threw him a glare and tried again: 'In all my considerable years I have never been on a case which has thrown up so little evidence. We haven't unearthed a single clue pointing us towards the kidnapper. It can't all be down to luck; he must be very clever. A lot of planning went into this one.'

'Or else he's been under our noses all the time,' Sparky suggested.

'I think Dave's right,' Gilbert said. 'We've plenty of circumstantial against Dewhurst, but it's hard to imagine what it would require to really put the finger on him. As far as we're concerned he's still the girl's dad, so finding a few fibres linking them together is a waste of time.'

I turned to DC Madison. 'Maggie, how did Dewhurst react when he ID'd the body?'

She shook her head. 'Distraught. He was wrecked. We were both in tears. If there was nothing else to go on he'd have convinced me that he didn't do it.'

'So what do you think?'

'I'm not sure. Maybe he did it but regrets doing it. It'd be the same emotion.'

'I can believe that,' said Gilbert. He went on: 'OK, on Monday the Acting Chief Constable's deadline runs out. I'm not interested in furthering his promotion prospects, and certainly have no intentions of jeopardising an enquiry to do so, but unless anybody comes up with a reasonable argument I'm suggesting we lift Dewhurst and his girlfriend, Parkinson, on Monday morning. Our main weapon will be surprise. Let's see how Ms Parkinson behaves when the cold light of reality hits her. Any objections?'

There were a few murmured no's and shaken heads. Gilbert turned to me, inviting my comments. 'Charlie? I know you're not keen.'

I pushed off the wall, dropping my chair on to all four legs. I felt weary about the whole job. I didn't know what we could hope to find that would incriminate him. The kidnapper had already demonstrated how clued-up he was about not leaving forensic evidence, and Dewhurst was hardly likely to break under cross-examination. He'd just play the grieving father and keep his mouth clamped shut. We'd be the villains. The girlfriend might sing to save her skin, if she knew anything. Probably would. And maybe our boffin could dredge something from the recesses of his computer's memory. There are specialists who can do that sort of thing, even though the information has been erased. It might be worth a try.

'No objections, boss,' I said.

'The ayes have it then. Let's organise the details now, and then maybe we can all have a day off tomorrow. We'll meet here six-thirty Monday morning. Now, who do we need and where are we going?'

He made it sound like a democratic process, which it wasn't. Going home I called in the pub for a sandwich and a couple of pints. I watched sport on television in the afternoon. England were struggling to avoid the follow-on against Gilbert and Ellice Islands. Later I rang Annabelle, but there was no answer.

On Sunday morning I called in the office and read most of the file on Miles Dewhurst. Then I shopped to restock the freezer and did a few of the more desperate chores around the house and garden. I urgently needed a cleaning lady, a gardener and a window cleaner. An alternative solution would be to move in with someone who either already had these or who managed to complete such menial tasks with consummate ease. I dialled Annabelle's number again. She still wasn't there. On a few occasions in the past Annabelle had disappeared for the whole weekend. Ah well, she was a big girl. It was none of my business how she spent her time. I had a shower and a sulk.

Gilbert and Ellice bowled underarm, so England managed to hold on sufficiently to save Monday's gate receipts. I had Sunday lunch at dinner time, in other words tea time, as is the modern practice. Roast beef, Yorkshire pudding, roast potatoes, peas, carrots, and sprout. Singular. All frozen. For pudding I had blackberry and apple pie from a local bakery. That was the best bit. I was settling down with a large pot of tea and *Biggles Flies East* when the phone rang. It was Gilbert. My superintendent, that is, not the island.

He said: 'Hi, Chas. You can go out and get rat-arsed tonight. Tomorrow is cancelled.'

'Great, I hate Mondays. Is this a one-off or will it apply to all of them from now on?'

'Just this one, sadly. You remember Terry Finnister?'

'Yes. Lorry driver from near Warrington who somebody fingered to us. Was delivering toilets or something when Georgina vanished.'

'That's him, except it was near Workington. Well, on Saturday he was arrested by the local fuzz for showing his own to a bunch of schoolgirls in the park. Apparently they laughed at him and he turned nasty, assaulted one of them.'

'I should think so, too. What's this got to do with us?' I asked.

'What it's got to do with us, Charlie boy, is that this afternoon he confessed to the murder of Georgina Dewhurst.'

Chapter Sixteen

I'd been standing by the telephone. I slumped into the easy chair alongside the low table and didn't speak for several seconds. Eventually I said: 'Is he being taken seriously?'

'North-West are taking him seriously. Apparently he asked to make a statement and it was all done with the duty solicitor present.'

'Golly gosh. Do you want me to get over there?'

'No, he's not going anywhere, they've already charged him. I've said we'll collect him at ten o'clock tomorrow morning. I think you and I ought to go. OK? That'll give them time to have the initial interview transcribed.'

'OK. Did he say how he killed her?'

'We might have a problem there,' Gilbert replied. 'His story is that when she struggled he put his hands on her throat to quieten her and she just went limp.'

'Like they always do.'

'Exactly. We'll have to check with the pathologist to see if it's a possibility.'

'What about his movements? I don't suppose he went anywhere near Capstick that Monday morning.'

'Suitably vague. He says he hid the body and went back for it one night. We'll find out more tomorrow. The good news is that Partridge gets his arrest to announce at the conference, and Dewhurst will think the pressure is off him.'

'So you're not convinced?'

'I've an open mind. Are you?'

'No.'

'Right. See you in the morning.'

It doesn't say much for a person's lifestyle when they want to claim credit for a murder they didn't do. It's a poor reflection on society when, for a few individuals, being a convicted murderer or child molester is a step up the social scale. Terry Finnister was on my mind when I went to sleep that night. He wasn't in my normal library of bed-time reveries. I cursed him and thought about Annabelle, but that only caused me to wonder where she had been all weekend.

Poor old Gilbert was called in to brief Trevor Partridge, the Acting Chief Constable, so DC Mad Maggie Madison went to Workington with me. We set off at eight, dodging the morning meetings. 'I'll drive there,' I told her. 'You can drive home, unless you'd rather sit in the back with lover boy.'

'Why not let him drive home,' she suggested. 'Then I could sit in the back with you.'

I tut-tutted. 'Any more talk like that, Margaret, and I'll have to report you for sexual harassment. You really will have to make an effort to control these animal urges.'

'Why?'

'Buggered if I know. We could always forget Finnister and book into a seedy boarding house in Blackpool.'

'Sorry, Charlie. It's the Holiday Inn or nothing.'

'No, it's got to be a seedy boarding house, much more romantic. People don't have affairs at the Holiday Inn. They go there for six hours' sleep and fifteen hundred calories of breakfast down 'em. Stay in bed too long and you'll wake up with a *Sanitised* label round you.'

Maggie said: 'Can you imagine the expression on Finnister's face if we said: "Do you mind driving,

Terence, old boy, while we have a session on the back seat?"'

'Can you imagine the expression on my face?' I answered.

It was harmless banter. I'd known Maggie, and her husband, a long time. She was a figure of stability to whom I'd turned once or twice when times were bad; especially when my marriage collapsed. Nothing heavy, just someone to talk to. She was a good cop, and I think she regarded me the same.

We fell to talking about the job. The latest policy scare that someone had dreamed up was called Tenure of Office. The theory was that we'd all have to rotate jobs every few years. Five years in CID and then it would be back into uniform. Maggie thought I'd have some inside information about it, but I didn't. She said she'd leave if it came about. I didn't know what I'd do. We both agreed it was crazy.

We had a comfort stop at the services on the M6. At Junction 36 I said: 'Let's take the scenic route,' and swung off the motorway. In Windermere I said: 'If we're taking the scenic route we might as well do the job properly,' and turned on to the Kirkstone Pass road, round the back of Helvellyn.

The tops were shrouded in the usual mist as we dropped down into Patterdale. 'They do good chicken legs in garlic there,' I said, gesturing towards the pub.

'Sorry, Charlie, we haven't time,' Maggie replied. She liked to play the mother hen with me. I accepted the roles.

'Just a thought,' I said.

The proximity of the mountains made me melancholy. Having to drive by them was like leading a small boy past a sweet-shop window. I'd done a lot of fell-walking and a small amount of climbing over the years, but hardly any recently, apart from the brief excursion with Annabelle a fortnight ago.

'When things quieten down maybe we should resurrect the CID walking club,' I suggested.

'CID boozing club, more like it,' Maggie replied. 'It was fun, though, maybe we should.'

Thirty minutes later we breezed into the station and identified ourselves to the custody sergeant. 'You're late,' he told us. 'We were expecting you an hour ago.'

'Traffic was bad,' I replied.

The sergeant passed me the detention sheet to sign. I noted that Finnister was in good health and bore no visible signs of bruising or other injury. I scrawled my name and the sergeant handed me a poly bag containing a few possessions. He removed a bunch of keys from a locked drawer.

'There's a transcript of the interviews for us, too, and I wouldn't mind a word with the detective who interviewed him, if possible,' I said.

'Sorry, they're all out. The interviews are here, though.' He retrieved a large manila envelope from another drawer. I could see from the bulge that it also contained a copy of the tape.

'Right, thanks. Let's go get him, then.'

The sergeant unlocked a door on to a short corridor between the cells. 'Has he been fed?' I asked.

'The prisoner ate an 'earty breakfast,' he answered. 'Full English, brought in from the takeaway next door. Should have set him up for the day.' We were outside his cell. The sergeant slid the hatch to one side with such force that it startled me. 'Wake up, Mr Finnister,' he bellowed. 'Your taxi has arrived.'

The door swung open, leading us into a standard eight-by-six room, painted magnolia after extensive research, with a bunk down one side. Finnister was invisible, huddled under the blankets. 'Wake up, Terry, time to go,' the sergeant called out, grabbing a handful of grey blanket and pulling it back.

The face he revealed was a death mask, little more than skin stretched over a skull. Finnister wore an expression like a snarl turning into a smile, as if, at the last moment, some great puzzle had been solved.

'Oh my God!' the sergeant mumbled, staggering back. 'Oh my God!'

'Ring for an ambulance,' I ordered, bundling him to one side. 'Maggie...'

I yanked the blankets away. From his chest down Finnister was lying in a big black pool of blood. It couldn't soak away because of the polythene sheet covering the mattress, protection against drunks pissing the bed. Maggie put her hand on his throat, feeling for a pulse. I found the slashes in his wrist and tried to hold them closed.

'Find something to bind these with, Maggie,' I said.

She shook her head. 'Waste of time, I'm afraid, boss. He hasn't a drop of blood left in him to save.'

It was their baby, so as soon as we decently could, we left them to it. I collected the manila, envelope and let Maggie drive us back. She drives with all the panache of the unimaginative, right foot hard down on one pedal or the other. Neither of us spoke much. I tried to read the interview notes, but concentration was difficult. Back at Heckley we played the tape in Gilbert's office.

The interrogation had been done with skill and patience. Finnister had freely volunteered the information that he had killed Georgina. The detective's tone was encouraging, and he had teased as much as he could from the prisoner about the details of the murder.

When Finnister realised he was saying too much, he clammed up. Otherwise it didn't tell us anything we didn't already know. Maggie made two coffees, and a tea for me, while we were listening.

'Thanks, Maggie, you make a good cuppa,' Gilbert said, taking a sip.

'That's sexist,' I declared.

'No it's not. It's appreciation. So what do you think?'

I took my time before replying. Then I said: 'We were late. I decided to take the picturesque route, through Patterdale. I think that if we'd been on time we'd have a prisoner in the cells now.'

'In which case,' he replied, 'Finnister would probably have topped himself on our premises, and we'd be taking all the flak.'

'If he'd had the means. We might have looked after him better.'

Gilbert said : '*If* you'd been on time. *If* we'd found whatever he used to cut himself. If your aunt had balls she'd be your uncle. It's not our fault, Charlie. It's not anybody's fault but his own. He'd have done it sometime, somewhere, however hard we'd tried to look after him.'

'OK, you're right,' I said. 'But I don't think we've done him any favours over the years. It would only have been common courtesy to have been on time.'

'No it wouldn't. He probably hadn't been told what time you were supposed to be there. Anyway, I have no qualms about not extending common courtesy to self-confessed child killers.'

'Nor have I, but I don't think he did it.'

Gilbert tapped the rim of his cup with a fingernail. 'No, I thought you didn't. So why did he confess?'

'It's common enough. Why do we do anything? Why did I join the police?'

'What about you, Maggie?'

'I'm not sure, sir, but I have my doubts.'

'Mmm. So the book stays open.'

Maggie and I nodded.

'That'll please the Acting Chief Constable,' he said, with the slightest hint of a smile.

Maggie volunteered to tell Dewhurst the latest developments. Just the bare facts, before he read about it in the papers. Down in my own office I rang Sam Evans, the police surgeon, to tell him I'd swished my hands round in someone else's blood. I'd washed them thoroughly immediately afterwards, and had no cuts or contusions, so he was able to reassure me. Normally we try to wear gloves in situations like that. I knew I wouldn't feel comfortable until I'd had at least one hot shower.

'Thanks, Sam,' I said. 'Try to keep out of paintbrush shops.'

It was a private joke. I'd met Sam about ten years previously after I'd fallen down a fire escape. When I admired the watercolours on the walls of his surgery he told me that his wife, Yvonne, had painted them. Unfortunately she'd suffered a slight stroke, leaving her with a tremor in her left hand, which was doubly sad because she was left-handed, and could therefore paint no more.

The pictures were typical of an amateur, tightly done and overbrushed, but the talent was obviously there. 'Why doesn't she paint right-handed, then?' I asked.

'I've suggested that, but she says she can't.'

'Would you like me to show her how? I'd be glad to.'

'Are you a painter, too?' Sam enquired.

'Well, I went to art school.'

'Great! That would be splendid. When will it be convenient?'

I went round a couple of nights later, armed with a large sheet of rag paper and the biggest sable brush available, purchased at massive discount during my student days. One of the secrets of watercolours is to use only the finest materials. I showed Yvonne how her pictures could be improved using a much looser, big-brush technique, and suggested she start by repainting all her old works. Using the wrong hand was a good way of enforcing this new discipline. Now she makes a steady income from art club exhibitions. I told Sam to buy her a size 12 pure sable brush, and specified the make. Poor old Sam breezed into the artists' suppliers and asked for one. He nearly had a cardiac arrest when the assistant said: 'That will be ninety-five quid, sir. Shall I wrap it?'

Our gossiping was interrupted by the other phone ringing. I said goodbye to Sam and hello to the new caller.

'It's Van Rees here, is that Inspector Priest?' said the voice on the line.

'Hello, Professor. Charlie Priest speaking. What can I do for you?'

'It's more what I can do for you. Could you possibly get over here, quickly as possible? I've found something that you'll be interested in.'

It was going-home time; I was tired and hungry and he was fifty miles away. 'Can't you tell me over the phone?' I asked.

'It's something I want to show you. Put your coat on, Inspector, and point your car in this direction. You know I wouldn't call you out for nothing.'

'I'm on my way. In fact... that's me knocking on your door right now.'

I hit all the rush-hour traffic, so it was an hour and a half later that I knocked on his door.

'Come in, Inspector Priest. Sit down, please. Coffee?'

'Thanks. I could murder a cup of tea.'

'Ah, murder. How we devalue the wickedness of the deed by everyday use of the word. Milk and sugar?'

'Just sugar, please. Do you ever go home, Professor?'

'Yes, of course, when I have to. But what could I find at home as fascinating as all this?' He gestured with the hand holding the teaspoon, splashing brown drops on to the papers on his desk.

I gave an inclination of the head, as if agreeing with him. He wasn't the type to be interested in football on the telly or to have a kind-hearted au pair.

I had a few sips from the mug he'd pushed across to me. It was coffee, with milk but no sugar. 'Mmm, just what I needed,' I lied. 'Now, what do you want to show me?'

He produced two ten-by-eight photographs from a folder. They were black at the bottom and white at the top, with a jagged line between like a badly sharpened saw-blade.

'What do you think of those?' he said, triumphantly.

I studied them for a few seconds, then said: 'You've taken up minimalist photography and want my opinion. Is that it?'

He peered over the tops of the pictures. 'You're holding that one upside down,' he replied.

I asked him to explain. When he'd finished I borrowed his sugar and put four spoonfuls in the coffee – champagne would have been more appropriate, but this would do.

'Well done, Prof,' I said, trying to hide the hotchpotch of emotions that was bubbling over inside me. 'Well done!'

I used his phone to ring Luke's home number. He was about to go out, as soon as he'd decided which earrings to wear.

'Luke, how long would it take to run off copies of all my reports of interviews with Miles Dewhurst?'

'Oh, about five minutes.'

'Good. Any chance of you calling in at the station and doing it, please?'

'What, now?'

'Mmm.'

'Er, yeah. No problem, Charlie.'

'Thanks. Leave them on my desk, I'll collect them in a couple of hours.'

On the way back I saw a fish and chip shop and swung into a vacant parking place. I was about to order when I remembered where my hands had been earlier in the day, and didn't feel hungry any more.

'Er, I've, er, changed my mind,' I said to the bewildered lady, and left empty-handed.

The reports were on my desk, as arranged. I took them home to read in bed, but not before I'd had a hot shower and a bowl of cornflakes, consecutively.

Ashurst Construction have premises on a bustling new trading estate in Stockport, Greater Manchester. Mr Black, their managing director and chief designer, welcomed me into his office at nine o'clock on Tuesday morning. I'd made the appointment earlier by ringing him at home.

'Sit down, Inspector. Can I order you a coffee?' he said.

'No thanks, Mr Black, I'd rather get straight on with it and I'm sure you're very busy.'

'Busy's the word. Still, it's preferable to the alternative. How can I help you?'

'First of all, could you tell me in a sentence what you do here and how well you know a company called Eagle Electrical.'

The genial expression slipped from his face. 'Ah, yes,' he said. 'The little girl. I read that you'd found her body. Dreadful. Dreadful.'

'Eagle Electrical...' I prompted.

'Yes, well, to answer your question, we are in the business of renovating property. Trading estates like this one, nursing homes, blocks of flats. We do a lot of work for local authorities. Eagle Electrical have supplied us with materials, and sometimes we've found it more expedient to subcontract the labour to them, too. Smaller jobs, though; we have our own teams of craftsmen. We use Eagle and others in preference to losing a contract.'

'So how well do you know Mr Dewhurst?' I asked.

'Miles Dewhurst?' He pursed his lips and shrugged his shoulders. 'I... know him, that's all. He comes in here about once a month looking for business. They haven't had a substantial order from us for quite a while. We try to put some stuff their way, to keep them floating. It's not in our interests for them to go under.'

'You think it might have come to that?'

'I really don't know. We're OK, but a lot of smaller firms are still failing in spite of all the talk of a recovery.'

'Could you tell me when you last saw Miles Dewhurst, Mr Black?' I asked.

'Yes. The morning his daughter disappeared. I'd presumed that was why you were here.'

'It is, but I need to hear it from your mouth. Is there any documentary proof that he was here that morning? You know what we say, sir: to eliminate him from our enquiries.'

He appeared quite eager. 'Well, yes, there is. It just so happened that he had a puncture in our yard. Very embarrassing for him – he drives one of those macho offroad vehicles. Something had gone through one of his sidewalls; ruined the tyre. Our mechanic took it round to ATS Tyres and had a new one fitted.'

'Took the wheel there or the whole vehicle?'

'The vehicle. He put the spare on and drove it there. Miles stayed in here with me. Only took half an hour. We put it on our account, so it's in the books, somewhere.'

'Good. Thank you. When it's convenient would you mind making a recorded statement in a local police station – everything you've just told me?'

'No, not at all.'

'I'll fix something up, then. Now, could I possibly have a word with the mechanic who took Dewhurst's car to the tyre depot?'

Nigel and Sparky were in deep conversation when I entered the office. Nigel was saying: 'So why was Prince Charles wearing this ginger hat with the tail down the back?'

Sparky rolled his eyes in a so-help-me gesture.

'Because,' he said, emphasising with a stab of the finger, 'because the Queen said: "Where are you going, Charles?" and he replied: "Heckmondwike," and she said: "Wear the fox hat."'

'Don't let Mr Wood hear you telling royalist jokes, David,' I said, endeavouring to keep a straight face.

'No, boss, it's not a joke. It's a true story.'

'So what's a fox hat got to do with Heckmondwike?' Nigel asked.

'Never mind that,' I interrupted. 'Where is Mr Wood?'

'Summoned to Division,' said Sparky. 'Apparently we've overspent on handcuffs.'

'So that means...' I stretched my arms wide, 'that I'm in charge. OK, boys and girls, gather round and Uncle Charlie will tell you a story.'

When I'd finished, there were smiles all round. I slid my diary, open at a list of phone numbers, across to Nigel and pointed at the phone. 'C'mon, Nigel, do your stuff,' I said.

He drummed his fingers on the handset for a moment, gathering his wits, then picked it up and dialled. After a few seconds he gave us a nod and settled back in his chair.

'Mr Dewhurst?' he asked. 'Oh, good. It's DS Newley here, from Heckley CID. Is it convenient for you to speak? You're not doing eighty on the motorway, are you?... Fine, fine. You've heard the latest developments, I presume? Yes... we've mixed feelings here, too.'

Nigel placed a hand over the mouthpiece. 'He's at home,' he hissed. He resumed the conversation; 'The fact is, Mr Dewhurst, we'd like to do a formal interview with you here at the station. As you know, it's a sad fact that in a case like this the closest members of the family always fall under a certain amount of suspicion. We need a taped interview describing your movements on the weekend in question; tie up a few loose ends, so to speak... Yes... Yes, I suppose it does seem rather pointless to you... How does four thirty, here, sound?... Oh, good. We'll see you then, Mr Dewhurst. Thank you for your cooperation. Oh, there's just one other thing. It's normal procedure for a solicitor to be present. Would you like me to arrange the duty solicitor or will you bring your own?'

Nigel replaced the phone and wiped his forehead

with the back of his hand. 'He's bringing his own solicitor,' he sighed.

Nigel had managed to squeeze all the key words into the conversation: under suspicion; taped interview; solicitor present. I said: 'Well done. Now, let's go to the pub and discuss tactics over a Steinberg's pork pie. I'm famished.'

These days we can't afford to have anybody manning the front desk. The public are expected to ring the bell for attention. We were looking out for Dewhurst, though. He arrived fifteen minutes late, in the Toyota, accompanied by Mr Wylie, his solicitor. The arrogant sod parked in the spot marked HMI again. They were shown into interview room number one, my lucky room.

Nigel and I joined them immediately. We noticed that Dewhurst's concession to grief was a black tie and matching cuff links. His designer stubble was as well groomed as ever, but he looked gaunt under his tan. Or was it worried?

'Thanks for coming,' I said briskly. 'This shouldn't take long.'

When we were seated, us on one side of the table, them on the other, Nigel said: 'This is a taped interview with Mr Miles Dewhurst.' He gave the time and date and went on: 'Could I ask those present to identify themselves. I'm Detective Sergeant Newley...' He pointed to each of us in turn.

'DI Priest,' I said

'Miles Dewhurst,' in an irritated tone.

'Oh, er, I'm Mr Wylie, senior partner with Dean and Mason, Mr Dewhurst's solicitor.'

I said: 'Thank you, gentlemen. Mr Dewhurst, you are no doubt aware that you have been under a certain amount of suspicion. I have to tell you that in spite of recent developments that suspicion still exists. It is my duty to inform you that you are not obliged to say anything unless you wish to do so, but anything you do say may be put in writing and given in evidence. Do you understand what I am saying, Mr Dewhurst?'

His indignation was on the verge of boiling over. He gathered himself together, considering whether to appear affronted or cooperative. Mr Wylie's hand reached out and fell on his arm. 'It's all right, Miles,' he said. 'Mr Priest is just doing it by the book.'

I repeated the question: 'Do you understand the caution, sir?'

He nodded.

'For the tape, sir.'

'Yes. I understand.'

'Thank you.'

Nigel took it up, as per the game plan. 'Mr Dewhurst, could you briefly describe your movements on the Friday before Georgina's disappearance?'

He shuffled and cleared his throat. 'Er, I had some appointments through the day. I'd have to look in my diary to be precise.'

'That's good enough. And in the evening?'

'Well, after work I picked Georgina up from the child minder's and we went to fetch Mrs Eaglin, her grandma. She'd prepared a meal for us. Afterwards we all came back to Heckley.'

He was talking. That was what we wanted. I said: 'And what did you do Saturday?'

He sat back in his chair, making himself more comfortable. These were easy questions; no problem.

'Saturday morning I worked. Paperwork in the office.'

'At the factory or an office at home?'

'The factory. I went straight from there to the golf club. Had a sandwich and a round of golf.'

'Where do you play, sir?'

'Brandersthorpe.'

Best in the area. You could buy a small car with the membership fee. I said: 'And in the evening?'

'Watched a kids' video with Georgina. Watched grown-up TV and had a couple of beers after she'd gone to bed.'

He was relaxing. Now it was Nigel's turn again. 'And on Sunday?' he said.

Dewhurst stretched his arms forward on to the table and interlocked his fingers. He stared at his hands as he spoke: 'Golf in the morning. Home for lunch. In the afternoon I watched sport on the box. Mrs Eaglin and Georgina went to the park to feed the ducks. Afterwards we took Mrs Eaglin home. Georgina and I left there at about seven and went for a pizza. It's... it was her favourite.'

'Which brings us to Monday morning,' I said.

Dewhurst pushed himself upright. 'For heaven's sake, Inspector. We've been through this a dozen times...'

He was getting cocky. He thought he'd survived the worst we had to offer. 'We'd like it down on tape, if you don't mind, sir. And you are still under caution, of course.' No harm in reminding him.

He folded his arms and addressed the table, speaking in short sentences as if addressing an idiot. 'I dropped Georgina off at the bus station. I bought a paper. I didn't see Georgina on to the bus because I was double-parked. Then I did my day's work. I came home to find you in my house.' He looked up and our eyes met briefly. I felt like Rikki-tikki-tavi, nailing Nag the cobra.

'Thank you. Could you expand on your movements after you left the bus station, please?'

'If you insist, Inspector.'

I did, I most certainly did.

He went on: 'I drove round the one-way system and headed out on the Manchester Road. I had an appointment at a company called Ashurst's, in Stockport, at nine o'clock. It was about ten past when I arrived. I had a puncture in their yard and had to cancel my next appointment. After that I think I went to Heaton's in Kidsgrove, but again I'd have to check my diary to be sure.'

'A puncture?' I said, raising an eyebrow like a bad thespian. 'That was unfortunate. Were you in the Toyota?'

'No, the Patrol.'

'So who repaired it for you?' I asked.

'Really, Inspector. Is all this necessary? It's my daughter's murder you're supposed to be investigating; not who repaired a puncture for me!'

'OK, let me put it another way. Were you anywhere near Capstick Colliery on that Monday morning?'

'No. Most certainly not!'

'Thank you. In that case is there any way in which you can verify your whereabouts?'

He gave a big sigh and sank back in his chair, saying: 'I'm sorry, Inspector. I didn't realise what you were getting at. The mechanic at Ashurst's put the spare on, then took the Patrol to the local tyre depot, ATS Tyres, and had a new one fitted. Mr Black, MD at Ashurst's, kindly offered to put it on their account. It should all be in their books, somewhere. I wasn't given any of the paperwork.'

Wylie, the solicitor, decided to earn his fee. He smiled and said: 'I must say, Inspector, you had me wondering where your questions were leading, but I'm sure my client has given a satisfactory account of his movements. Both Ashurst's and the tyre depot will have details of the transaction.'

'No doubt,' I agreed. 'So let's get this clear, and I would remind you that you are still under caution. You went to Ashurst's and had a puncture. Their mechanic took the Patrol to ATS Tyres and had a new one fitted. When it was returned to you it had five good tyres with the spare in its proper place under the back of the vehicle. Is that what happened?'

'Yes.'

'You're certain of that?'

'Well, yes.'

'Have you or anybody else removed or touched the spare since then?'

'No.'

'Has the vehicle been in for a service?'

'No.'

'Good.' When I'd entered the interview room I was carrying a folder. So that it didn't cause a distraction, I'd placed it on the floor, leaning against the leg of my chair. Now I reached down and retrieved it. 'In which case,' I said, 'perhaps you could explain this.' I removed the two black and white prints that Van Rees had given me and shoved them across the table.

Wylie leaned forward, interested. Dewhurst looked scared. 'I... d-don't understand,' he stuttered.

'Let me make it easier for you then, Mr Dewhurst.' I had a pair of scissors in the folder. I used them to cut across one of the prints, as close as possible to the jagged saw-teeth. I placed the cut-down print over the first one.

Dewhurst kept silent, his face a mask of fear and

contempt. Wylie said: 'I'm afraid you've lost me, Inspector.'

'I'll explain, then. This one' – I indicated with a finger – 'is a photograph of the black plastic bag in which poor Georgina's body was found. It's the type that comes in a continuous roll. You just tear them off at the perforations, as required. This other one' – I pointed again – 'is the next bag on that roll. The edges are a perfect match, as you can see. It was removed from under Mr Dewhurst's Nissan Patrol, wrapped round the spare wheel.' I turned to Dewhurst: 'Would you care to explain how it came to be there, sir?'

Chapter Seventeen

Dewhurst's suntan was rapidly losing the struggle to keep some colour in his face. Beads of sweat formed on his forehead and an eyelid developed an involuntary twitch. He said: 'I don't know what you are talking about.'

'It's called infanticide, Mr Dewhurst. I'm suggesting that you murdered Georgina.'

'You're mad.' He spat the words at me.

I expanded on my accusation: 'You'd planned the whole thing for a long time. We know all about your financial situation and the love nest in Todmorden. The ransom notes were made well in advance of the deed. To make them you bought envelopes, notepad and glue from Woolworths. What you didn't use you discarded, probably by simply placing them in a litter bin or skip whilst on your travels. You murdered Georgina on the Sunday night, giving her a massive dose of your mother-in-law's sleeping tablets and helping them along with a plastic bag over her head. You carefully opened the roll of bin-liners you had previously purchased and tore off the first one. You hid it at Capstick Colliery, with Georgina's body inside. The rest of the roll was placed between the front seats of the Nissan and you disposed of them sometime on the Monday.'

Wylie was sitting bolt upright, his eyes switching from me to his client and his mouth hanging open.

I pressed on: 'To give yourself an alibi for Monday morning you faked the puncture. That was when your luck ran out. Mechanics in general have a bad reputation. Unfortunately for you, the one at Ashurst's is

very conscientious. The spare wheel he removed was
filthy with dirt from the road. When he put the other
wheel back under your vehicle he remembered seeing
the roll of bin liners between the front seats. He carefully removed the next bag from the roll and used it to
wrap around your spare, replacing the remainder of
the roll back where he'd found it. I removed that bag
from under your Nissan Patrol four weeks later.'

I turned to Nigel and gave a jerk of the head towards
the shattered figure sitting opposite. Nigel said: 'Miles
Jonathan Dewhurst; I am arresting you for the murder
of Georgina Alice Dewhurst. Do you wish to say anything? You are not obliged to say anything, but what
you do say may be put in writing and given in evidence.'

We should have noticed the warning signs earlier.
Dewhurst hunched his shoulders forward and I briefly
saw that his lips had turned blue. Then he clutched the
front of his shirt and pitched head first on to the table.

'He's having a heart attack,' I cried, and heard
myself ordering an ambulance for the second time in
two days. Nigel dashed out while I loosened Dewhurst's
collar and supported his head. Within seconds the
room was filled with helpers. The uniformed boys
have more experience at this sort of thing than we
have, so I let them take over. The tape was still running. I said: 'Interview terminated at... twelve minutes
past five,' and flicked it off.

The custody sergeant didn't share our euphoria. He
said: 'Aw, bloody 'ell, Charlie!' when I told him that the
invalid now on his way to Heckley General had just
been arrested for murder, and that I wanted him
charged. 'Do you know what this means?' he protested.

'Well, let's see,' I replied. 'He'll need round-the-clock guarding, more for his own protection than anything. Then you'll have to comply with the requirements of PACE: read him his rights; arrange a solicitor; allow him to phone a named person; give him a copy of the code; ask him his eight favourite records... That's about all, isn't it? Should make for a touching bedside scene.'

'All! All! Where do I get the staff?'

'Look on the bright side,' I answered. 'He might die.' I probably meant it.

Walking through the foyer I saw a hunched figure heading towards the doors. I called after him: 'Mr Wylie?'

He stopped and turned. As I approached he looked to have aged ten years in the last hour. We faced each other in silence for a few moments, then I said: 'This must have come as a terrible shock to you.'

'Yes, Inspector, it did.' His voice trembled as he spoke.

'There was no other way we could do it,' I told him. A more clued-up brief would have frustrated my line of questioning. I'd taken advantage of him because he couldn't believe that his client could do such an evil deed. His only consolation was that he hadn't impeded justice.

'You did your job, Mr Priest, and did it well. I, on the other hand, cannot profess to have represented my client to the best of my abilities.'

'You couldn't have known...'

He stopped me, raising a manicured hand that had never done anything heavier than lift a conveyance. 'It's all right,' he said. 'I don't mind. I really don't mind.' There was the merest trace of a smile on his face as he turned to the door. He'd lost a case, but he'd be able to sleep at night.

'Goodnight, Mr Priest.'
'Goodnight, sir.'

It was hand-shaking, back-slapping time in the office. We interrupted Gilbert's meeting so that he could break the news to most of the top brass who weren't at the conference. The press office released a statement giving as little information as possible: a man was helping with enquiries...

Dave Sparkington had gone to Ashurst's to take Mr Black and the mechanic to their local nick and record their statements. It was after seven when he returned with the tapes. Gilbert arrived while we were playing everything through for the custody sergeant, so we had to play the first one again. They agreed that we had enough to charge him; the only cloud was whether the bin-liner from under the Nissan was admissible. I'd retrieved it without the help of a search warrant.

'It still proves he did it,' I claimed, 'even if he does get off on a technicality.'

'I doubt if he will,' Gilbert reassured us, 'but we'll let the CPS legal boys worry about that.' He looked at his watch. 'I reckon we've just about time for a celebratory snifter down at the club, eh?'

Sparky, surprisingly, was the first to object. 'Not for me, thanks. I said I'd try to be early tonight. Can we make it tomorrow?,

'It's, er, a bit awkward for me, too, Mr Wood,' said Nigel.

Gilbert looked at me. 'Tomorrow then. Eh, Charlie?'

I said: 'Yeah. Let's have him charged first. If he survives. Then we'll have the full team in the club, tomorrow.'

They drifted away. Dave said: 'You coming, Charlie?'

'Not just yet, Dave,' I replied. 'You go. I just want to tidy up.'

I watched out of the window as they left. We are on the first floor, the main body of the station being down-stairs. One by one their cars paused at the exit before pulling out into the sparse traffic and heading home. The streets were quiet, partly because of the rain, part-ly because Tuesdays in Heckley have never been a rival to Mardi Gras.

Some of my best thinking is done alone in the office, with everybody's light off except mine. The building creaks and whispers as it settles down for the night. Outside, a siren warbled as a Traffic car left the yard to witness someone's misery.

I picked up the phone and tapped the numbers. From memory. I'd remembered Annabelle's number from the very first time I dialled it. Not bad for some-one who never mastered the Lord's Prayer. Wonder what the wife of a bishop would make of that?

She answered immediately, repeating the number in her warm, rounded vowels.

'Oh, hello Annabelle, It's Charlie,' I stumbled.

'Hello, Charles. This is a pleasant surprise.'

'Glad you think so. How are you keeping?'

'Very well. And you? How is the crime-fighting going?'

'It's going well. I was wondering, Annabelle... if you are not doing anything, would it be all right if I popped round to see you?'

'Of course it would. Are you coming now?'

'If you don't mind. I'm feeling a bit... what's the adjective that means anticlimaxed?'

'Fed up?'

'That's it. I wish I had your way with words. I feel a need for some TLC.'

'You poor thing. Come and tell Auntie Annabelle all about it.'

'Half an hour?'

'Fine. Shall I bring a bottle of gin up from the cellar?'

'A cup of Earl Grey will do.'

'I'll put the kettle on.'

'Bye.'

And now I felt happy. Like Father Christmas must do at the end of his round.

The batteries in my razor were flat so I retrieved Nigel's toilet bag from his bottom drawer and swapped batteries. His weren't much better but I scraped most of the stubble from my face. My aftershave had congealed to a jelly so I borrowed that from Nigel, too. When I looked at myself in the mirror I wasn't sure that visiting Annabelle was such a good idea. Ah well, what you see is what you get. I rinsed my face and dried it on the roller towel. The aftershave smelt like Culpepper's dustbin.

Annabelle looked really pleased to see me. 'Come through into the kitchen,' she said. 'The kettle won't take a moment.' As she turned away I gazed appreciatively after her. Hungrily and longingly, too. She was wearing a white blouse and black trousers, with no jewellery. As she filled the kettle I wished I knew her well enough to go up behind her and slip my arms around that waist.

We sat at opposite sides of the refectory table. I waffled something about her kitchen being nice.

'Yes,' she agreed, 'I'm very lucky to live here.' She went on: 'So, what's the reason for this deflated feeling, or are you not allowed to tell me?'

I said: 'It'll be common knowledge by tomorrow. We've just arrested Miles Dewhurst for the murder of Georgina.'

Her face darkened. 'Her father?' she gasped.

'Yes.'

'But... but that's monstrous. Who on earth would have thought he did it?'

'Well, I did,' I replied.

After a pause she asked: 'How do you know it was him?'

I said: 'I've known right from the beginning. Well, from the second day, when we had the TV appeal.'

'I saw that,' said Annabelle. 'The poor man looked devastated. I can't believe he was acting.'

'I don't suppose it was all a sham. But just before we went on the air I saw him go to the gents' toilet I thought I could do with one myself, so I followed him in. He wasn't having a pee, though. He was fixing his hair; running the comb under the tap and inspecting his reflection in the mirror. Hardly the behaviour of a grieving parent. When I came out I decided to perform a little experiment with Gilbert. Use him as a control group type of thing. I told Gilbert that his hair was sticking up and he ought to go and comb it. He nearly bit my head off. Not exactly enough to convince a jury, but it made me think. We had to wait until we found the body for the proof.'

'I read about that,' she said. 'Somewhere up in County Durham, wasn't it? What led you to it?'

'He sent us a note with various instructions. He thought he'd got away with it, and was impatient to tie up the loose ends; put it all in the past and start his new life. I just followed the instructions.'

'*You*, Charles? Are you saying *you* found her?'

I nodded.

Annabelle reached across the table and put her hand over mine. 'Oh Charles, that must have been horrible. That poor little girl,' she sighed. She looked across at me, a new determination illuminating her face. 'And poor you,' she said. 'I wouldn't normally have commented, Charles, but you look a wreck. I bet you're not sleeping, are you?'

'I don't need much sleep.'

She studied my crumpled shirt and realisation struck her. 'Have you come here straight from the office?' she demanded.

Another nod.

'Without eating?'

Nod.

She jumped to her feet. 'Charles, you can't go on like this. It's bad for you. What would you like? It won't take a moment to rustle something up.'

'Sit down, Annabelle. A cup of tea and a biscuit will be fine. Most of all I just want some pleasant company. I feel as if I've been living in a sewer lately.'

She sat down again. 'It's all getting to you, isn't it?' she said, quietly.

'Yes,' I replied, 'I think it is. It must be something to do with growing older. Or else I'm getting sensitive. Either way, I think the time is coming for the police force and Charlie Priest to part company.'

'Maybe it's something to do with being a human being,' she replied, adding quite firmly: 'There is some home-made soup in the freezer and I am going to heat a bowl for you. Understood?'

I smiled and said: 'A bowl of your home-made soup would be extremely welcome.'

She rummaged in the deep freeze for a few moments before emerging with two plastic containers. She frowned as she looked for labels on them, her nose wrinkling with concentration. 'This one,' she pronounced, 'is *soup du jour*. This one is *soup de la maison*. Any preference?'

It was chunky vegetable with lamb and a few secret ingredients. The alternative had been carrot and orange with coriander. They both sounded delicious. Annabelle cut me a huge chunk of bread and gave me a cup of tea for support while the soup defrosted in the microwave. I nibbled the bread and had a sip of tea.

I said: 'Is this bread home-made?'

'Yes.'

'It's wonderful. Can I order two loaves per week, please.' Now I felt ravenous. I could easily have eaten the whole loaf.

Annabelle said: 'The soup will be about ten minutes. I wish you would let me make you something more substantial.'

I shook my head. After a few moments of silence I said, right out of the blue: 'Tell me about Peter.'

She looked taken aback for a second, and I wondered if I'd dropped a big one, but she said: 'Peter? What would you like to know?'

I decided I wasn't walking on broken glass after all. 'Everything,' I said.

'Where shall I begin?'

'Where else? How did you meet? No, before that. First of all tell me about yourself. Dispel the mystery that surrounds this beautiful lady I know as Annabelle Wilberforce, while I... finish this bread.'

She blushed and settled back in her chair. After inspecting her fingernails for a few seconds she took a deep breath and it all spilled out: 'I was born in a little village in Oxfordshire. Father – Daddy, as we called him – was something in the City. I can't be more specific than that. I have an older sister and a younger brother, Hugh. He's an engineer, somewhere in India I believe. We don't have much contact. My sister, Rachel, is married to a Harley Street charlatan. I have no contact with her at all. At first, things were idyllic, although you don't realise it at the time, do you?'

Now her gaze was fixed on the top right-hand corner of the ceiling. She went on: 'Then, when I was about eight, it all turned sour. Daddy vanished. Years later I learned that he ran off with a female colleague. First the pony had to go. I changed schools and we moved to a smaller house. Mummy hit the bottle. We'd come home from school and find her drunk, with the house like a refuse heap. The day after I passed my eleven-plus she took an overdose of painkillers and died.'

I'd been nibbling the bread. Now I pushed the plate away and listened.

'The three of us were spread amongst relatives. I went to live with Aunt Grace, in Cheltenham. At first it was much better there, and I was sent away to school, which I enjoyed. Then one Christmas I came home to find that Aunt Grace had married again. He was called Alec. Uncle Alec. He seemed to take a shine to me. He... took me for walks, to the pictures, bought me special treats. I thought he was wonderful.' She paused. I saw her swallow before she took up the story again: 'One night, in the dormitory, the girls were talking. The older girls were telling us about... well... about sex. I suppose it was all invented, the product of girlish imaginations, but suddenly I realised that Uncle Alec's affection wasn't as innocent as I had believed.'

Annabelle had drawn up her knees and was embracing them with her arms, still staring at the ceiling. She continued: 'After that it was horrible. Once he realised that I knew what he was after and had not told Grace, he became crude and persistent. I hated going home for the holidays. I would make excuses and stay behind for an extra week, and always went back for the new term a few days early. Half-term holidays I stayed at school. I visited as many friends as I could. I became quite a proficient little liar, I'm afraid.'

'Understandably,' I said.

She put her feet back on the floor and looked at me. 'The net result was that I did well at school. I was determined to, so I could get away from them as soon as possible. I was accepted for Lady Margaret Hall when I was seventeen. They suggested I do a year's voluntary work, so I packed my rucksack and went to Biafra. It was quite a shock to a little girl from the Home Counties. But Peter was there to help me. He was thirteen years my senior and I fell hopelessly in love with him. I thought he'd hardly noticed me, but towards the end of the year he was transferred to Kenya and asked me to go with him.'

The microwave beeped four times. Annabelle jumped up and served the soup. 'Would you like some more bread?' she asked.

I shook my head. 'No thanks, but I'd like you to continue the story.'

After serving the soup she resumed her seat and began again. 'Kenya was wonderful. You must go, sometime. Peter insisted I continue my education, so my degree certificate says Nairobi University. Not as prestigious as Oxford, but more colourful.'

'Mine says Batley College of Art,' I admitted between mouthfuls.

'We married when I was nineteen and stayed in Kenya for another eight years. I've been back a couple of times.' She was smiling now, a faraway look in her eyes. 'I miss Kenya. Those were probably the happiest days of my life.'

'So why did you leave?'

'Peter was taken ill. Malaria, a particularly persistent

strain. He regarded it as God's will and we came back to England. He threw himself into his ministry and the rest, as they say, is history.'

'You never had children?'

The clouds came back. 'No. It wasn't to be. Something else that Peter put down to God's will. Understanding what is willed by God and what isn't is a science known only to a few.'

For the first time I detected that things had not always been sunshine and roses between the bishop and his lady. 'What happened to him?' I asked.

'Cancer. He wouldn't see the doctor because he thought it was the malaria and it would just run its course. When he did go for tests it was too late. It took him two painful years to die.' She fixed me with her blue eyes. 'My faith was never as strong as his, Charles. What I experienced in Biafra saw to that. But I'll never forget how brave Peter was; right to the end. If faith can do that I wish I had more.'

It was my turn to reach out and place my hand over hers. She turned her hand over so that our fingers intertwined. I couldn't help comparing her childhood with my own: an only child of doting parents who took exaggerated pride in my modest achievements. 'You've had some rough times,' I said. 'It hasn't all been bedtime cocoa and Winnie the Pooh, has it?'

'No. Did you think it had?'

'Yes,' I confessed. 'I probably did.'

'C'mon,' she said, rising to her feet. 'Let's go where it is more comfortable.'

We went through into her sitting room. It was a tasteful amalgam of the modern and the traditional; bold prints and lots of dark wood. I sank into the settee while Annabelle searched for a CD.

'Any requests?' she asked.

'Something light and breezy,' I suggested.

'Vivaldi?'

'Perfect.'

She came to sit alongside me and we waited for the first crystal notes to fill the room.

It wasn't really a Zen experience. Exactly the opposite, I suppose, but the feeling was similar. All of my senses were switched off except my hearing, as if I were floating in a bath of liquid so perfect that I couldn't feel its presence. Maybe my eyes were closed, or perhaps they were open but there was a complete absence of light to trigger the optic nerve. This was the state of grace that drug-takers and religious fanatics crave. The music was Mozart.

I appreciated him as I had never done before. Perfection. Maybe he was the master, after all. But why Mozart? I thought. Where am I? Ought I to be going somewhere? Has the alarm gone off? Surely it was Vivaldi a minute ago.

Oh Carruthers! I remembered where I was. It's at unguarded times like this that the real inner you expresses itself. I sat up and blurted out: 'I fell asleep!' Not very bright but it could have been a lot worse.

Annabelle clutched her sides with laughter. She was sitting in one of the easy chairs. I held my head in my hands and said: 'Oh God, what must you think of me?'

'I think you must have been exhausted,' she said, still giggling at my discomfort.

I looked at the clock. It was nearly midnight. 'I'm sorry, Annabelle. You must think I'm dreadful company. I just felt so relaxed and...'

'Don't worry about it, Charles.' She'd regained her composure. 'You were tired. Actually, it was quite nice to have a man snoring on the settee again.' The giggling erupted once more.

'I didn't snore!' I exclaimed in horror, adding: 'Did I?'

'Mmm... just a little.'

'Oh no! It gets worse.' I slipped my shoes back on, not remembering having taken them off, and rubbed the fur from my teeth with my tongue.

'Would you like a drink before you go?' She was in full control again.

'No thanks, Annabelle. I've already overstayed my welcome. It's been a lovely evening for me, if not for you.' I retrieved my jacket from the kitchen and we walked towards the front door. I said: 'Annabelle, I'd like to see you at the weekend. There's a few loose ends to sort out in the office, then I want to change my priorities; sort out my life. May I, see you?'

'Yes, Charles. I'd like that.'

'Saturday? I'll book a table somewhere.'

She, shook her head. 'No. I'll cook us something. You bring the wine.'

'That sounds nice,' I said. It was my entry for the Understatement of the Millennium competition. We were at the door. 'Thanks for putting up with me.'

'It should be me thanking you, Charles.'

'For what?'

'For asking about Peter.'

She'd opened the door slightly, allowing a blast of cold air into the hallway. I pushed it shut again and took her in my arms. I could feel the heat of her body as it moulded to mine. She was so slim my arms easily encircled her, and her ribs were a gentle ripple beneath my hands. Her lips were strong and mobile... and she took them away far too quickly.

'You smell nice,' she whispered. 'What is it?'

'Oh, it's er, called... Nigel's,' I croaked, tracing her spine with my fingertips. 'Nigel's aftershave.'

'I think you ought to go, Charles,' she sighed.

'Me too,' I lied, adding: 'Saturday,' as I gave her a farewell peck on the cheek.

The rain had stopped. Or maybe a blizzard was raging – I forget. I drove away from the Old Vicarage as quietly as I could. At the end of the street I mixed up the gears and stalled the engine. Then I switched on the wipers when I tried to indicate.

The wind and rain had scrubbed the air clean, so you could see for ever. All the lights of the valley were stretched out below, prickly bright against the blackness of the night. Just above the horizon, barely broken free from the earth, was the slenderest arc of a new moon I had ever seen. It was red, like the imprint of a thumbnail dipped in blood. The thumbnail had belonged to a madman called Purley, the blood to the late Michael Ho. Bad memories came pressing in, trying to dislodge the good ones, but I didn't let them.

Chapter Eighteen

Dewhurst didn't die. He was charged with murder and transferred to the hospital wing at Bentley Prison. CPS didn't envisage any problems with my evidence. We have some good friends in the Chinese community, so instead of going to the police social club and getting rat-arsed I suggested we have a speciality banquet at the Bamboo Curtain. To my surprise, everyone agreed.

It was a memorable meal. Ten of us sat round the table and the dishes kept coming until we could eat no more. Sparky earned our displeasure by snaffling all the wontons. He said he liked junk food. Nobody laughed. Then we went to the social club and got rat-arsed.

Houses were still being burgled in Heckley. Old ladies were having their pensions snatched and cars were being taken from unconsenting owners. Three tortoises had been stolen from different addresses.

'Tut tut,' I said. 'We can't have this, can we? Three tortoises purloined. What has the world come to while I've been busy? We'd better send a posse out.' We were in the Super's morning meeting and I was looking at the print-out of offences.

'Don't mock,' rebuked Gilbert. 'They're an endangered species and mean a lot to their owners. Ask the pet shops to look out for them. Apparently it's an offence to sell one these days.'

'Yessir!'

'I've heard it said,' Sparky informed us, his face a mask of solemnity, 'that some members of our immigrant population like to gamble huge sums of money on tortoise fights.'

Gilbert removed his spectacles. 'Listen, you cocky sods,' he said. 'While you've been swanning around at vast expense to the force looking for a murderer who was under your noses all the time, everybody else has been up to their ar... ar... ar...'

'Arseholes?'

'... armpits in proper crime. Earning their bread and butter. So go to it!'

Getting back to normality was difficult. I sent the troops out and settled down to writing thank-you letters to various people. Towards the end of the morning DI Peterson called in to offer his congratulations. He wanted to sit and talk, and had a defeated air about him. The library trail had grown cold so he was retreating back to Trent Division. The Mushroom Man had dropped out of the newspapers, until the next time. As Peterson left, Sparky came in.

'Morning, sir,' said Sparky, holding the door for him.

'Good morning, Constable,' he replied.

I rocked back on my chair and scratched my head with the blunt end of the ballpen. 'What was it that Oscar Peterson played?' I asked.

'Don't ask me,' Sparky answered. 'I'm useless at sport.'

The best phone call of the day came in the middle of the afternoon. '*Carmina Burana*, Carl Orff,' said the voice on the other end.

'Er, er, let me think... Schubert, *The Trout*,' I answered.

It was Bill Goodwin, a DI at City HQ. They are based in the town hall, and Bill is my source of concert tickets. He has a standing order with the box office for first refusal on any cancellations, and sometimes lets me know about them, although I hadn't done business with him for a long time.

'Congratulations, Charlie. I hear you did a good job.'

'Aw shucks, it was nuthin',' I replied.

'Well done all the same. What about these tickets?'

'What tickets?'

'For *Carmina Burana*.'

'Are you serious?'

The concert season lasts six months and normally all the tickets go in the first week of sales. For a big showpiece concert like this there would be a waiting list longer than a wet Wakes Week in Morecambe.

'I'd love them, Bill. When are they for?'

'Friday.'

'Tomorrow? Someone's left it a bit late.'

'They're mine. Joyce was rushed into hospital yesterday. Appendicitis. They operated this morning. The tickets are yours if you want them.'

'Oh. I'm sorry to hear about Joyce. How is she?'

'The op went off OK, but she's still groggy. I'll go to see her straight from here.'

'Good. Good. Give her my love, Bill, and I hope she's fit and well before too long. Can I ring you back in five minutes about the tickets?'

Annabelle was at home, fortunately, and *Carmina Burana* was one of her favourites, although she had never heard a live performance. 'It sounds wonderful, Charles. They were sold out months ago. How on earth have you done it?'

I told her that when I said I needed two seats they promised to kick two students out of theirs. 'What's the point in being a fascist if you don't reap the benefits?' I said.

'Oh, absolutely,' she replied.

I was saying the usual goodbye formula when Annabelle interrupted me. 'Food,' she said. 'I expect you intend grabbing a pork pie or a bowl of breakfast cereal, so I'll prepare something for afterwards. We can come back here and eat. All right?'

'Oh, are you sure? It seems a lot of trouble...'

'Nonsense. See you tomorrow.'

I rang Bill and accepted his offer. After a few quiet moments I said a little thank you, to no one in particular.

First thing Friday morning I announced that I would be leaving at five p.m. come fire, flood or assassination. Three nasty muggings were done during the day by a gang of steamers. Two youths make the initial grab while five or six others hover nearby ready to combat any attempt at resistance. They were all Afro-Caribbean, so descriptions were sketchy. 'He was black,' they say, and expect us to recognise them immediately. I put everybody I had on the streets looking for them. Knives are only a grasp away in these cases. Mugging turns to murder as easily as spring snow turns to slush.

Myself, I went shopping. I thought about a haircut but decided it would look as if I were trying too hard. Besides, it had just reached that indolent bohemian stage; good for my new image. I bought a bottle of Glenfiddich for Jimmy Hoyle – he deserved the credit for retrieving the bin-liner from under Dewhurst's car – and some aftershave for myself. I searched high and fairly low but couldn't find Nigel's anywhere. I settled for some called Charlie. The biddy who served me was wearing enough make-up to grout a shower cubicle.

On the way home I topped up the petrol tank and bought a bunch of salmon-pink roses. After a quick cup of tea and a slice of toast I set both alarm clocks and grabbed an hour's nap. I was taking no chances. In the shower I used the last of the blue jelly stuff that somebody bought me about ten Christmases ago. Choosing which suit to wear wasn't a problem. I mated it with a dark blue shirt and a bold tie in a Picasso design. He's my favourite painter. I considered the socks with little clocks on them but settled for a diamond pattern in the same colours as the tie. I brushed my hair and looked in the mirror. Fan-bloody-tastic.

Annabelle answered the door immediately. I thrust the roses forward.

'Oh Charles, they're lovely,' she said. 'They are my favourites; how did you know? Come in, I'll put them in some water.'

I followed her through into the kitchen, where she filled a large plain vase and arranged the flowers in it. She was wearing a suit in an unusual lilac colour, with a very short skirt which I quickly realised was a pair of culottes. The jacket had three-quarter-length sleeves and her blouse was a deep blue in a curious material. It had a bloom to it, like yeast on a grape, that exactly matched the colour of the suit. Her tanned legs were bare and she wore high-heeled shoes. Annabelle never tried to disguise her height; she rejoiced in it.

The effect on me was like a kick in the stomach. The pain was physical. I wondered what the other bishops' wives had thought of her. And the other bishops.

I didn't start the engine immediately. Faith might move mountains but compliments work better on people. 'You look absolutely wonderful,' I told her, shaking my head in disbelief.

'Oh, just a few rags I threw on,' she declared with obvious delight, adding: 'You don't look bad yourself.'

We hit the usual Friday-evening traffic but I'd allowed plenty of time.

'Will you be able to find a parking place?' Annabelle asked.

'Leave it to Uncle Chas,' I reassured her, with a conspiratorial wink. At the town hall I drove round the back and through the entrance to the police station private car park. All the top brass were at home, tucking into their quiche, so I pulled up in a spot marked CH. SUP. 'Tonight,' I announced, 'you are in the company of an honorary chief superintendent. I told them it was a special occasion, so they've promoted me. It runs out at midnight, though.'

'Will the car turn into a pumpkin?' she asked.

'Oh, a pumpkin. A lay-by. It'll turn into something.'

The tickets were at the front desk. During the drive I'd told Annabelle how we'd acquired them. I led her in and pressed the button. A WPC appeared.

'My name's Priest,' I told her. 'DI Goodwin has left some tickets for me.'

'Yes. Mr Goodwin is still here. He asked me to let him know when you arrived.' She picked up the phone and dialled his number. He was with us in seconds. I introduced him to Annabelle.

'I'm so sorry to hear about your wife, Bill. How is she?' Annabelle asked.

She was doing well, so we didn't feel too bad about deriving so much pleasure from her misfortune. Bill was going straight round to the hospital. He handed me the tickets and I slipped him a cheque.

Annabelle said: 'Well, give Joyce our best wishes, and as soon as she's better we will try to repay you by inviting you both round for dinner, won't we, Charles?'

'Yes, of course,' I said. We. I liked the sound of that.

There's a passage leading from the nick into the

main body of the town hall, with a door locked on this side. Prisoners are transferred to the courts that way. I said: 'Any chance of using the private entrance, Bill?'

'Sorry, Charlie,' he replied. 'No can do. It's a fire door now; emergency use only. If you open it you'll start the sprinkler system. That'd make you popular.'

'You mean we've to walk round the outside, with the *hoi polloi*?' I sounded hurt.

"'Fraid so.'

'This is no way to impress a lady. C'mon, Annabelle, let's go.'

They said their farewells. At the door I turned to give Bill a wave of gratitude and he made an approving nod of his head.

The tickets said Row D. Because of the size of the orchestra and all the choirs involved, rows A, B and C had been removed. We were in the front row.

'The front row!' Annabelle whispered, incredulously. 'We're in the front row!'

'I don't muck about,' I told her. 'I just hope the conductor is not too enthusiastic with the baton. I could easily lose an eye.'

'Watch out for the trombones,' she warned.

'Maybe we should have brought an umbrella,' I replied.

The warm-up piece was a Stockhausen. The orchestra plinked and clanged through it with concentrated enthusiasm that wasn't matched by its reception from the audience. A few know-alls cheered and everybody took too many bows. Then the removal men came on and reorganised everything. When the stage was set for the new piece the orchestra began to filter back. The percussionists tuned the big timpani, hinting at what was to come. Line after line of choristers filed on, recruited from every choral society in the North, plus a couple of school choirs. Slowly the huge stage filled and everybody coughed and tuned instruments and fidgeted for the last time. Then, as if to a signal from the back of the hall, a hush came over the auditorium.

I winked at the cello player. He winked back.

Annabelle leaned towards me. 'I think the cello player fancies me,' she whispered.

'No. He fancies me. I fancy you,' I hissed, taking her hand.

The leader entered and bowed and was applauded. Then the conductor. He was popular. Not everyone had my view of him. His shirt looked as if he'd worn it all week and his suit needed cleaning. He turned to the stage, raised his baton, and, a few seconds later, the first crashing chords of Orff's greatest hit shook the fabric of the building.

I'm a lowbrow when it comes to music. Decent melodies and plenty of biff-bash are what I like. Sitting there, next to the most beautiful woman in the place, I'd probably still have been as happy as a sparrow on a chimney if they'd just tuned up for the next hour, but the music engulfed me. Carmina Burana is based around a collection of medieval verses written mainly in Latin. Some are sacred, others profane. It could have been written for us, I thought. All too soon the orchestra began the relentless build-up to what must be the longest finale in the repertoire. At the end every pair of lungs on stage was at full extent, fiddlers' elbows, were going like mating rabbits and the drummers were flailing their arms as if attempting flight. And then it was over.

After a moment's breathless silence some courageous soul shouted: 'Bravo!' and we erupted into applause. I turned to Annabelle and she was as delighted as a schoolgirl. The leader and conductor had more bows than the Royal Navy and she clapped every one.

We joined the throng shuffling up the aisle, the rhythms and tunes and *wa-wump*! of the big drums still pulsing through our bodies. 'That was wonderful,' Annabelle told me. 'It's so nice to have an influential friend.' She took my left arm in both of hers and rested her head on my shoulder. I buried a kiss in her hair.

In the foyer we merged with a sea of excited, smiling faces and were borne slowly towards the exit, which is a revolving door, flanked on each side by a swing door. Coming from the centre aisle we were in the stream of people heading towards the revolving door.

I remember wondering what etiquette demanded in such situations, but it was out of my control. When it was our turn the pressure of bodies propelled me in first and Annabelle squeezed behind me. We shuffled forwards, and she placed her hands on my hips. It didn't feel right – I ought to be following her. I made a few movements with my feet, as if doing a party dance, and felt her echo my steps.

We moved round in a semi-circle and slowly a gap appeared and enlarged. Eager to make amends for my slip of manners, I stepped briskly out and skipped to one side, raising my arm in an extravagant gesture, like a bullfighter making a pass.

Both barrels of the shotgun roared simultaneously.

The blast passed between my body and my arm, taking bits of my jacket with it, and I felt the heat of the muzzle-flash on the side of my face. Glass shattered and Annabelle jerked backwards against the panel of the door behind her, before flopping to the floor in a tangle of arms and legs, like a discarded marionette, after the curtain has fallen.

Chapter Nineteen

I tried to get to her, but the people in the segment behind were screaming and yelling and trying to get back into the building. I heard a voice, my own, shouting 'No! No!' somewhere outside my head. When the people behind were safely in the foyer I attempted to pull the door open but Annabelle's body was jamming it. Eventually I made a gap and squeezed through to her. I grasped her under the shoulders and reversed out on to the town hall steps, her long legs unfolding as I retreated and broken glass crunching under my feet. I sat there on the top step, with Annabelle cradled in my arms, trying to stem the blood, until the ambulance came and they took her from me.

They lifted her on to a stretcher with infinite gentleness and wrapped her in a bright blue blanket. The stretcher fitted on to a trolley which was exactly the same height as the back of the ambulance. It slid straight in and the wheels folded up. The paramedic closed the door and swung the handle to fasten it. I watched the ambulance slip away into the night, lights flashing, as sirens and other blue lights converged on the town hall.

Inside the station everyone was running around like ants on a pan lid. An exasperated sergeant kept asking me for a description of the gunman, and couldn't believe that I hadn't seen anything. I sat hunched on a hard chair in an interview room, feeling like a figure of ridicule, while officers ran in and out, shouted instructions and cursed. Bill Goodwin appeared and rescued me from further harassment by taking me to his office.

He found a West Yorkshire Police sweater and I swapped it for my jacket and shirt.

'I should have gone with her,' I said.

'No, you'd only have been in the way. You did the right thing.'

I picked up the phone to ring the hospital, but he put his hand over it. 'Give them a few more minutes, Charlie, then I'll ring. They won't know anything yet.' He asked a constable to make us two teas, but I didn't touch mine.

Gilbert arrived, closely followed by Sam Evans. 'Are you all right, Charlie?' Sam asked.

'I'm OK, but I wish I'd gone with the ambulance. Will they know how she is yet?'

'Have you tried ringing?'

'No,' Bill replied. 'I thought we'd give them a bit longer.'

'They might tell me,' said Sam, picking up the phone.

He asked for the sister in Casualty and introduced himself. He listened and nodded and looked grave. We heard him ask: 'Could you let me know as soon as there's any further news?'

I sat up; that meant she was still alive.

'They're taking her to surgery, they'll let us know.'

'I'm getting over there,' I told them, jumping to my feet.

'I'll take you,' Gilbert said. 'You're in no fit state to drive.'

Sam came with us. A police car was parked outside the hospital entrance, its lights switched off. Gilbert and I recognised it as an ARV.

Sam led us expertly down various dimly illuminated corridors until we were in the casualty department. It was rush hour. The place was filled with Friday-night boozers, suffering stab wounds, broken arms and sundry minor-injuries. Somebody in a cubicle made gurgling noises as a pipe was passed into his stomach to drain its alcoholic contents. A youth with a Mohican haircut and gold rings in his nose and eyebrows was complaining that his girlfriend was having a bad trip.

The sister had no further information for us. I supplied her with Annabelle's name and address for the admission forms, but wasn't much help with next of kin. When she asked me my relationship to her I just said: 'Friend.'

A policeman from the ARV, wearing a bulletproof vest over his shirt, was sitting on a chair in the middle of the corridor that led to the operating theatres. He nursed a Heckler and Koch automatic in the crook of his arm. Another cop stood surveying the scene in the waiting room, arms folded, legs apart; as implacable as the Colossus of Rhodes. Gilbert approached him cautiously and showed his ID. They talked and nodded, and Gilbert pointed to me, obviously telling him who I was.

When he rejoined us I said: 'Look, I'm staying here for as long as it takes, but you two might as well go home. I'm grateful to you both for coming.'

It made sense, so they left. The sister suggested I use the staff canteen, but I declined. She let me wait in her office, and a male nurse brought me a coffee.

Every thirty or forty minutes I stretched my legs in the waiting room. New faces replaced the ones who were either patched up and sent home or admitted into a ward. The place grew slightly more quiet as the night passed. The occasional boisterous drunk fell silent when he saw the police presence. Several clients appeared to be regulars. A down-and-out who said he had blue spiders crawling all over him was dealt with patiently and then propelled out through the door. Everybody called him George. I wandered down a corridor, between the cubicles, and found myself in the resuscitation room, where the ambulances bring the serious cases. Annabelle would have passed through here. The victim of a hit-and-run was being attended to. Through a gap in the curtains I saw the doctor pull the blanket over the man's head, then wipe the sleep and the sweat from his own eyes.

I went to the bathroom. The walls were covered in graffiti and most of the taps had been left running. When I washed my hands flakes of dried blood from under my fingernails went down the plughole. Back in the sister's office I watched the sky growing grey over the chimneypots and high-rise flats. A porter on the next shift arrived, and left his newspaper on the desk. I glanced at the folded bundle – today was the first day of the new football season.

'Mr Priest?'

I turned towards the voice. It was the sister.

'Mrs Wilberforce has been taken to the ICU. You can see her for a few moments.'

I jumped to my feet. 'How is she?' I demanded.

The sister held up her hand to curb my haste. 'I have to warn you,' she said, 'that she is very ill, and is likely to remain on the critical list for some time.'

'But she'll live?'

'This way. I'll take you.'

She led me back through the resus. room to the intensive care wards. We entered one and she introduced me to Annabelle's nurse, but I never heard her name. There were six beds in the room, with Annabelle in the end one.

She was laid out flat, with just a thin sheet over her. A blue device was sticking out of her throat, with a corrugated tube leading to a ventilator machine that was doing her breathing. A thick orange tube came from under the sheet and ended in a bottle on the floor. There was a drip leading into her arm and a battery of instrumentation alongside her bed that wouldn't have looked unreasonable on the flight deck of Concorde.

I couldn't take it all in. What had I allowed to happen to the beautiful, vivacious woman I was with a few hours ago? Last night she'd been giggling like a schoolgirl for the first time in years, and I had congratulated myself for bringing about the change in her. Now she was being kept alive by electrical impulses and motors and pumps, and I was to blame for that, too. Two years ago I had been shot by another madman. I wished it was me again this time.

'What's happening to her?' I whispered.

The nurse tried to tell me, but I didn't catch much of it. She used words like intubated and pneumothorax. Annabelle had a punctured lung and damage to various other organs. She'd lost most of her blood. The nurse said she was responsible solely for caring for Annabelle.

'Please look after her,' I whispered. 'She means a lot to me.'

'We will,' the nurse promised, assuming it was her I was addressing.

'Can I come back later and sit with her for a while?'

'Yes, of course.'

'Thank you.'

I gazed into the gas fire until my eyes burned. When I couldn't keep them open any longer I swung my feet on to the settee and fell asleep. Sam Evans woke me, tapping quietly on the window. He was carrying the bottle of milk from my doorstep.

'You look a mess,' he declared. 'Have a shower and put some clean clothes on, while I make coffee.'

My resistance had vanished, so I asked him to ring the hospital for me and did as I was told. In the bathroom I stripped naked and bundled everything together, for throwing in the dustbin. I was under the shower when he poked his head around the door. 'She's still critical but there's no deterioration in her condition. I would say that's good news.'

'Good. Thank you, Sam.'

The clock inside me didn't know what time of day it was, so I had a big bowl of cornflakes for lunch. Surprisingly, Sam approved of my diet. Shortly after he went, Nigel and Sparky arrived, in different cars. Nigel was returning mine, but he left it out on the road. Sparky dropped his into the drive.

'I've been thinking,' he said as I let them in.

'In that case you'd better sit down,' I told him. Nigel asked if he could make coffee.

Sparky went on: 'The press are asking questions about Annabelle. They've found out who she is and have decided she's the latest victim of this Mushroom Man. It's only a matter of time before some kind soul earns his forty pieces of silver by telling them about your involvement, so we're swapping cars. It might throw them off the scent until the story dies. I think you ought to bugger off somewhere – you can't do anything here – but I don't suppose you will.'

Nigel agreed with him, but I shook my head. 'I'm staying,' I said.

When they left I walked outside with them and we stood talking in the garden for several minutes. Sparky knows about gardening. He told me what to do with the perennials, but I didn't listen. Listening has always been one of my problems. The housemartins were gathering on the phone wires, and a blackbird was gorging itself on the berries on next door's mountain ash. The man over the road was dismantling his barbecue.

I nodded in his direction and said: 'That marks the official end of summer.'

'It's still only August,' Sparky protested. 'What happened to all this global warming. It's more like November.'

'Ah,' said Nigel. 'That's the strange effect of global warming. We'll actually get cooler. The weather in Britain is governed by the temperature of the Atlantic Ocean. As the icecaps melt, due to the warming, the meltwater cools the seas, so we'll have cooler weather.'

Sparky gave him the scowl he usually reserves for burglars who swear blind that they were drunk and were convinced that the penthouse they were stripping really was their own squat. 'Are you 'aving us on?' he said.

I was shivering when I went back inside. Nigel had given me an envelope containing stuff from the bloodstained jacket I'd left in the City nick. It was my wallet and some loose change. And the ticket stubs and programme for the concert. I opened the programme and read from the translation of the ancient verse:

O Fortune, variable as the Moon.
Always dost thou wax and wane.

My mind flashed to the new moon I'd seen the previous Tuesday as I drove away from Annabelle's, but this time I had no defence against the bad memories it invoked.

I sat all that night in the corner of the intensive care

unit. A different armed policeman was on duty outside the door. Two patients had moved out, another was brought in. I watched the ventilator rising and falling, and the green blips moving across the ECG screen. The nurses had an office area in the middle of the room. They were constantly checking their charges, moving quietly and efficiently. They read dials, made notes, felt brows and changed drips. I could understand why intensive care nursing was so satisfying.

When I wasn't in anybody's way I held Annabelle's hand and tried to talk to her. I whispered in her ear that she had to get better. She just lay there, as if in the deepest sleep, breathing with the rhythm of the machinery. Her face was pale, with dark smudges under her eyes, but she still looked hauntingly beautiful, like some aristocratic lady who'd fallen under a spell.

I heard voices outside the door and looked up. Through the porthole window I could see Nigel remonstrating with the armed policeman and showing him his ID card. I went out to them.

'What's happening?' I said.

'Sorry, Mr Priest,' said the uniformed PC, 'I didn't know who he was.'

'That's OK. Nigel?'

'Morning, boss. How is she?'

'No change. It's a bit early for you, isn't it?'

'It certainly is. I didn't know it was light at this hour. Unfortunately the press have found out about you. It's all over the Sunday papers. They've been camped outside Dave's all night, but now they're here, at the hospital. We've come to get you out, when you're ready.'

'Thanks, just give me a minute.' I had a word with the nurse and a last look at Annabelle. I squeezed her hand and told her I'd be back later.

Nigel radioed Dave, telling him to bring the car to the entrance. The other uniformed policeman walked out with us. The press were gathered in the foyer, like jackals at a kill, waiting for any scraps that they could make a meal out of. Nigel and the PC positioned themselves on either side of me and we headed purposefully towards the door.

Cameras flashed. A whizz-kid newshound with eyes in his backside and a huge video camera hiding his face cleared a path for us without once looking where he was going. Several microphones were poked towards me, their owners firing questions simultaneously.

'Was this another Mushroom Man shooting?'

'Are you and Annabelle lovers?'

Nigel tried to parry the questions. 'You've been given a statement,' he told them. 'We've nothing to add.'

'Is it true you didn't see anything, Inspector?'

'Are you expecting him to strike again?'

A tired hack at the back of the group shouted: 'Apart from that, what did you think of the concert?'

I clenched my fists and swung towards him, but the big PC's fingers clamped around my arm and propelled me through the door.

They trotted after us towards the car, their sound men running behind like poodles on leads. Sparky hadn't unlocked the passenger door so I couldn't get in. My car doesn't run to centralised locking.

A microphone was thrust under my nose. 'Do you love Annabelle?' the girl holding it asked. She was about nineteen and had an editor to please.

I could imagine the exclusive that would be claimed if I gave the wrong answer. Sparky leaned over to lift the catch and I pulled the door open. As I climbed in she poked the mike into the side of my face and repeated the question: 'Do you love Annabelle?'

I turned so my lips were touching the microphone and said: 'No.'

I slammed the door. If you tell a lie, might as well make it a whopper. That was the biggest I'd ever tell.

Our press office prepared a statement to get them off my back: we were just good friends; she was still on the critical list; and yes, the shooting was being investigated by the Mushroom Man team. When they realised there was no more, they drifted off. The headlines weren't very flattering: 'Top cop never saw a thing,' they said.

I had some kip and tried eating Sunday lunch at the local pub, but I didn't enjoy it. In the evening I went back to the hospital and sat with Annabelle all night. She was just the same, and I left as dawn broke. I asked to be informed of any change in her condition, but I wasn't next of kin, so they were reluctant.

When I drove into Heckley nick car park later in the day, I half expected Sparky to have commandeered my parking space as well as my car, but he hadn't. I used the back entrance and ran up the stairs to Gilbert's office. He was expecting me.

'Hello, Charlie. I'll just put the kettle on,' he said.

'Not for me, Gilbert, if you don't mind. I'll be looking like a pot of tea soon.'

'Oh. Something stronger?'

I shook my head.

'Fair enough. So how are you then?'

'Not bad.'

'Good. Did we tell you that we've traced Annabelle's sister and her husband? They live in Guildford. She has a brother, too, but he's somewhere in Africa.'

'He's in India,' I said.

'India?'

'Mmm.'

It was Gilbert's turn to shake his head. 'Isn't that typical of the FO?' he declared. 'Scouring the wrong bloody continent.'

'Friday night,' I said, 'when I met Annabelle...'

'Yes?'

'I've been thinking about it, racking my brain. I believe we may have been followed.'

Gilbert's brow furrowed with interest and he sat back so hard his chair protested. 'Go on,' he encouraged.

I picked up his ballpen and turned it over and over in my fingers. 'When she came to the door she... she looked beautiful...'

'She's a lovely lady, Charlie; one in a million. Everyone who knows her is devastated. Take your time.'

'We were talking. When I drove out of her street into the Top Road I looked in my mirror. There was a car close behind me. I hadn't seen it when I stopped at the junction, it came from nowhere. Maybe I wasn't concentrating and hadn't looked properly. I gave myself a reprimand and took more care. It followed us all the way into town. Now I can't help wondering if it had been waiting for us.'

Gilbert said: 'Well done, Charlie. Well done.' He wasn't crass enough to ask the obvious, and waited for me to volunteer the information.

'It was a little car, possibly a Fiesta, although it could easily have been something else. Colour? Possibly one of those insipid beiges that you wonder why people buy. Sorry, Gilbert, your last Granada was a similar colour, wasn't it?'

'They gave me a good discount. It was called catshit. If it was a Fiesta, what mark would you estimate?'

'I'm not sure, but one of the older, more angular ones.'

Gilbert picked up the phone and dialled. 'Hello, Maggie. Charlie's with me. Could someone bring the Ford colour charts up to my office, please.'

Maggie brought them herself. I stood up and she gave me a hug. She said: 'Oh, Charlie, we're all so sorry. How is she?'

I gave her an extra squeeze and told her that Annabelle was still unconscious but holding on.

Gilbert waited until we were through before saying: 'Peterson's in the building somewhere. Do you mind if he sits in on this?'

I didn't, so he asked Maggie if she could round him up. When she left he said: 'I know one thing, Charlie. You certainly have the knack of getting the best out of your WPCs. They never throw their arms around me.'

'Treat them all the same, Gilbert. That's the secret.'

'What about sexual harassment?'

'I've learned to put up with it.'

Peterson came puffing in, complaining about the number of stairs and how cold it was in this godforsaken part of the world. He looked embarrassed when he saw me, but didn't offer any words of sympathy, for which I was grateful.

Gilbert told him about the car and we examined the colour charts. There was coral beige, sierra beige, cordoba beige, nevada beige, sahara beige and tuscan beige, and I only thought it might be beige. Peterson wasn't impressed by the standard of my evidence, and I offered a silent apology to all the useless witnesses I'd cursed over the years.

He pretended I'd given him the big breakthrough he was waiting for. After a few transparent nods of approval he said: 'What can you tell me about Mrs Wilberforce?'

'Nothing,' I declared. 'Nothing relevant.' Nothing that was any business of his. I didn't want to discuss her with him. The little I had was precious to me, not for writing in notebooks before going on to the computer, to be picked over by hard men looking for a murderer. Let them read someone else's entrails.

The tone of my voice didn't deter him. 'She had no enemies that you know of? Were her views regarded as controversial within the Church?'

'Of course not!' I snapped. 'And could I remind you that she is still alive, if only just.'

Gilbert said: 'Mr Peterson, if Mr Priest had any information that would help this enquiry, don't you think he would have offered it?'

Peterson ignored him. 'Did you know,' he announced, for it wasn't a question, 'that Mrs Wilberforce was – is – considering ordination?'

'No, I didn't,' I hissed, gripping the edges of my chair.

'Well, she is. I had a long talk with the Bishop. He suggested it to her and she said she'd think about it. Apparently her ex-husband was a hell-fire-and-brimstone man.'

I took deep breaths while he was talking. When I felt I was under control I sat back in my chair and folded my arms. 'Inspector Peterson,' I began, 'first of all, Mrs Wilberforce's husband died after a long illness. He was her late husband, not her ex-husband. Secondly, he was a traditionalist, not a hell-fire-and-brimstone man, as you put it. And to say that Mrs Wilberforce agreed to think about ordination is hardly the same as saying she is seriously considering it.'

'Mmm. Perhaps.' He stood up to leave. There was a

knock at the door and Nigel entered, carrying a piece of paper and looking smug.

Peterson said: 'This car. I don't suppose you managed a glimpse of the driver?'

I shook my head.

'Or the number?'

'No.'

'Of course not. Silly question. Still, I have to ask.'

Nigel was holding the door open. Peterson was almost out when he changed his mind. 'Oh, nearly forgot,' he said. 'Nine people have contacted various newspapers confessing to being the gunman – eight Mushroom Men and one Destroying Angel. I think we can safely say that a religious nut is on the loose.'

When he'd gone, Gilbert said: 'We'll have that coffee now, with a drop of lotion in it. Yes, Nigel. What can we do for you?'

He stepped forward, face glowing with enthusiasm. 'Message for Char... er, Mr Priest. It reads: "Mrs Wilberforce conscious and breathing without the aid of the ventilator. Taken off critical list." Message timed fifteen thirty-seven.'

My prayers were being answered.

Chapter Twenty

Gilbert had misjudged me when he told Peterson that I would have offered any information I had. They'd put an armed guard on Annabelle in case the attacker came back, but they were guarding the wrong person. The one vital piece of information I had withheld was that Annabelle was not the intended victim. The shot in the town hall doorway was aimed at me, not her. Annabelle had been directly behind me, her hands on my hips. She was hit because I skipped to one side as the trigger was pulled. I wasn't running away or hiding; maybe he'd come back.

I bought chocolates and salmon-pink roses and made myself look smart. I was back in my own car, thank goodness – the kids' stickers in Sparky's had been ruining my image. The hospital car park was crowded. I thought about sweet-talking my way into a parking spot inside the grounds but decided not to. It's not my style. I cruised round until a place became vacant and slotted into it, narrowly beating a taxi carrying a family of Asians. Three people were getting out of a top-of-the-range Rover a couple of spaces away. The man was wearing a camel overcoat with an astrakhan collar. The younger of the women was tall and stooped, but the other one was quite small and elderly. They walked towards the hospital as I went to collect a ticket from the machine. The driver of the taxi hadn't the right money, so I changed a pound for him.

First of all I visited Casualty and had a word with the sister, to thank her for their efforts, and gave her the box of chocolates. She told me that Annabelle was still seriously ill, but as strong as a swan's wing. Now she was in Ward 4B, upstairs.

I followed the signs and found the ward. Each patient was in her own little room, with open fronts on to a central corridor. I wandered along, looking in at various stages of suffering, but didn't find Annabelle. As soon as a nurse appeared I asked.

'She's in here, sir,' she said, gesturing, 'but no more than two visitors to a patient, *please.*' The three people from the Rover were already in there, which was why I'd walked by twice.

They looked up as I entered. 'I, er, didn't know she had visitors,' I said. Nobody spoke. 'How is she?'

'She's asleep,' the man answered. He was leaning forward in his chair, elbows on knees and hands together. The old lady was arranging a bunch of mixed flowers, with her back to me.

I gazed down at Annabelle. She looked peaceful, and all the tubes had been removed except for the drip, but an impressive array of instruments were still flashing and beeping alongside the bed. 'Good. That's good. My name's Priest, by the way. Charlie Priest.'

'Newton,' said the man, hardly taking the trouble to look at me.

'Right. Well, I'll, er, come back later.'

I was drifting aimlessly down the corridor, still carrying the roses, when a voice shouted: 'Excuse me!'

I turned to see the younger of the women coming after me, and suddenly realised who she was. Rachel was about ten years older than Annabelle and the bone structure was the same, but a different disposition had moulded her features to the wrong side of plain. Maybe she'd always lived in her kid sister's shadow, always been regarded as the unattractive one. Fate can be cruel.

She didn't introduce herself, just launched straight into what she had to say. 'You're the policeman Annabelle was with when this happened,' she told me.

'Yes.'

'And apparently you didn't see a thing.'

'No.'

'So meanwhile he walks free while you do nothing.'

'We're doing everything we can,' I said, feebly.

'Well, it just isn't good enough. First thing tomorrow I'm having words with a friend at Scotland Yard. I'll get something done if you can't.'

She turned on her heel and stalked off. I said: 'And it's nice to meet you, too, Rachel,' to her retreating back and recommenced my wanderings.

I knew which was their car, so I sat in mine and waited for them to return. According to the radio it was the coldest August day for a hundred years, so I used the car heater a couple of times. Drivers kept assuming I was about to go, and queued for my space. I shook my head at them and sank down into the seat. I was there two hours.

When they came back it's fair to say I wasn't in a good mood. I got out and retrieved the roses from the passenger seat. Newton was carefully folding their coats and placing them in the boot. I didn't have one, and it was a long walk to the front entrance. Flurries of rain splattered on the windscreen. The women saw me, and words that I couldn't hear passed between them. The little old lady looked from me to Rachel and back again, before she started towards me. I waited for her, holding the flowers and feeling foolish.

She was very old, with a white face and a little red button of a nose. I gave her the best smile I was capable of.

'You're... Charles,' she stated. 'Rachel has... just told

me who you are. We've... kept you waiting all this... time.'

'You've come a long way,' I said, as if that excused bad manners.

'Well, yes, I... suppose so. And they... did have to pick me up... in Northampton.'

She had difficulties with her breathing, and I had to wait for her words. 'Don't get cold,' I said, partly because I was shivering myself.

'I'm so... sorry I didn't speak to you... earlier.' She held out her frail little hand. I took it between my thumb and fingers as she said. 'I'm Mary... Wilberforce.'

I blinked and stared at her. 'So you're–'

'Annabelle's... mother-in-law.'

'–Peter's mother.'

'Yes.' A smile lit up her face. 'Annabelle told you... about Peter?'

A gust of wind, straight from the Arctic icecap, blew across the car park, cutting through my jacket. I moved round and bent over her, to shelter her from it. 'Yes, she did. I don't think I ever saw her happier than when she was telling me about Peter and their time in Kenya,' I said.

'That's lovely... of you... to say so.' Her eyes were watery, perhaps with the dust blowing about, perhaps with memories of a son who rose to be a bishop but died before his time. She gripped my hand in both of hers, 'And now I'd like... to tell you something.' She paused and took a deep breath. 'Annabelle... comes to stay the weekend... every few weeks. She came... two weeks ago. I thought she had... something on her... mind, so I asked her. She... told me that she would always... love Peter; that he would always be... special to her. But now she had met someone else who was... special. She wanted to know if I... if I minded.'

She seemed impervious to the cold. I pulled the front of my jacket together as she continued: 'I told her to... snap you up, before someone else... did.'

I wanted to tell her how much her words meant to me, but my teeth were chattering and nothing intelligible came out.

'And now, when Annabelle is... better, you'll both be able... to visit me.'

I nodded. 'I'd like that.'

A nurse admired the roses and placed them in a vase beside Annabelle's bed, relegating the other bunch to the windowsill. Annabelle was still sleeping. Once or twice she stirred restlessly and shook her head from side to side. I jumped to my feet, ready to fetch help, but she settled down again within a few seconds. The drip bag was nearly empty and I hoped that someone would come to change it soon.

All I could do was sit beside her bed and stroke her long fingers. She still wore a wedding ring, a thin silver band, possibly the best they could afford on their meagre African incomes. I wasn't jealous of Peter for being married to her, but I wished I'd met her when we were both broke, so we could have built something together. I envied him for that.

'You look tired,' she whispered, very softly.

I looked up from her hand, into those eyes. She smiled, and her nose crinkled in the way that cuts the legs from under me and paralyses my tongue. I squeezed her hand, and when the power returned to me I said: 'Welcome back.'

She tried to speak again, but her throat was obviously sore from all the tubes that had been poked down it. I put my finger to my lips and shushed her. 'Don't talk,' I said. 'There'll be plenty of time for that. Just get better first.'

She sank back for a few moments, but was not content. 'Charles?' Her voice was a faint croak.

'Sssh.'

'We were... at a concert.'

'Sssh.'

'Did I have an accident?'

'Yes, something like that. But you're safe now, and you'll soon be well again. Then, if you'll let me, I'm going to look after you better than you've ever been looked after before. That's a promise.'

She squeezed my hand. 'Do I look a mess?' she asked.

'As if you've been dragged through a hedge. Longways. But that's still lovely.'

Her mouth opened; but before any words came out I raised a finger in disapproval and said: 'Ah! If you don't stop talking I shall leave. I'm only staying if you promise to be quiet.'

She clamped her lips together in an exaggerated grimace and sank back against the pillow. I poured some fruit juice and held it while she drank. She silently mouthed the words: 'Thank you,' and gave me a smile so warm the central heating switched off. She was going to make it, and so, God willing, was I.

There was still a round-the-clock guard at the hospital, but they were protecting the wrong person. It was reassuring, though, to know that Annabelle was safe. Peterson was convinced that the so-called Mushroom Man, or Destroying Angel, was responsible, but I couldn't see it. The Angel name could easily have leaked out. It was just some lunatic with a gun having a go at Charlie Priest. I have plenty of enemies. I found a new writing pad and fibre-tip and settled down in front of the fire with a mug of tea and a packet of custard creams. An hour later I had a list of ten possibles, with stars in double circles against the first three.

The winners were, in order of preference:

> Don Purley
> ABC (Bradshaw and Wheatley)
> Eddie Grant

I had a bowl of cornflakes, to save time in the morning, and went to bed. As I closed the curtains I noticed a car about a hundred yards up the road. It was out of place. I sneaked into the spare bedroom in the darkness, and took a longer look at it. While I was watching its lights came on. It made a U-turn and drove away. It was nearly one a.m., and for once I slept like a doorstep.

'Mornin', troops!' I hollered as I breezed into the office at about ten o'clock, chirpy as a barrow wheel.

'Morning,' grumbled assorted voices.

'God, you look rough, Dave,' I said to Sparky, reaching across his desk and giving him a chuck under the chin.

He swiped at my hand as I pulled it back. 'It's this lot,' he complained, waving at the paperwork. 'Back to TWOCs and burglaries. Nobody told them to behave themselves while we were otherwise engaged. I thought Doc Evans had given you a sick note.'

'He has. This is a private visit. What's happening with Dewhurst?'

'Not much. Nigel set up a bedside interview in Bentley, but he refused to speak. He's going for the sympathy vote.'

'That won't do him any good.'

Maggie wandered over. 'How's Annabelle?' she asked.

'Loads better, thanks. I called in briefly this morning and they'd had her out of bed for a few minutes. Far too soon, in my opinion. She's still in a lot of pain. Actually, I've something to ask you. Come into the office.'

When we were out of earshot of the others I said: 'Annabelle's asked me to take her some clothes from home. I haven't a clue what she needs. You wouldn't do the necessary for me, would you?'

'If I can. What have you in mind?'

'Well, if I take you to her house, could you fill a suit-case with stuff? Underwear, nightdresses, you know.'

Maggie started laughing. She snorts when she laughs, making it impossible not to join in. 'You're the limit, Charlie,' she giggled.

'Well, I'd be embarrassed, rummaging through her underwear.'

'But you'd like to, wouldn't you?'

'Er, yes, I suppose I would. I'd just prefer her to be there at the time.'

'You're blushing!'

'No I'm not!'

'Yes you are!'

'It's one of my endearing traits.'

She blew her nose and shook her head. 'When do you want to go?'

'To suit you. I'm not working.'

'Neither am I – the boss is off sick. Are you going to be here a while?'

'Probably.'

'Give me the key and her address and I'll go now.'

'I've got friends I haven't used yet,' I said, fishing the key for the Old Vicarage from my pocket.

Don Purley was a mean hombre. I put him away for

life, with a fifteen-year tariff. Last night I couldn't remember the name of his wife, but as soon as I looked at the list again it came back to me. Rhoda. I wrote it next to his. They were a weird couple – into body-building and martial arts. She was only five foot two, but had striking red hair and bigger muscles on her nipples than I had on my arms. They ran a health club just outside Heckley. He was my favourite for bearing a grudge, but he still had three or four years to serve – there's no remission on the judge's tariff. Unless he'd escaped, of course.

Purley murdered the Ho twins, Michael and David. They were Hong Kong Chinese, who'd come over here with a suitcase that rattled and a kilogram of heroin strapped to their bodies. Something had panicked them, and they'd dumped the drugs down the plane toilet. That left them in a strange land with no source of income. Being as enterprising as most of their country-men, they were soon in business again. They cashed in on the fearsome reputation of the Triads and started a protection racket. We were watching them, but not closely enough. I was called to their flat and found one of them strangled and the other one's head kicked to a pulp.

The doctor who attended the scene pointed to a crescent shaped imprint behind the Adam's apple of the strangled one, who happened to be David. He'd been killed by a karate grip to the throat. It's easy enough – you just strike out and grab the other fellow's windpipe. He stands there, arms and legs free, but so paralysed with pain he can't do a thing about it. An agonising death follows if you don't release him. David's bulging eyes and lolling tongue were testimony to the effectiveness of the hold.

'That's where his thumbnail dug in,' the doctor said,

pointing at the scarlet arc. Ever since then my first glimpse of the new moon had resurrected the ghost of David Ho.

'In that case,' I declared, 'there's a thumbprint just behind it.'

The doctor looked at me as if he were examining the contents of a bedpan. 'Skin on skin,' he sniffed. 'You're wasting your time.'

When the SOCO and the photographer arrived I gave strict instructions that nobody else was to enter the room. We'd just started using superglue in fingerprint work. Something in the fumes given off by the glue reacts with the constituents of the dab to leave a white deposit. It's called polymerisation, but I don't think anybody fully understands why it works. The SOCO shook his head but agreed to give it a try. Trouble was, you're supposed to place the object in question, usually a knife or a gun, in a fume cabinet. We were talking about a human head, still attached to the body. I took the biggest plastic bag we had and pulled it over David's head. The SOCO put the glue inside and I sealed the bag as best I could with Sellotape. It wasn't pleasant work. The photographer stood by with his array of fluorescent lights. Images often show up better under ultra violet.

We waited and watched, half expecting the bag to steam up with the products of respiration, but it didn't. Across the room a bluebottle buzzed around the bloody head of Michael Ho.

Periodically SOCO looked inside and renewed the glue. The photographer tried his various lights and took some 'before' pictures. We were breaking every rule in the Health and Safety at Work handbook. We should have been wearing protective goggles,

breathing apparatus, and diving suits. I closed my
eyes when he used the ultra violet.

It didn't work.

I said: 'There's a print behind that mark, and I want
it. What can we try next?'

'Ninhydrin?'

'OK. Give him a squirt.'

'It'll turn him pink.'

'He won't mind.'

'What will the pathologist think?'

'Scarlet fever? Give him a squirt.'

Ninhydrin comes in an aerosol, and reacts with
blood as well as the amino acids and proteins found in
fingerprints. The SOCO sprayed some on David's
neck. Splatter from the aerosol fell on to his unblinking
eyeball. I turned away.

SOCO said it would work better if it was warmer, so
we switched on the three-kilowatt electric fire that the
room boasted. As the temperature rose, so too did the
smell of blood. He was wrong about the colour – it
turned the body purple.

We were looking for a transitional stage. Hopefully
the spray would react with the prints before it reacted
with the skin of the deceased. It seemed a long shot.
The photographer took some more 'before' pictures.

'There's something there!' SOCO gasped, offering
me his magnifying glass.

I shook my head. 'Just get it on film.'

We were locked in that obscene room for over two
hours, but next morning I had on my desk a picture of
a fragment of a fingerprint. Others didn't believe it, but
I was convinced. The skin of the fingers and hands is
characterised by the ridges that create prints, but the
rest of our skin is relatively smooth. I highlighted the
lines with my pencil, producing what I suppose was

an artist's impression. In fingerprint jargon it was only part of a whorl, with a fork and a lake nearby, but it was a start.

I drew a quarter-mile-radius circle around the Hos' flat and we listed every small business within it. Everyone, that is, who might be a victim of their protection racket. We checked criminal records and fingerprinted those who had stayed clear of the law. We found plenty of whorls, forks and lakes, but none were in exactly the same relationship as those we were looking for. It would never be enough to make a conviction, but it could point us in the right direction.

I expanded the circle. And again. And again. At two miles it encompassed six sheep farms, ten derelict mills, a Yorkshire Water reservoir and the Fighting Fit Health Club, owned by a certain Donald Purley. He had a criminal record for dealing in drugs, mainly steroids, and the print of his right thumb matched our picture.

We raided his flat and club at seven a.m. one Wednesday morning. A pair of trousers were newly dry-cleaned, but still had blood in the fibres. In a wardrobe was a pair of snazzy shoes with brass tips on the toes and heels. They shone like a choirboy's face, but a stick-on sole was coming away slightly at the toe, and under it we found a hair that had once grown on Michael Ho's head. Later, two people ID'd him as coming down the stairs from the flat at the time of the killings. We had him.

On tape and in court he protested his innocence. Off the record, when I was alone with him, he swaggered and bragged that we'd never make it stick. We did, for fifteen years.

But he should still be in jail. I dialled the number for Bentley prison and asked to be put through to records.

I didn't know which prison he was in, but they were computerised. A convict keeps his number throughout his sentence, and it moves around with him.

'Do you know his date of birth, sir?' asked the female warder.

'No, I'm afraid not. He's not a teenager, though.' I gave her a rough guess.

'Sorry, sir. We don't have a Donald Purley at all.'

'You must have. He was a lifer. Should have about four years still to go. Maybe he died.'

'Let me check.'

Another phone was ringing in the background as I waited.

'Found him, sir. Donald Purley, DOB seven, nine, fiftythree.'

'That sounds like him. Where is he?'

'He was released, sir, nearly three years ago.'

'Released! Does it say why?'

'Compassionate grounds. Presumably he was terminally ill.'

'Oh. Is there a release address?'

'No. It just says: "Released into the supervision of Heckley Probation Service."'

'Right. Thanks. I'll contact them. Could you give me another release address, please?'

'We'll try. What name?'

'Eddie Grant.'

He'd moved to Leeds. I wrote the address next to his name on my list and rang Heckley Probation Office.

'Good Morning. Could I speak to Gavin Smith, please?' I asked.

'Mr Smith is off sick. Would you like to speak to anyone else?'

'Yes, someone who might know about a lifer out on licence.'

'I'll put you through to Mrs Pettit. Who's calling, please?'

'Inspector Priest, Heckley CID.'

Mrs Pettit came straight on. 'Yes, Inspector. How can I help you?'

'I need to know the whereabouts of a lifer who was released into your custody. Donald Purley. Can somebody fill me in about him?'

'Don Purley. Can I ask why you need to know?'

Probation officers are very protective towards their clients, but I had a right to know. It was just a matter of being patient. 'I'm conducting an enquiry, and his name is in the frame.'

'In that case,' she said, somewhat haughtily, 'I suggest you take him out of the frame. I was his supervising officer. Don Purley died less than a month after he was released.'

'Oh. What did he die of?'

'Tuberculosis and pneumonia.'

'Right. Thank you.'

'Goodbye.' Click. Have a nice day, Mrs Pettit. I replaced the handset.

TB, often called consumption. Once one of mankind's great killers, it has largely been eradicated by improved sanitation and the discovery of antibiotics. As standards of living rose, the incidence of the disease fell away. But now it was with us again, and our prisons were often where it chose to make its comeback. I ruled a line through the top entry on my list. That left two naps and seven also-rans.

A fresh-faced DC popped his head round the door. 'Would you like a sandwich fetching, Mr Priest?' he asked.

'Yes please.'

'What sort?'

'Prawn and avocado, in granary bread.'

'From the canteen!' he gasped.

'Oh. In that case make it two sausage rolls and a custard.'

The ABC on my list referred to a business empire run by a man called Cakebread. He had organised the theft of a few Old Masters and traded them for about fifty million quid's worth of heroin. He'd been killed trying to escape, but a couple of his colleagues had only received short sentences, and we'd only touched the tip of the iceberg. There'd been a police involvement, too, which was never fully resolved. The more I thought about it, the more sinister it looked.

I rang Oldfield CID, in Lancashire, where the investigation had been centred, and asked to speak to the inspector who'd helped me with the enquiry. He promised to ring me back in a few minutes. A mug of tea arrived with my sausage rolls, so I put my feet on the radiator and lunched. The radiator was warm. The cold spell must have induced someone to have the central heating restored a few weeks early. Unnecessarily, because the wind had swung to the south, and the pundits were now forecasting an Indian summer. The custard looked like last week's. Its filling had dried and shrivelled and come away from the pastry, like a cowpat in a plastic bucket.

The DI rang me just as I was wrestling with a mouthful of it. I mumbled a greeting. First of all he wanted to know more about the shooting. I answered his questions and told him that I wasn't on the case, but was looking into the possibilities of someone bearing a grudge, namely Bradshaw and Wheatley, or other, unknown, members of the gang.

'See your point,' he said, 'but I doubt if it's either of those two. They were given eighteen months and two years, but they're both out now. As you know, they also received hefty fines, courtesy of the Drug Trafficking Act, and were virtually stripped of everything they possessed.'

'As you said, I know all that.'

'Sorry, I'm just building up to the big finish. Cakebread was never charged, so his fortune remained intact, but now in the name of Eunice, his wife.'

'So?'

'So Bradshaw, the pilot, has moved in with Eunice. A nice little catch for him, if you don't mind mascara all over your breakfast. Brian Wheatley is back in his old business, property development, courtesy of sponsorship by the other two. We're watching them like shitehawks, but they're keeping squeaky clean. I don't think it's them, Charlie. They're probably quite happy with the way things turned out.'

'I see what you mean. I'd be grateful if you could give some thought to what I've said, though.'

'Will do. Good hunting.'

'Cheers.'

Maggie came in, humping a large Samsonite suitcase and grinning like a Cheshire dog. That's very similar to a Cheshire cat, but more politically correct.

'Charlie!' she gushed, eyes wide. 'She's some gorgeous things.'

'I know, she always dresses well.'

'Wowee! I wish I had her wardrobe. And her taste. I think that's everything she'll need. I put some make-up in, too.'

'Oh, God!' I said, putting my hand to my head. 'I forgot to mention make-up.'

'I felt like trying on some of her suits, but sadly' –

she patted her hips – 'I'm two sizes too large. Here's the key. Everything is safe and secure.'

'Thanks, Maggie. What would I do without you?'

'Probably send Nigel,' she laughed.

Chapter Twenty One

I drew a question mark next to ABC on my list and memorised Eddie Grant's address. The case weighed a ton. Lugging it down the stairs, three people asked me if I was going on my holidays. I wished I'd told Maggie to meet me in the car park.

I showed my ID to the gateman at the hospital and asked if he'd look after the case while I parked. It would save me carrying it about quarter of a mile. He suggested I park inside the grounds, so for once I abused the privileges of power.

Annabelle was propped up by pillows. 'Twice in one day,' she croaked. 'I am honoured.'

I kissed her forehead. 'Is your throat still sore?'

She nodded.

'Well, don't try to speak.' I refilled her glass with juice and passed it to her. I nodded towards the case. 'I asked Margaret Madison, one of my WPCs, to help me with the clothes. I think she'd like to borrow some of your outfits.'

'She's welcome...'

I interrupted her: 'Unfortunately she's slightly broader across the beam than you are.'

It was more comfortable for both of us if I sat on the edge of the bed. I could see her and she didn't have to crane sideways to watch me. She took my hand and said: 'Charles?' A puzzled expression was on her face.

I put my other hand over hers. 'What is it, love?'

'I... I was shot, wasn't I?'

I nodded. 'Yes, you were.'

'Who did it, Charles?'

'We don't know. There's a maniac loose; some sort of religious fanatic.'

'Will he come back?' She sounded frightened.

I squeezed her hand. 'No, he won't come back. There's a guard in the corridor, but he won't come back. I know how his mind works, and I promise he's not after you any more. You're completely safe here.'

She relaxed, and I stayed with her until she fell asleep. The sister told me that she was tired, after being out of bed for a couple of short spells, but was making good progress. She estimated another three weeks in hospital if there were no setbacks. Apparently Rachel had suggested that Annabelle stay with them to convalesce. I reluctantly accepted that it might be for the best.

Eddie Grant lived at 23, Chesterton Court, in the Towncroft district of Leeds. I plotted my route in the A to Z and set off. There was a hold-up in the tunnel section of the inner ring road, so traffic was heavy. Away to the right the sun was shining on the massive bulk of the NHS building, but it only illuminated its ugliness. I wondered if the architect had ever heard of the Parthenon. Stalin would have loved it.

Towncroft isn't one of the areas of the city that civic visitors are shown around. Unemployment, drugs and lethargy have taken their toll. I stopped on one corner, looking down a hill, and wished I had my camera. The street was littered with broken bricks and a burnt-out car sat at the edge of the road. The detached house facing me had recently been one of a pair of semis. Its partner had been demolished, or blown up, leaving a jagged line where the join had been. It was like a scene from Bosnia, and I was Kate Adie.

I trickled along in second gear, reading the street

names, steering round the litter and scavenging dogs. Dickens Avenue. Kipling Drive. Tolstoy Grove. Tolstoy? How did he get in here?

There it was – Chesterton Court. Number 23 was marginally better than the average: the gate worked, the windows were made of glass and grass managed to exist in the garden. A few broken kids' toys were scattered about.

A heavily pregnant girl answered the door. I said: 'Is Eddie in?'

She looked scared. 'I dunno, I'll see,' she said, starting to close the door:

'Are you Marie?' I asked.

'Er, yeah. Who are you?'

'Inspector Priest. I arrested Eddie six years ago. Met you then. Let me in, love.'

Eddie was slumped in an armchair, watching a black American woman tell her shrieking audience about the time she was date-raped by the spiritual leader of the Mississippi Morons. A little girl aged about six was sitting next to him. He looked up as I entered.

'Hello, Eddie. Charlie Priest. Nice place you have here.' It was reasonably tidy inside.

'What do you want?' he grumbled morosely.

'Mind if I sit down? Just a little chat. Could we have the telly off, please?'

Marie followed me in and sat protectively alongside him, as if she were his mother. When I'd first seen her she was sixteen, and looked like an angel. She could have gone in any direction she chose, had she known the options. But she didn't, and fell into the same one as all her friends: get married to the first yob you meet with a prick bigger than his IQ and have kids, not necessarily in that order. Now she was twenty-two, pushing fifty, and lumbered with a short-arsed layabout who had all the personality of a used tyre. It depressed me. Given another chance, I think I would dedicate my life towards steering sixteen-year-old girls away from idiots like him and towards a loftier lifestyle. The sugar daddy could have an important role to play in society; he should be sponsored by the community tax. I didn't understand what it was, but maybe I was also a little jealous of the attraction Eddie held for her.

'This is your daughter?' I said, nodding towards Marie mark two, already doomed to a life of poverty and hardship.

'Yes.'

'Hello.'

She glowered at me. Ah, well, you can't woo 'em all.

'Do you think she could go up to her room?' I suggested.

Grant patted her backside, pushing her towards the door. 'Go play outside, Shelley,' he told her.

When she had gone I said: 'You must have brought her up yourself, Marie.'

'Yes, I did, until she was four.'

'That can't have been easy.'

She shrugged, as if to say: You didn't think of that when you banged her daddy up for ten years.

Eddie Grant had robbed a series of banks and building societies at gunpoint. It was only an airgun, but he'd fired it once or twice, and a young girl cashier had lost an eye. He'd also pistol-whipped a customer who'd had a go at him. He was a vicious piece of work. When the judge sent him down he left the dock swearing to kill me and my wife and kids. He said he knew where I lived, and he'd hunt me down for as long as it took. As I was in the middle of expensive divorce proceedings at the time, it didn't perturb me. But he'd

served his five, after time off, and was back on the
streets again. And somebody was trying to kill me.

'Right, Eddie,' I said. 'Where were you at nine
o'clock on Friday night?'

'Friday night?'

'Uh-uh.'

'Dunno.'

'You'll have to try harder than that.'

'Er, Mr Priest?'

'Yes?'

'I read about the shooting in the paper. You don't
fink it was me, do yer?'

'You said you would kill me, so convince me you
weren't having a go. Where were you on Friday?'

'I s'pose we was 'ere. Together.'

'That's right,' Marie announced. 'We can't afford to
go out, and can't get no baby-sitters since we moved
'ere.'

'Can anybody else confirm this?'

They shook their heads.

'Why did you move here?' I asked.

'To get away from 'Eckley,' he replied. 'We was in
wiv a bad crowd. Drugs an' stuff. That's why I did the
banks. All that I said in court – them freats – I was off
my 'ead at the time. I'd 'ad some stuff the night before.
Pills. Don't ask me what they was. An' Marie was
pregnant. And when 'e said ten years it just blew my
'ead. I didn't mean anyfing.'

'Have you a job?'

'Now and again.'

'What doing?'

'Roofin'.'

It's always roofing.

Marie said: 'Would you like a cup of tea?'

I shook my head. 'No thanks, Marie.' I turned to

him. 'There's plenty of drugs around Towncroft, Eddie. Are you managing to stay away from them?'

He nodded. Marie said she made sure he did. We made small talk, mainly about how they were settling in a strange town. After a while Eddie said: 'Mr Priest?'

'That's me.'

'When I was inside, this last time, they put me wiv this old lag; 'e was about forty. I was braggin' about what I'd do to you, playing the big man. He told me to shut up. 'E said that if you deserve it, you should serve it. Then 'e said that 'e knew you. 'E said you was all right; not bent like all the rest. It wasn't me, Mr Priest, I promise it wasn't.'

I stood up to leave, saying: 'I'm touched, Eddie.' At the door I added: 'But I'm not impressed. If you think of anything, anything at all, let me know. Maybe we can do business.' I pointed a finger at Marie's belly and smiled. 'Good luck,' I said. She didn't smile back, and why should she? I'd only accused her husband of attempted murder and given him a veiled invite to become a grass, to add to their other problems.

Shelley was drawing pictures in the dirt on my car. I winked at her and drove off, back to my world, on the other side of the universe.

My intention was to call at the General and see Annabelle again, but I reluctantly decided not to. She wasn't expecting me, and I only encouraged her to talk, aggravating her sore throat. Rest would do her more good.

Two reporters were waiting on my doorstep. They were local, and were hoping for an update for the *Heckley and District Weekly*, due out on Thursday, although I knew that anything juicy that they gathered would immediately be syndicated. I invited them in for a coffee and repeated what they already knew. They had nothing to tell me.

My appetite had returned. A new takeaway was open on this side of town, so I gave it a try. I had chicken bhuna, with pilau rice and a couple of chapatis, washed down by a brace of lagers. The list was on the table. I drew a line through Eddie Grant, then modified it with a question mark. I put another next to the one already against the ABC entry and scanned the also-rans, but nothing obvious jumped out at me.

When I looked out of the bedroom window the car was parked down the road again. I slipped my trainers on and went outside, through the back door. I climbed over the fence and sneaked down my neighbour's garden, narrowly avoiding falling into his new goldfish pond. Back on the street, I turned right, and right again at the end. I was now approaching the car from behind. When I reached it I opened the passenger's door and got in.

'Evenin', Dave,' I said.

'Evenin', Charlie,' Sparky replied.

'Does Gilbert know you're mucking up his overtime allowance?'

'This is extra-curricular.'

'Good. Seen anything?'

'Yeah. The woman next to you doesn't draw the curtains when she goes to bed.'

'Well, thank God there isn't a window at my side. She frightens me to death when she's fully dressed.'

We sat in silence for a while. I said: 'You're getting on better with Nigel these days. I'm glad about that.'

'He's OK,' Sparky concurred. From him it was the equivalent of an Academy Award.

'I forgot to ask. Did Sophie get the results she wanted?'

He chuckled. 'Let me down. She got five As and three Bs. I'd told her straight Ds, or else. Looks like she's going to cost me a fortune.'

'Hey, that's brilliant. I'll have to find a decent CD for her.' Sophie was my goddaughter, and at Christmas and birthdays I tried to manipulate her musical tastes. Maybe a Janis Joplin this time.

After another silence I said: 'So, you don't think he was' trying to shoot Annabelle?'

He looked across at me. 'Do you?'

I shook my head. 'No. He was having a go at me. And I never told Peterson.'

'Peterson's a twat. He wouldn't have believed you.'

'What about this Destroying Angel? Do you think it was him?'

'Not sure. Probably not. Apparently the first two killings weren't him, he just claimed them. Who's to say he isn't doing the same again?'

'Good point, Dave. I hadn't thought about that.' I told him about my list, and the visit to see Eddie Grant. 'How tall is he?' Sparky asked.

'Grant? He's only a squirt. About five foot five, no more. Why?'

He shuffled in his seat, lifting himself more upright. 'I've been sitting in on Peterson's meetings,' he told me. 'Liaison officer. There's been a slight development. Everybody who attended the concert is in the process of being interviewed, plus all the staff at the town hall. Usual stuff – asked to describe everybody they saw. One of the women who looks at tickets probably saw him.'

'Go on,' I urged.

'It was after the concert started. A few people were hanging around in the foyer; latecomers who'd been hoping for a ticket, that sort of thing. She says she particularly noticed one character because he was carrying a sports bag. A black and red Adidas. She was quite the little detective, this lady. She said he must have been a tennis or squash player.'

'Why?' I queried.

'Because there was a hole cut in the end of his bag, for his racket handle to poke through.'

'Or a shotgun,' I murmured.

'Or a shotgun. She described him as being small – five two to five six – wearing a baggy suit and a hat. That's about it.'

'So you reckon Eddie Grant's back in the frame?'

'I'd say so.'

'No. It's not him. I can feel it in my wobblies.'

'You've told me often enough never to trust hunches.'

'That's true. But it's late. I want to go to bed and you're going home. That's an order. Otherwise I'll report you for pimping on the lady next door.'

'I think you ought to carry a gun,' Sparky said.

'We don't carry guns, remember?'

'You could always book one out for yourself.'

'I'd get the sack.'

'Mmm, probably. What about the radio? Do you have one?'

'No.'

'Bloody hell, Charlie! What's the matter with you? Some madman's out to kill you, so you keep it to yourself and don't even carry a radio. Not to mention visiting the main suspect without telling anyone. Do you want him to succeed?'

I sighed. 'When you put it like that, it does seem a bit stupid.'

'Here.' He reached over and grovelled in the glove compartment, producing a personal transmitter/receiver. 'Take mine.'

I accepted it and opened the door. 'Cheers,' I said. 'And, er, thanks.'

'Bugger you, Charlie,' he called across to me before I closed the door again. 'I'm looking after that ten-pound bet we have.'

I walked the hundred yards home. As I unlocked the door I heard his engine cough into life.

The hospital has fairly liberal visiting hours, and they didn't mind me calling in at any time. I was making toast for a quick breakfast before going there when the phone rang.

'Is that Mr Priest?' asked a female voice.

'Yes. Who's that, please?'

'It's Sister Williams, on ward B. Will you be able to visit Annabelle this morning, please?'

'Yes, why? What's happened?' My heart was pounding.

'Nothing to panic about, but she's had a restless night and has asked me to call you. She wants to see you and is worrying herself into a state. I don't know what it's about, but she says it's important.'

'OK. I'm on my way.'

I poured my untouched mug of tea down the sink and grabbed my jacket. I wanted to race there, but I regularly hear of the results of such impatience and went with the traffic flow. I parked in the big car park, stuffed some money in the machine and ran to the hospital.

Annabelle was sitting up. Someone had done her hair and she was wearing one of her own nightdresses, but her face was lined with worry.

'Oh Charles, I've been so worried about you.'

I bent forward to give her a kiss and she flung her arms around my neck, almost pulling me off balance. I extricated myself and sat on the bed, holding her hand.

'Worried about me?' I said. 'You're the one everybody is worried about.'

She sank back against her pillows. 'I've remembered what happened,' she said, the words tumbling out. 'The man with the gun...'

'Look,' I interrupted. 'We know all about him. He's a long way away now, so don't you concern yourself about him. He won't come here.'

'But I saw him.'

'You saw him? When?'

'When he fired. He wasn't shooting at me, Charles. He was shooting at you. It was you he was trying to kill.'

I stroked her long fingers. The wedding ring was made of silver wires, twisted together in a local design by some Kenyan silversmith. It looked so simple against her suntanned skin, its elegance representing everything about her that I loved. 'Yes, I know,' I said. 'We have a good idea who he is. He'll be arrested soon.'

She shook her head in agitation. 'But you don't understand. I saw him. He was wearing a man's hat, a trilby, but I don't think it *was* a he. I think it was a woman. A woman in men's clothing.'

I couldn't hide my incredulity. 'Are you sure?' I demanded.

'No, it was just an impression. But that's what I think I saw. Please be careful, Charles.'

A nurse came and put a thermometer in Annabelle's mouth. 'I will,' I said. She couldn't speak, so I told her that I had a bodyguard, that Sparky was following me everywhere I went and armed police were never far away. It wasn't true, but hopefully it eased her mind.

The nurse read the thermometer and entered the result on the chart. When she'd gone I said: 'I understand you're staying with Rachel to recuperate. It's a good idea.'

She sighed. 'Yes, I said I would. I'm not so sure about it being a good idea, though.'

'I thought he was a doctor?'

'He's an osteopath. He manipulates the bank balances of the wealthy. Qualified by correspondence course with a college in Medicine Hat, Nebraska, or somewhere.'

'Gosh. That's worse than Nairobi.'

The old smile came back, enslaving all before it. 'Not to mention Batley College of Art,' she chuckled.

A frond of hair had fallen across her left eye. I brushed it aside and said: 'Have you forgiven me for falling asleep on your settee?'

'You really know how to make a woman feel wanted, Charles, but you are forgiven.'

'Oh, you're wanted,' I stated. 'Believe me, you're wanted.'

It was a struggle, but I tore myself away. From home I rang the office, but nobody was in, not even Gilbert. I made some fresh toast and a pot of tea, but restlessness blunted my appetite. I carried breakfast through into the front room and placed it on a low table at the side of my favourite easy chair, in front of the gas fire. There was still nobody in the office, so I dialled Control.

'Where is everybody, Arthur?' I asked.

'Hello, Mr Priest. Out on the job; we had three ram-raids last night. Plus I understand you have a couple off sick.'

'Sick? It's not allowed. What's wrong with them?'

'Virus going round. It's called one-day flu.'

'So they'll be back tomorrow?'

'No, it takes about a week to get over it.'

'Well, why do they call it one-day flu?'

'Don't ask me, that's just its name.'

'I see. If anybody comes in, ask them to ring me at home.'

'Will do. Do you want me to chase them?'

'Er, no, I don't think so. Bye.'

I finished the toast and tea. I was just reaching over to switch on Radio Four when the phone rang.

'Priest!' I snapped.

'Hello, Charlie. It's Gav Smith. I hear you were after me.'

'Hi, Gavin. Yes, I was. Thanks for ringing, but I spoke to Mrs... Petty, was it? She answered my question.'

'It's Mrs Pettit, actually. Yes, she told me, but I've just had a look at the file and she didn't give you the full story.'

'Oh, go on.'

'She said Purley died of TB and pneumonia, but what she didn't tell you was that they were AIDS-induced. I don't suppose it makes much difference, but Don Purley had fullblown AIDS.'

'Jesus, thanks. What was he doing – injecting?'

'Probably, plus a bit of shirtlifting.'

'Shirtlifting? Bet you didn't put that in your report.'

'Not in those words, so don't quote me. Anything else?'

'Yeah. His wife, Rhoda. What happened to her?'

'Still in Heckley, as far as I know.'

'We tried her name alongside the electoral roll and she didn't show.'

'Oh.' He was silent for a few moments before he said: 'What name did you try?'

'Well, Rhoda Purley,' I answered.

'Hang on a second.' I could hear the rustle of sheets as he riffled through the file. 'Here it is. Name of spouse or partner – Rhoda Flannery. Common-law wife, as we called them in those days. They weren't married.'

'Bugger!' I spat the word out. 'You've been a little treasure, Gavin. Give me his release address, please.'

'Forty-nine, Attlee Towers.'

'Got it. I owe you a pint.'

'You're welcome. I know you don't believe it but we are supposed to be on the same side, you know.'

I rang Heckley Control and spoke to Arthur again. 'Bring up the local electoral roll,' I told him, 'and check for a Rhoda Flannery. Then find out what car she drives, please. I'm at home.'

He rang me back in a few minutes. She still lived at Attlee Towers and drove a 1988 Ford Fiesta, colour grey. Ah, well, I wasn't far off. He told me the registration number. I grabbed my jacket and picked up Sparky's radio from the hall table, where I'd left it the night before. The rain had started again.

Attlee Towers is on the mean side of town. Once, rows of terraced houses stood there; two-up, two-down and back-to-back. No hot water, shared closets, and washing strung like bunting across the cobbled streets. But now people remembered them with affection, for there had been a sense of community that vanished when the bulldozers moved in. They'd been replaced by vertical warrens with unlit stairwells and cardboard walls.

There are four blocks on the estate, all named after giants of the Labour movement. It was a lot worse than I remembered: Attlee Towers was in its death throes.

It reminded me of some eccentric art gallery, with all the paintings on the outside, like a forerunner of the Pompidou Centre. Most of the windows and doors were covered by sheets of plywood, on which the graffiti artists had demonstrated their talents with enough stolen aerosols of paint to give Heckley its own private hole in the ozone layer. The wooden sheets were portrait-style over the doors, landscape on the windows, and the artists had worked with a flair and urgency that showed in the results. Some of them were bloody good, but I'd never admit it in front of the Super. Here and there dingy curtains indicated an occupied flat.

Forty-nine is on the fourth floor, but it was a coincidence, not good planning. Four floors is about the limit of my endurance these days, but I didn't trust the lift. The stairway was narrow and dark, and stank of urine. An empty drinks can clattered away from under my feet, the noise echoing unnaturally loudly as it rattled down the concrete steps.

Huddled on the landing of the third floor were two youths. They stared at me with blank expressions on their spotty faces. The air was pungent with the smell of solvent and one of them was trying to hide a plastic bag.

'Put that where I can see it,' I told him.

He made no effort to do so. I fished my ID from my pocket and held it in front of his nose. 'Now!' I yelled. He placed the bag on the floor, alongside where he was sitting.

'OK, now let's see what you're using.'

He produced a tube of glue big enough to make a full-scale replica of the *Spruce Goose*. Half of it was gone.

'Now you,' I told the other one.

'I 'aven't got anyfing, mister,' he said.

'No? So open your jacket.'

He reluctantly unzipped his bomber jacket. I put

my hand in the inside pocket and found a cylinder of lighter fuel.

'How old are you?' I demanded.

'Fifteen,' they replied, not quite in unison.

'Well, if you keep on using this stuff you won't make sixteen. Now get out of it.'

They sidled off down the stairs, backs to the wall as they looked up at me. As they vanished round the landing below, I shouted: 'Stick together,' after them, and immediately hated myself for it.

They inhale the lighter fluid – butane – by operating the valve against their teeth. It is under pressure in the cylinder and injects straight into the lungs, reaching the brain in seconds. It's an act of desperation, with no safety margin between a good trip and an OD. I pressed the cylinder against the metal banister until it was empty, the tube growing icy in my hand as the pressure inside dropped and the smell of the gas nearly knocking me over. Then I squeezed the rest of the glue out. Neither container had a price ticket indicating which shop had supplied it.

The fourth floor. External corridors radiate out from the main structure, each with three flats along it. I chose the wrong one first: 44, 45 and 46.

Forty-seven, this was more like it. All the windows were boarded up and defaced. Forty-eight, just the same. Window, door, window, all covered and spray-painted; but the design on the last sheet of plywood stopped me in my tracks.

It was a skull, done in red on a white background and edged in black. It was the artist's *tour de force*, the prize exhibit in the gallery. He'd captured that grin that mocks the living surprisingly well, for the teeth were comprised of four letters. They spelt: AIDS.

Chapter Twenty Two

Rhoda Flannery would have to pass that skull every time she went out, every time she came home. I edged by it, and found myself outside number 49.

All the curtains were closed. I knocked on the door. Something told me that nobody was in, the same mysterious sense that tells you that nobody will pick up a telephone. It can be wrong, though. I hammered, again and again, but I couldn't conjure her up.

Fictional detectives carry little bundles of bent wires that enable them to bypass the most sophisticated products of the lockmaker's craft. Or if it's a Yale lock they just slip a credit card in and *hey presto!* But this wasn't a Yale. My own preferred method is to borrow a key.

It's common knowledge that there are only about ten different keys for all the locks on these flats. An old customer of mine, called George Dunphy, lived in one of the other blocks. He was also an old-style cat burglar; no bricks through windows for him. I radioed control and asked for his address. It took a couple of attempts as the radio was on the blink.

He was in. 'Hello, George. Remember me, Charlie Priest?' I said when he answered the door.

'Mr Priest? Well, blow me down. What can we do for you?'

'Well, you could invite me in.'

He lived in Bevan Towers, and the council had elected that this block should house the more responsible tenants. Attlee Towers was reserved for rent defaulters, immobilised travelling people and rehoused single-parent families. George led me through into a cosily cluttered living room. The gas fire and telly were at full blast, and Mrs Dunphy did not look pleased to see me.

'I need to break into a flat, George, over in the Attlee block. I was wondering if you could help me.'

It wasn't the most tactful way of putting it. 'No, he can't,' stated Mrs Dunphy. 'All that's behind him.'

George gave me a look that said he'd love to, but his wife held more terror for him than any judge had ever done. 'Well, Mr Priest, it's like the missus sez. I ain't done nothing like that for years.'

'I know that, George. What I mean is: can I borrow your key? Or can you tell me how to get in?'

'Oh, we can do that. Wait a minute, let's see what we 'ave.' He went to the sideboard and took an ancient biscuit tin from the cupboard. There was a picture of George VI and Queen Elizabeth on it, in their coronation finery. He tipped the contents on to the table.

It was a treasure chest. Hundreds, possibly thousands of buttons spilled out, in every design and material imaginable. Other items were mixed in with them, like marbles and foreign coins and campaign medals. I fingered a couple of medals.

'Are these yours?' I asked, with genuine interest.

He was rummaging through the pile. 'Them? Yeah, they're mine.'

'Where did you get them?'

'An 'ouse in 'Eckley,' he said, throwing his head back and roaring with laughter. I had to join in.

'I was in the army nine years,' he explained, wiping his eyes, 'when they was needing 'em, not feeding 'em. This is what we're looking for.'

He'd found a master key. The end was a simple T-shape. Soon he produced another two of slightly different designs. 'One of them'll get you in,' he stated.

'Great, thanks.' I couldn't resist asking: 'Do you, er, want them back?'

'Not me, Mr Priest. Been straight ten years now. You keep 'em.' He nodded towards his wife. 'But I'd love to come with you.'

I thanked him and left. Five minutes later I was trying the keys in the door of 49, Attlee Towers.

None was a perfect fit, so I tried them all again, using more force. One felt as if it was doing something, so I shook the key about in the lock and twisted harder. It worked, I was in.

I closed the door behind me, slid the bolt across and switched on the light. 'Anybody home?' I shouted, although I was certain the place was deserted.

The room was a dump. The dralon suite was threadbare and the wallpaper bore black marks where the furniture had rubbed against it for years. Discarded clothing was flung about the place and a plate bearing the relics of a meal was still on the table. A well-used flypaper hung from the ceiling; didn't know you could still buy them. I tried not to breathe.

Against the far wall was what I took to be a Welsh dresser. The shelves were filled with cheap little trophies and shields. I walked across to examine them. Most had been awarded to Rhoda, for her body-building exploits, but were mainly bronzes, with an occasional silver. Even at her chosen sport she was always the bridesmaid, never the bride. On the mantelshelf were several photos of the pair of them in various poses, bodies glistening like porpoises. They must have thought they looked good, and that was all that mattered.

I started opening drawers and cupboards, not sure of what I was looking for. The dresser was filled with all sorts of household items, glass and crockery, some of it good quality. Nothing for me, though. A sideboard contained all the documents that we acquire and hoard in our passage through life: like insurance policies, old gas bills and the instructions for the microwave. The cupboards in it were stuffed with clothes, mainly woolly jumpers. I turned to a writing desk in the corner.

Like a professional burglar I opened the bottom drawer first, and when I saw the contents my stomach convulsed, as if it had been clawed by a polar bear. The drawer held a pile of newspaper cuttings, and smiling at me from the top sheet was the face of Annabelle. In a corner lay an unopened carton of shotgun cartridges. I'd found what I'd come for: Rhoda Flannery was the Mushroom Man.

I sat on the floor for several minutes, back to the wall and staring at the carpet. There were plenty of questions, but I couldn't come up with any answers. God willing, when Annabelle was well I'd spend the rest of my time with her. Marry her, if she'd have me. And I'd leave the police force. All it offered was a front-row seat at a Greek tragedy, and I'd paid in full.

Outside it was raining again, or was it still raining? I stood in the doorway to the flats and tried to radio Control.

'Priest to Control.'

No reply.

'Charlie Priest to Heckley Control. Acknowledge.'

Silence.

'I say again, this is Charlie Palooka with an urgent message to Heckley Control. Answer the goddamn radio, Arthur.'

I flicked the switch off and on and pressed the 'speak' button, but wasn't even rewarded with a hiss of static. I'd have to use the mobile phone in the car.

As I stepped off the curb my left foot went into a pothole filled with water. It came over my ankle and filled my shoe.

'Bugger!' I cursed, shaking my soaking foot. 'Bugger-bloody-damn!'

'And fuck!' I added for good measure.

'Arthur, why can't I reach you on my radio?' I snapped, when he answered the phone.

'Sorry, Mr Priest. We could hear you. You must have another faulty radio. The transmit button sticks in when it's wet. What was all the cursing about?'

'I stepped in a puddle. Up to my knee. I'll have to go home to change my shoes. Look, Arthur, these radios should have been sorted weeks ago.' I was annoyed about it, and having one cold foot didn't help.

'We thought they had been. All the new ones were sent back and modified.'

'It's not good enough. I'll have words with the supplier. A fault like this could cost someone's life.'

'You're right, boss. Put it in your pocket, then it won't get left in the car.'

I retrieved it from the glove box where I'd tossed it. 'OK. Now listen to this. I want an APW broadcasting for Rhoda Flannery, home address: forty-nine Attlee Towers, Heckley; driving a grey 1988 Ford Fiesta. You've got the number.'

'Will do, Mr Priest. What's it about?'

'She's the Mushroom Man.'

'Sheest! Are you sure?'

I ignored the question. 'Suspect is armed with a shotgun, and very dangerous. On no account to be approached by unarmed officers. I'm outside Attlee Towers now. Can you have someone here as soon as possible? Oh, and inform Mr Wood.'

Five minutes later a local patrol car joined me, and said that an ARV was on its way. I pointed out Rhoda's flat to them and gave strict instructions that they were to wait for the armed officers if she came back. I said I was going home to change my shoes and would then go to the station. It could be a long day.

I reversed the car into my drive, so I could make a fast getaway if anybody rang. It felt cold inside the house, and I was chilled through. The radiators weren't on at that time of day, so I turned the gas fire fully on and pulled the easy chair closer. I kept my jacket on, but removed my shoes and socks so I could toast my feet. There was a draught on my neck, so I sank lower into the chair. When I'd thawed out I'd make a drink and a sandwich. Meanwhile, I'd just relax and let the others do the running around. It was out of my hands.

Well, I thought it was.

This was my parents' house, inherited by me after they died. Dad was a do-it-yourself freak. He'd installed the central heating, years ago, and made a good job of it. Except for one small thing. In the hallway, under the carpet, there is a trap door that gives access to the circulating pump. It creaks every time you walk over it. He'd tried to fix it and so had I, but without success. As I sat there, warming my feet, it creaked. Somebody was inside the house.

That was why it was cold: one of the windows was open. I reached out and picked the phone up from the coffee table alongside my chair. It was dead. I delved into my inside pocket for the radio, but just as I touched it the door flew open.

The ridiculous and the terrifying are sometimes just a hair's-breadth apart. She was wearing a man's suit that was two sizes too large for her even before her body had been wasted by disease, topped off by a trilby hat. She would have looked as if she were auditioning for the Artful Dodger had it not been for the gaunt face, dotted with sores that would never heal because her immune system was gone. And the sawn-off shotgun. The Dodger never carried a shotgun.

'Who the hell are you?' I said. I knew the answer, but would never have recognised her.

'Put your hands where I can see them,' she croaked, 'and say a quick prayer, before I blow your fucking head off.' Her voice was a cackle, like she had a throat full of eggshells.

'It's Rhoda, isn't it?' I said.

'And you're the late Charlie Priest.' She pointed the shotgun at me. It focuses the attention like nothing I'd experienced before. Keep 'em talking, the book said.

'Why?' I asked. God! Was that the best I could do? 'Don't you think I deserve an explanation?' Marginally better.

'What explanation did you give Don?' she hissed.

'Don committed murder,' I told her. 'He knew what was coming; bore no grudges. It was my job to put him away, and I did it.'

'He was innocent. He wouldn't lie to me. You didn't get him life, you gave him a death sentence.' She was shrieking now. 'Do you know what it was like? A hundred men sharing a needle, passing it from cell to cell for a month until someone brought a new one in? He didn't deserve what he got in there.'

I was hopelessly off balance, sprawled in the armchair with my arms dangling over the sides. I pulled my feet back against the seat as I spoke: 'Nobody deserves that, Rhoda. Least of all you.'

'What do you care? Look at this!' she screamed, flinging her hat into the corner. The red mane had gone, replaced by a patchwork of weeping lesions. I felt myself recoil at the sight. 'Well, we got it, whether we deserved it or not, and now you get yours.' She levelled the gun at me.

'What about the others, Rhoda? Did they deserve what they got?'

'Ah! Them,' she scoffed. The gun swung a couple of degrees away from me as she threw her head back and laughed. I drew my hands in, placing them on the chair arms.

'Yes, them. What had they done to you?'

She could barely control her laughter, the gun waving about alarmingly, sometimes pointing at me, sometimes not.

'Nothing!' she declared. 'They'd done nothing to me. Don't you see, that's what makes it so perfect.'

'I don't understand.'

'You're the fucking detective. The *Top Cop*.' She taunted me with the words. 'Tell me, then, Mr *Top Cop*, what's the perfect murder?'

'Er, I don't know. One that nobody knows has been committed, I suppose.'

'Close, but not quite. One without a motive, that's the perfect murder. I had no reason to kill them. You were just the next in the line. Four proper priests, then you. I was going to kill another person called Priest, just to sew things up, then I could die happy. Unfortunately that stuck-up bitch you go out with got in the way. That was a laugh when I found out she was a bishop's wife.' She chuckled and grinned, revealing brown teeth with gaps at the sides of her mouth. She reminded me of the skull on the window of number 48. I flinched at her words, but used the movement to curl my fingers over the ends of the chair arms. I was as poised as I'd ever be.

'Rhoda,' I said, as softly and calmly as I could, 'there's been too much killing. You've had a raw deal, but this won't solve anything. You could have treatment. They've drugs now that could help you. Put the gun down.'

'There's no treatment for this!' she cried, pointing at her head. She leaned back against the wall and I could see that her cheeks were glistening with tears. 'I said I'd wait for him. I had a job and a flat. We could still have had kids, that's all I ever wanted. It wasn't much, was it?'

'Kids,' I sighed. 'That's all I ever wanted, too. But it wasn't to be.'

'Still...' she said, and the steel was back in her voice and the gun wasn't wavering any more, 'killing you will make me feel better for a couple of days.'

'What about the first two? Were they really you?' The words tumbled out and I wondered if any of our conversation was being transmitted. It would make riveting listening in the control room.

'Ah!' she snorted. 'I saw a headline over someone's shoulder. It said: 'Priest killed. Was it murder?' For a glorious moment I thought it was you. My heart leapt. I got off the bus a stop early to call at the newsagent's. I wept when I read it was only some crumby vicar.'

There was a scrunch of gravel under tyres from the road outside. A look of panic flickered across her face and the gun steadied, pointing at my head. 'Neighbours,' I said. 'They come and go all the time.' I eased myself up slightly. 'So what about the second one? Did you do him?'

'No, he just fell down the tower. That's when I got the idea, though. I liked the thought of some religious nut knocking off priests.' Her shoulders bobbed up and down with amusement.

They'd surround the house; listen at the windows; then try to make contact, probably by ringing the door-bell. 'But the next two were all your own work,' I said.

'All my own work,' she boasted. 'And now it's your turn.'

'Where did you get the name, Destroying Angel?'

'I know all about mushrooms. Which are good, which are bad. I've always liked that one.'

'I thought they were poisonous?'

'No more talking.' She levelled the gun. 'Kiss your arse goodbye, Charlie Priest–'

TRIIIING! The doorbell!

I went in hard and curving. First to the right, towards her but away from the gun, then up for it. Her eyes had flickered towards the sound of the bell, and for a tenth of a second she couldn't decide whether to swing the gun away from my grasping hand or try to blast me with it. It was all I needed. My body hit hers and bounced her back against the wall. The fingers of my left hand curled round her wrist, thin as a robin's leg, and lifted it and the gun towards the ceiling. She went for my eyes with her free hand, clawing ribbons of skin from my cheek. I jerked my head back and managed to grasp her other wrist. I was a foot taller than her and a few stones heavier. I stretched her arms apart and pinned her to the wall as if she were a petulant child. She was still holding the shotgun.

'In here! I've got her!' I shouted.

Then her knee hit me in the balls.

Forget childbirth – the knee in the balls is the most excruciating pain known to mankind. A fireball exploded in my stomach and my knees buckled, as if a scythe had gone through them. I was blinded by agony, but the threat of a twelve-bore is a powerful anaesthetic. Teetering on the edge of blacking out, I concentrated with all the power I possessed on gripping that right wrist. Outside, the door glass was shattering and wood splintering. With a desperate effort I swung her away from the wall and kicked her legs from under her. She fell over backwards. As she hit the floor I collapsed my legs so that my entire weight fell mercilessly on top or her. Our faces were touching as I did so, and her breath erupted in a volcanic torrent into my face. I turned my head sideways to escape it, and she sank her teeth deep into my ear.

The cavalry rushed in. They found us on the floor, as if crucified face to face, with my blood and her saliva intermingling and dribbling down her cheek, on to the carpet.

Chapter Twenty Three

Sparky prised her jaws open with a spoon handle. Once she was off me she allowed the boys in blue to take her away. Sparky cleaned up my ear with a wet cloth whilst I put a tentative hand down my Y-fronts and gingerly explored the contents. He handed me a tea towel and told me to keep it pressed against the side of my head.

'Well, at least we know what to call you from now on,' he said.

'What?' I groaned.

'Van Gogh,' he replied.

'I'd have thought Goebbels,' suggested Nigel.

'It's not funny,' I snapped, somewhere between laughing and crying. 'And if you've knackered my front door you can bloody well pay for a new one.'

'You're right, Charlie, it's not funny,' Sparky admitted, hooking his hands under my shoulders. 'C'mon, let's get you to hospital. Can you stand up?'

They did some nifty microsurgery on my ear and told me it would soon be as good as new. When they learned that the person who'd bitten me had advanced AIDS they handled me with rubber gloves and spoke in whispers. My right testicle looked reasonably normal, but its partner resembled a ripe aubergine. No treatment was offered. 'We'll just see how it goes,' the doctor said, adding that he'd have another look at the ear in a week. Two nurses, female, said they'd check my goolies again tomorrow morning.

In the afternoon a woman in civilian clothes with a comfortable face came to visit me. She had a permanent smile, as if she were dosing her HRT patch with cocaine. She introduced herself and told me she was an AIDS counsellor.

The gist of it was that I should think carefully before I decided to have a test. Even if it proved negative the fact that I had been tested might lead to difficulties with life insurance or obtaining a mortgage. I should ask myself if I really needed to know.

'Of course I bloody well need to know,' I growled at her.

In which case, she reassured me, the news was not all bleak – it was possible to be HIV positive and not develop the disease for as long as twenty years. As nobody had heard of AIDS that long ago I took this information with a pinch of scepticism. When she went into the bit about anal and oral intercourse I told her I was tired and pulled the blankets over my head. Her parting shot was that everything we had said was confidential. Who told you? I thought. She scared the willies out of me.

Modern NHS hospitals have a menu system for mealtimes. Every day you are given a list of the following day's dishes, upon which you tick your selections. Unfortunately this means that on your first day you have to have what the previous occupant of the bed chose on his last day. I was following a diabetic rabbit on hunger strike. I vowed revenge on the next hapless soul to lie here.

Sam Evans came in the evening, bearing a magazine on trout fishing. He looked tired.

'How did you know I was interested in trout fishing, Sam?' I asked.

'I didn't. Are you?'

'Not especially. Wouldn't mind having a go, though.'

'That's what I thought, so it's what I'm prescribing for you. How are you feeling?'

'Worried.'

'I guessed you might be, so I've been doing some swatting.'

'Just make me one little promise, please,' I begged.

'What's that, Charlie?'

'To be honest with me.'

He nodded. 'OK. Well, the news is not too bad, although it could be better. The basic facts are that if she infected you it will take about eight weeks for you to make sufficient antibodies to be detected by a blood test. That's what we look for, antibodies.'

'So I won't know for another eight weeks?'

'Afraid not. Plus another week for the test. However, the bright side is that there is no documented case anywhere in the world of AIDS being contracted through a bite. As you know from your work with DNA, there are blood cells in saliva, but the quantity of virus present is infinitesimal, and there is also an agent present that inactivates it. That's the good news.'

'However...'

'However... I've just examined her, Charlie. She's in the hospital wing at Filton Green.'

'You have been busy.'

'It's in a good cause. I can't say I'm happy about what I saw. The disease has affected her brain – dementia – although I suspect she was on the way before she caught it. You saw the lesions on her face; well, the inside of her mouth is just as bad. Her gums are ulcerated and bleeding. The truth is, Charlie, we know so little about it. Up to today I knew next to nothing. I'd be a liar if I said I thought you were in the clear.'

I pursed my lips and focused on the big paper clip holding my notes at the foot of the bed. 'So we sit tight and take the tests in eight weeks,' I said.

'That's right. The risk is slim, extremely slim, but in my judgement it's there.'

He told me that the incidence of HIV and AIDS was relatively low in Yorkshire, and I might receive a more educated assessment from a London doctor, but my brief experience with the counsellor had taught me that peddling optimism was part of the treatment. The biggest part. I trusted Sam.

There were other illnesses she could have passed on to me, some serious, but they faded into insignificance compared with the big A. As a precautionary measure a cocktail of exotic chemicals was injected into my bloodstream.

I asked the nurse for something to make me sleep, and it worked. It was only a pill, unfortunately. After breakfast I made it to the toilet without too much discomfort and removed the bandage from around my head. The ear didn't look too bad, so I put my clothes on and inched my way to the front entrance. I saw a sign pointing to Ward 4B, where Annabelle was, but didn't follow it. In the foyer is a bank of payphones, with the numbers of taxi firms prominently displayed. I rang one, and asked him to take me home. The two nurses were due for a disappointment when they came to make their examination. One of them was black, the other white. How appropriate, I'd thought at the time.

I locked my door, pulled the phone out and went to bed for nearly two days. Gilbert came round and gave me a telling off and progress reports on my two murderers. Dewhurst was pulling round but not saying anything, Rhoda was sinking fast and doubtful for standing trial.

'He came out of jail and passed it on to her. Can you believe it?' I asked.

Gilbert shook his head.

'And she still loved him. He did that to her and she still loved him.'

'It's affected her brain,' he said. 'Apparently it can do that, in a few cases. I don't think she was all there to begin with. And what about you? How do you intend spending your enforced rest?'

'I think I'll go away for a few days, as soon as I can get about OK. Have a change of scenery.'

'Good idea, but what about Annabelle?'

'Annabelle? She's making good progress. I rang about an hour ago.' I didn't tell him that I hadn't asked to be put through to her.

'What about seeing her? I'll take you, if you want.'

I sat and inspected my fingernails for a couple of minutes, before saying: 'Gilbert, there's an outside chance that I've been infected. It'll take eight, nine weeks before we know, one way or the other. I've... I've decided not to see Annabelle again until it's all over.'

He sat up, looking shocked.

I was quite calm. I said: 'I'll never let it affect me like it did Rhoda. If I've got it, it's better we finish right now.'

'Does she know?' he asked.

I shook my head. 'When Sam came to see me I asked him to deliver a message. That the woman who shot her was in custody and I was safe, but I'd gone down with this flu bug that's going round, so I was staying away from her. It didn't sound so cheap at the time.'

'You're right, it sounds cheap.'

'Don't give me a hard time, Gilbert. I'm doing my best.' After a silence I went on: 'My dad died of cancer, as you know. In the two years that he had it my mother never once said the word. She'd never admit that he had cancer. In her eyes there was a stigma attached to it that I couldn't understand. Cancer didn't happen to nice people. I don't understand now, but I'm closer. Annabelle nearly died because of me. AIDS is a sordid disease, Gilbert, and I'll never inflict any part of it on her.'

He stood up to leave and I walked with him to the newly repaired door. As he went out he turned and said: 'You're a selfish bastard, Charlie.' I knew he was wrong – it was the toughest decision I'd ever made.

At the motorway I made a snap decision and turned right. Two and a bit hours later I booked into the Balmoral Guest House at one of the smaller east coast resorts. It would be unfair to say which one. The chief amenity of the town was a golden beach, criss-crossed with groynes to stop the tide washing the sand away, and blessed with a half-mile sewage outlet to keep things sanitary. A First World War defensive position was preserved for the children to play on through the day and for their slightly older brothers and sisters to screw each other goggle-eyed in during the evenings, while their parents played bingo. The morning tide washed the discarded condoms out to sea, where they choked the occasional passing cod.

Breakfasts were full English, but most mornings I settled for toast and cornflakes. Afterwards I wandered up and down the beach, keeping my left ear to the wall, although anyone who saw it probably assumed I was an injured rugby union player. I drank a lot of tea, seated at formica tables, and pecked at some respectable fish and chips. The Salvation Army band gave concerts from a bandstand in the middle of a grassy area. The girl with the collection box had blonde hair tied severely back and hidden beneath her hat. She reminded me of Grace Kelly in *High Noon*.

I spent a lot of time sitting on benches. It was the most popular pastime in town. One evening a girl of about fourteen with a Bardotesque pout came to sit alongside me. She was wearing an indecently short skirt and an unzipped biker jacket, revealing a T-shirt that looked as if it were concealing two bottles of Tia Maria. When she asked me for a light I told her to go away. She called me a fucking wanker and went. Later I saw her getting into someone's car. There wasn't a lot there for the kids to do.

They play bingo at the Balmoral in the evenings. I fell into the role of mystery guest and avoided everyone. I would have done so whatever the circumstances. People were enjoying themselves in a way that was incomprehensible to me, but I couldn't condemn them for that. Maybe I'm a snob. I sneaked past the laughing faces and went up to bed. The sheets were crisp and the pillows stuffed with feathers. If I'd had the odd pint I fell asleep reasonably well; any more and I lay awake, thinking about Annabelle.

I stuck it for a week then went home. The goolies were a matching pair again and appeared to be functioning properly. I saw Sam and he removed the stitches from my ear, so I was back to normal – if you ignored the time bomb ticking away inside me.

The weather was good, as predicted, so I did a lot of walking and visited art galleries and museums that I'd been meaning to see for years. I had afternoon tea in country cafes and chatted to shop girls and people in the street. The weeks crept by.

I rang the hospital almost every day. Annabelle was still making very good progress, they said. Halfway through the fifth week they told me that she had been discharged, and a few days later a letter arrived in a long white envelope. It carried a Guildford address and was very brief. It said:

> Dear Charles,.
> What went wrong? If it has to end, please don't let it be this way.
> Love,
> Annabelle

Sparky called now and again, and Nigel came a couple of times. 'When are you coming back?' Sparky asked one day, as he sat consuming my chocolate digestives.

'I might not,' I replied.

He froze in mid-dunk. 'Seriously?' he said.

'Yeah. Doc Evans says he'll swing it for me, if I want. There's still a couple of shotgun pellets floating about inside me from way back, or I can jump on the stress wagon. Post something-or-other trauma. Take your pick.'

I didn't want to tell him about the AIDS risk. I had no objection to him knowing, but I couldn't face the shocked expression or the stumbled words of support. I assumed Gilbert would have told him, but it didn't look as if he had.

'I don't blame you for getting out, Charlie, but it doesn't sound like your style.'

'It's not, Dave, but I've had enough.'

'Why not go for promotion, cruise through the next couple of years like Mr Wood does?'

'Gilbert would be delighted to hear you say that,' I chuckled.

'There's one good thing. If you do go, the community charge should come down.'

'How do you make that out?' I asked.

'Well, there'll be a lot less work for the prisons and hospitals to do. Without your regular contributions they'll be able to close one of each.'

'Yes, we do seem to have been keeping them busy recently, don't we?'

Dave looked thoughtful and said: 'If you're about to become a pensioner I feel embarrassed about asking you for that tenner. Call it my contribution to the collection.'

'Gee, thanks, Dave.'

A ferry capsized in the Far East, drowning a hundred and thirteen souls. A dog in Essex had a heart valve replaced and a Pro-Life supporter shot dead three doctors in Arkansas. On the fifty-sixth morning I presented myself at Sam Evans's surgery to give a blood sample.

'Where would you like me to take it from?' he asked.

'You,' I replied.

'The choice is left arm or right arm.'

'Oh. Left, then.'

I looked away. When it's my blood, I'm squeamish.

'We'll take a couple of samples,' Sam was saying as I studied the pattern on the curtains. 'They do a test called ELISA to detect the presence of any antibodies, then a more specific one called WBT, which is really a confirmatory test, but I've persuaded them to do it, anyway.'

I flinched as the needle went in.

'Sorry,' Sam said. 'Did I hurt you?'

'Yes. Badly,' I replied.

'Well, that should do it. Tell my delightful receptionist to give you the first appointment in seven days' time. How are the testicles?'

I rolled my sleeve down. 'Feeling unwanted. How are yours?'

'Mind your own business. You seem to be back to your old cheerful self, Charlie. It's good to see.'

'It's all a front, Sam. Inside I'm scareder than a kitten on a clothes line. See you next week.'

The weather was still good so I decided that the outside of the house would benefit from a lick of paint. I dragged the ladders out of the garage and set them up against the back bedroom window. The neighbours came out to watch.

'Painting your windows?' said the man.

'Er, that's right,' I answered.

He sucked in a long breath. 'Bit back-endish for painting, if you ask me,' he declared.

I scraped the loose paint off and gave the frame a good coating of white gloss. The neighbours have a little sun lounge attached to the back of their house, where they like to sit and read or drink tea. It looks very pleasant. Just as I was finishing I noticed that they were both in there, but had swivelled their wicker chairs round so that they could sit watching me.

'Right, you buggers,' I muttered. I clambered down the ladder and rummaged about in the garage until I found what I wanted.

Back up the ladder I painted the big pane of glass bright blue, the next one red. The little one that opens received a coat of canary yellow. Well, they did ask if I was painting the windows, I said to myself.

The two of them stared at me as if they had just discovered that a psychopathic monster lived next door. I pointed with the paint brush. 'Mondrian,' I shouted, but they couldn't hear me through their double glazing.

It's more difficult to be cheerful when there is no

audience. I tried to eat decent food, to keep the resistance high, but had little appetite for anything. Gilbert was right, I decided – I should have told Annabelle the truth, right from the beginning. I wished I had a photograph of her.

A politician was assassinated in Spain and England were walloped by Romania at football. An airliner crashed in Russia and Rhoda Flannery died in the prison hospital. Maybe she had the last laugh, after all.

The seventh morning dawned bright and frosty. I showered and dressed in comfortable clothes: jeans, woollen shirt, leather jacket and trainers. I scraped the ice off the windscreen, put a load of stuff in the boot that I might need later and drove to the surgery.

It was ten to nine and Sam's car was already there. I was OK until I parked the car, then I started shaking and had difficulty locking the door.

Three patients were already waiting, huddled within themselves like starving peasants awaiting an audience with the laird. The receptionist switched her smile to main beam and started saying: 'Dr Evans says you're to go straight...' but I was already knocking on his door.

'Good morning, Charlie. Take a seat,' he said, placing a letter he was reading back on his desk.

'No thanks, Sam. Are they the results?'

'Yes, they are.'

'So what do they say.'

He turned the letter towards me and pushed it forwards. Bless you, Sam, you didn't make a drama out of it. A huge smile split his face as he said: 'The tests confirm that you are not HIV positive. Congratulations, Charlie, you've beaten it.'

I flopped in the chair and threw my head back, gulping in great draughts of beautiful fresh air like a man dragged out of the quicksand in the nick of time.

Sam was rabbiting on, but I was hardly listening: '... so if you haven't used a dirty needle or had unprotected sex since you were in hospital, we can safely say you are fit and healthy.'

I didn't remember having unprotected sex when I was in hospital. Must have been asleep for that bit. I gave him the grin and just nodded my appreciation of what he was saying.

He delved into one of the drawers at his side of the desk and produced a bottle of champagne. 'Have a celebratory drink on me,' he said.

'Now?' I suggested, taking it from him. It was the first word uttered by the new Charlie Priest.

'Er, no. I don't think my patients would appreciate it. Better make it some other time. By the way, Yvonne said I've to invite you to lunch on Sunday. Can you make it?'

I held up the bottle. 'I'll bring the booze,' I said.

'Good. Smashing.'

I stood up to leave. 'Thanks for everything, Sam.'

'You're welcome, Charlie. It's good news for all of us, you know, not just you.'

He walked to the door with me. 'So what are you going to do next?' he asked. We were down to the small talk.

'Next? Good question. Suddenly there's a next. Back to catching villains, I suppose.'

'I meant today.'

'Oh, today. Driving,' I replied. 'I've got to go to Guildford.'

'Guildford. That's a long way.'

I looked at my watch. 'Yes, and I'm running late.'

'Well, take it steady.'

'No chance. Flat out all the way. See you Sunday.'

I pulled the door closed behind me. The number of grey faces in the waiting room had doubled and the receptionist had removed her spectacles. We exchanged warm smiles. I thrust the bottle of champers forward and hollered: 'Next!' as I strode towards the exit.

Try to leave 'em with a smile, that's my motto. It's not always this easy, but if it was, anybody could do it.